The Senator's Daughter

E.P. Livingston

N

Published by Next Chapter Stories, LLC

ISBN: 9798391092834

DEDICATION

To my Aunt Evelyn who was so excited that I was writing a novel. We miss you so much and I wish you were here to see this all come together.

AUTHOR NOTE

Throughout this novel, you will find that I have used terms in reference to marginalized groups that were common in the 19th century. Indigenous people are sometimes referred to as Indians and African Americans are sometimes referred to using a racial slur. I do not condone the use of this language but I also wanted to maintain the novel's historical accuracy. The use of this language may be offensive to some readers.

ACKNOWLEDGMENTS

A heartfelt thank you to Tim Vickey at Next Chapters for taking me on and helping to make my long-held dream of publishing my first novel come true! I'm so grateful.

To all of the fellow students who I workshopped this piece with four years ago and who all gave such thoughtful feedback and encouragement. You helped me get through a tough bout of writer's block and jump start this book again. Another special thank you to the writing group I've been a part of for the last handful of years. It's been wonderful working alongside you all on our various projects. Thank you!

To the early champions of this novel (Jeff Bloodworth, Berwyn Moore, Carol Hayes, and Sabrina Kauffman) who read the drafts and gave invaluable advice. Thank you all for helping this novel become what it is today!

To my talented cousin, Tracy Ratliff, for designing such an exquisite cover! You are so talented and I'm grateful that you put your heart into creating this amazing design.

To my wonderful group of friends for their love and support. Thank you for putting up with my constant updates on the progress with this book!

To my parents and my entire family, particularly my Aunt Shirley. Thank you all for always being there for me and believing in me. I love you all so much.

To my boys for teaching me so much about love and patience. You are my world and I can't wait to see what the future holds for each of you!

And, last but not least, to my partner, Jason Ramsey. Thank you so much for believing in me and being my constant sounding board in everything. I love you more than words can express. Let's continue to be adventurers, darling!

PROLOGUE
JULY 1825

"Grace, I'm so glad you're here. I'm afraid many of the other ladies won't be joining us," Mrs. Whittle exclaimed, rushing over to where Julia Webster stood with her mother, Grace, in the wide arched doorway leading into the matron's small ballroom. Julia had been distracted by the archway's ornate carvings of roses interspersed with plump, beaming cherubs and turned her attention to Mrs. Whittle who was rather spry in her old age. The tiny spectacles that sat on the bridge of her nose magnified the older woman's perceptive green eyes and her graying hair was neatly pulled back into a no-nonsense bun. "It seems that they, or rather their damned husbands, don't care about equal rights for all minorities. How can they offer so much support to Negro abolition and neglect the other groups who are marginalized?"

Lingering respectfully behind her mother, Julia felt mild curiosity toward the cause her mother and Mrs. Whittle were championing this season. Mrs. Whittle was the head of one of Boston's most influential charity networks and had taken a liking to Grace's giving nature immediately. The older woman had been a frequent visitor in the Webster home over the years. She always seemed intent on enlisting her mother's help in organizing the salons she put on to foster awareness about the plight of underrepresented groups to the wives of Boston's sea captains, politicians, and wealthy businessmen.

Julia had been too young to really appreciate what the two women had to discuss. Even now, she was more intrigued by Mrs. Whittle's towering home that overlooked the harbor than she was in what the impassioned woman had to say. However, she was twelve now and her mother had determined that Julia was ready to be initiated into the fold, dragging her along on this sweltering day when she would have much rather gone down to wade in the Charles River with her younger brother, Edward. He always seemed to find the eels sunning themselves between the rocks and they would watch, simultaneously fascinated and poised to run if one of the slippery creatures decided it was time to slink back into the river.

"Not that abolition for all Negros should be minimized," Mrs. Whittle went on hurriedly, bringing Julia back into the present. "That cause will always be our top priority. It's just that we simply can't ignore the other groups who have no voice!"

"You're right of course, Lydia," Julia's mother responded in her small, though clear, voice, nodding in agreement. "You have to understand, though, that the native tribes don't affect the other women and their husbands directly. They are far removed from Boston's interests." Julia's mother visibly softened when Mrs. Whittle hung her proud head a little. "But I'm sure some of the others will come. Perhaps they're running late. We saw a carriage accident behind us on the way and everything is sure to be backed up for some time. I've brought Julia with me, too."

"Oh, Julia dear, I'm so sorry. I didn't see you there," Mrs. Whittle blanched, adjusting her spectacles as if this would help her to better see people she was too distracted to notice. "I'm glad you came today."

"Thank you for having me, Mrs. Whittle," Julia answered politely, coming forward to stand next to her mother. She was slightly annoyed that Mrs. Whittle had overlooked her but such was the life of a daughter with a dainty, raven-haired mother.

The conversation her mother was now having with Mrs. Whittle faded into the background as Julia made her way further into the sunlit ballroom. At least twenty upholstered dining chairs were arranged in a semi-circle in the middle of the cold marble floor, the swirls in the stone dancing off of one another. Julia looked up into the high ceiling and found a mesmerizing painted likeness of a ship at sea in a storm, waves of steely gray and iridescent green threatening to pummel the great merchant vessel's hull. A crack of lightning shot out of one of the ominous black clouds and Julia could almost feel the sizzle of electricity in the air.

Looking around, she found that her mother and Mrs. Whittle had moved to the chairs and were now sitting with a tall, lanky man dressed in a muted gray waist coat and breeches, the leather of his boot tapping a nervous rhythm on the floor. Julia caught her mother's eye and tilted her head toward the open doors that led toward the outdoor terrace. Her mother nodded her permission and Julia scurried outside, the humid air hitting her instantly. When her eyes again adjusted to the white light of the sun, she looked out toward the ocean's mighty expanse in the distance, the tiny islands just outside the harbor dark blips in a sea of aquamarine. She could just make out the masts of countless ships piercing the hazy air, some of their sails billowing in the stifling breeze.

"It is a lovely sight, isn't it?" a deep voice said behind her and Julia wheeled around. The man who stood just off to her right was like none she'd ever met before. He had an air of elegance about him, his straight inky black hair with tiny flecks of gray was parted smartly down the center of his scalp and falling down to his shoulders. Two bright red, silky feathers were interwoven into his hair at the crown of his head and the sunlight glinted off a number of small metal hoops that curved down the rim of his exposed ear. His complexion was at least three shades darker than hers and an exquisitely crafted blanket of sky blue and leafy green geometric shapes was draped over his left shoulder, providing a stark contrast to his white cotton shirt.

Julia could feel her mouth gaping a little and snapped it shut quickly, at a loss for words. She had heard what native people looked like from her mother but had never been this close to one before. All she could do was nod mutely, her cheeks growing warm from embarrassment. Luckily, her mother came out on the terrace with the tall man, who was introduced as Mr. Williams, a missionary who was accompanying the distinguished Indian in front of her.

"Julia, I see you've already met Wohali. He's from the Cherokee nation down in North Carolina and is going to be speaking to us today," her mother explained, her eyes darting between her daughter and Wohali.

Finally seeming to realize Julia's words had escaped her, her mother turned to Wohali and introduced herself. "I'm Mrs. Grace Webster. This is my daughter, Julia. We're looking forward to learning about your way of life and message for us, sir."

"The pleasure is mine, Mrs. Webster. I'm very happy that I will have such a captive audience," Wohali returned. He gave a kind wink to Julia before the four of them re-entered Mrs. Whittle's ballroom, Julia trailing behind the others sheepishly. Two other women had come in that short time and when they were all settled, Wohali began to tell all of them of his life in the south, switching seamlessly between English and Cherokee.

What he said didn't really matter to Julia; it was the way he spoke that enthralled her. The warmth of his voice and gentleness in his eyes made her feel as if she had known him forever. Julia didn't want the afternoon to end but in no time at all, she was striding toward the family's carriage beside her mother, the pressure of Wohali's handshake still shooting tingles up her palm and through to the tips of her fingers. *I will always remember you,* Wohali, she thought as she settled next to her mother inside the carriage and pulled away from Mrs. Whittle's estate.

CHAPTER 1
BOSTON, 1829

The soft morning light of an increasingly muted November sun filtered through the window pane of Julia Webster's second-floor abode. Typically strewn with half-read books and dresses thrown haphazardly over furniture, the room was uncommonly organized for its inhabitant. The bed was stripped of its sheets, the latter stacked neatly at the foot of the bed on top of the quilt. A large trunk, fully packed, rested on the floor next to the bed. Despite the initial calm the sun found in this scene, it had only to shine on the opposite side of the room to encounter a flurry of anxious activity.

Julia's full skirts hissed softly as she continued to pace over the expanse of floor, her eyes continually darting toward the window which looked out on the small front lawn of the Lee home. She was torn between staying in this comfortable, familiar place and the excitement she felt at being able to see her brothers again. Fletcher would surely raise her spirits with anecdotes from his first term at Harvard and Edward, always an obedient lamb, was her favorite partner for a stroll around their estate. Her father and this woman he was about to appoint as the replacement for her mother . . . that was a much more complicated matter.

She had only met Caroline Le Roy once when her father, the highly regarded Senator Daniel Webster, had come into town for a brief two-day stay earlier that month on his way to accompany the fashionable and very single lady to New York. In none of their correspondence to each other had her father mentioned anything about Caroline and yet there she had been, seated across from Julia in Cousin Eliza Lee's parlor, sipping tea and sporting a ridiculously large, feathered hat. Julia had even joked with Eliza after her father and Caroline had departed that the hat could have made an excellent centerpiece for the dining table if they ever had the prop master for the theatre over. Eliza had quickly admonished her with a good natured *shush.* The encounter had been brief, not more than an hour, and Julia had thought nothing of it afterward. Until she had received the invitation in yesterday's post . . . to her father's wedding.

Of course, she did not expect her father to be alone for the rest of his life; he needed companionship as much as anyone else would, especially on those grueling excursions down to Washington that often stretched into months at a time. But the ache she felt from her mother's passing almost two years ago was still needle sharp more often than not. Perhaps she was holding on too tightly but Julia was hesitant to move beyond her family's loss and she felt her father's courtship of this woman was far too hasty. She wondered if her father even knew what Caroline's favorite shade of blue was. Her mother's had been cerulean.

Julia ceased her pacing when she heard a soft knock on her door and swung it wide open to find Louisa, Eliza's young maid, in the hallway. Louisa was accompanied by Peter, the Lees' brawny cook. "Your brother will be here for you soon," Louisa informed Julia with a quick bob of her head. "Is that the trunk yer takin' with you?"

"Yes, thank you," Julia confirmed and the two young women moved aside to allow Peter in to retrieve the heavy trunk. He maneuvered it onto his shoulder with effortless dexterity, nodded his head silently, and turned out of the room and into the narrow hallway. Julia could hear his heavy footfalls as he made his way down the stairs followed by a heavy thud as the trunk met the hardwood floor of the atrium below.

Julia turned her attention back to Louisa. "I hope Fletcher is well. It's been months since I've seen him last. Harvard must keep its pupils unnecessarily busy," she rambled, reaching for her gloves beside the kerosene lamp on the mahogany writing desk.

"Yes. It'll be good ta see him again," Louisa answered, a faint blush creeping across her plump cheeks, making her look much younger than she was. Julia had connected with Louisa almost instantly when Eliza had taken her on last spring and admired her for her kindness and willingness to always listen. What exasperated Julia about her was this maddening fascination Louisa had with Fletcher. There could be no chance for her, Julia was certain of that. Even if Louisa hadn't been the hired help, Fletcher would never consider courting and marrying a colored girl, however educated she was.

"Yes, it's always good to see family," Julia replied kindly, attempting to catch Louisa's averted eyes. Setting her gloves back on the desk, Julia took Louisa's small, rough hands into her own and tilted her head so that she could look into her friend's still flushed face. "Speaking of brothers, have you seen Quentin recently? I know working on the wharf must be strenuous."

Louisa did not talk about the perils Quentin faced often but Julia had heard enough to know that the life of a dockworker involved backbreaking work in a dangerous environment. Whenever she accompanied Eliza to Faneuil Hall to find the best fish and they walked the short distance to Long Wharf, she would see the tiny figures of men up in the sails, securing rigging or trying to patch holes in the fabric. She often wondered if Quentin was one of the poor lads up there with nothing to catch him should he fall.

"Oh, Julia, I haven't heard from him in a couple of weeks," Louisa answered and her dark eyes widened a little in worry.

Quentin and an overworked uncle were the only family Louisa had in Boston. Julia knew that Louisa's parents had passed on some years before, leaving her and Quentin to essentially make their own way. When Louisa had told her that Quentin had learned how to write to keep track of some of the supply logs on the ships, the evening lessons in Julia's bedroom had commenced. She wanted to help Louisa in any way she could and figured if Louisa knew how to write to Quentin that would give her friend some peace of mind.

"Well, that's why we must keep practicing your letters in the evenings when I return. That way, you can begin writing back to Quentin. And I need you to be able to write to me while I am away the next time or I will go mad with boredom." This, at least, got Louisa's mouth to pull up into a small smile.

Julia heard a sudden rap on the front door and knew Fletcher had made his grand entrance when she heard his booming greeting to Eliza shoot up the staircase.

"That would be fine," Louisa murmured. Then, seeming to remember where she was, she gently extricated her hands. "You must be goin' now. I'm sure there is a pile of things for you to do afore you leave."

"I suppose . . ." Julia trailed off. The thought of briefly touring her own home before being whisked off to New York in a rickety stagecoach to help plan a ceremony she was less than thrilled about seemed suddenly very daunting. She would rather stay here, conjugating French verbs with her tutor, Miss Searle, or tidying up the garden with Louisa before the ground froze completely than being forced to be on her best behavior to impress a woman who at their last meeting had slurped her tea.

"Best not to put this off, then. I hope you have a lovely Christmas, my dear." Julia squared her shoulders, turned into the hallway, and made her way down the stairs, knowing that she must take the first step in order to get things over with. Ideally, the trip to New York would pass quickly and she would be back with Eliza and Louisa before the start of the New Year.

A tinkling laugh was the first sound that wafted over to her as Julia opened the parlor door and entered. Eliza sat near the front window, her back to the bustling street on the other side of the paned glass. She was blond, pale, and petite, beautiful in an understated way that snuck up on a person. Her sharp blue eyes lit up when she saw who had entered the room and her kind smile added to her ethereal quality.

"Julia, love, Fletcher has been regaling me with some of his adventures at Harvard," Eliza explained, nodding to the figure in the ornate winged back chair opposite her.

Eliza was her mother's cousin and Julia had stayed with her on and off for as long as she could remember. Since her mother's death, Julia had spent increasingly more time in the Lee home rather than her own just a few miles away. The only time she could recall leaving for an extended period was to travel to New Hampshire for her uncle's funeral that previous spring. It had been awful; her father's family was so stiff and removed that it had made this additional loss even worse. Julia had practically leapt at the chance to return to Boston before her father and brothers, wanting to return to a household where people didn't flinch at the sound of a choked sob. Eliza had seen her through this tragedy as she had seen her through the loss of her mother. With sympathy, understanding, and more than a few tears.

Eliza and her husband Thomas, a quiet, hardworking tradesman, had provided what Julia knew her father wanted for her: security and an environment to flourish in. She could not have been more grateful to them.

"I'm sure he has," Julia replied wryly, coming around and finding her older brother quite content in his own revelry. A cup of coffee in one hand and a copy of the *Boston Courier* newspaper in the other, Fletcher had made himself right at home. "So what wisdom have Harvard's professors imparted on you in your first term, Fletcher? Do you know the difference between a state and a country now?" She feigned interest in her fingernails and could sense the smirk creeping over her brother's face.

"Cheeky, cheeky, little sister. Better to get that out of your system here rather than in New York," Fletcher countered, folding up his paper and pushing himself up to his full height.

"Well, you can expect many more aspersions to your character then," Julia quipped, looking at her brother as if for the first time. He seemed to have grown taller in their time apart, though she knew that couldn't be possible. She wasn't sure if it was his newly acquired knowledge or the prestige associated with attending law school but he seemed more at ease with himself, as if his chest couldn't puff out any more than it already was. Perhaps she was being sentimental but she missed the lanky, determined boy with a mop of dark hair who used to weave between the sand dunes, chasing after her on sticky summer afternoons in Cape Cod.

"I'll prepare myself accordingly," Fletcher said, winking at her. Then, seeming to notice that it was already after noon, he set the paper and cup down on the small table to the side of his chair and gallantly offered her his arm. "Shall we be off, then? I could only get a few days off to see that you make it to New York all in one piece."

"Fletcher," Eliza admonished, her thoughts seeming to turn to scenarios involving impassable roads and the thieves that were surely canvassing them. Julia gave Fletcher a pointed look, motioning for him to make things right. When it came to Julia, Eliza was very protective.

"Oh, we'll be fine, don't you worry, Eliza," Fletcher backtracked, having at least the decency to turn a faint shade of red. "I'll keep our Julia safe. After all, she has a bride to help prepare." Fletcher's face had become unreadable so that Julia had no idea what her brother really thought about their father's upcoming nuptials. Perhaps there was more to Caroline Le Roy than feathered hats and tea slurping, though Julia doubted it.

"I know, Fletcher," Eliza replied, taking Julia from him and enveloping her in a warm hug that reminded her far too much of her mother. "Just please keep her safe. I have big plans for her in the New Year!" Julia gritted her teeth as Eliza released her and Fletcher led her from the parlor, out the front door, and to their waiting carriage. Her love for Eliza was unwavering but her cousin's quest to find Julia a husband had begun early and was evolving at an alarming rate. Eliza's motto when it came to such things was 'it's never too early to start looking.'

Once James, the Websters' stocky stable hand, had hoisted Julia's trunk atop the carriage and he had climbed up into the coachman's box to take up the reigns, the time for dawdling was over. Eliza embraced Julia again silently, rocking her back and forth almost imperceptivity as if she couldn't stand on her own. "Be safe. I'm sure you'll have a wonderful time. And if you don't, don't hesitate in coming back. We'll see each other again before you know it," Eliza whispered in Julia's ear before she released her. Fletcher helped Julia into the carriage's plush interior, closing the door behind them, and the carriage bucked to life a few minutes after they had settled themselves. Julia looked out the carriage's window at Eliza waving at the wrought iron gate and didn't turn back to Fletcher until Eliza faded from view.

* * * *

"Edward, I can't believe how tall you are now! What is Achsah feeding you in Portsmouth?" Julia exclaimed later that evening as the three siblings sat together in the parlor of their own home after supper. Julia was still trying to wrap her brain around how much her younger brother had changed in the three months they had been apart. The top of his fair head now reached Julia's shoulder and his shirt seemed too small for him, the cuffs of his sleeves stretched tight against his wrists.

A faint shade of crimson spread over Edward's cheeks as he murmured something about how their uncle's widow was a stickler for vegetables. Edward had always been introverted; someone was bound to be even in the outspoken Webster family. He and their mother had been particularly close; she had coddled the baby of the family without shame and she was the only one who could coax him out of his shell at the supper table or comfort him when he awoke to terrifying nightmares that frequently brought on asthma attacks. To lose a mother was a terrible thing; to lose her at seven years of age was particularly tragic for a boy who had relied on her so.

He had retreated deeper into himself after her death and Julia wished there was some way to extricate him from his thoughts so that she could help him grieve. The only thing she could think to do was to be brightly cheery whenever she was around him. She was hopeful that their aunt, Achsah, and her daughters provided Edward a nurturing environment while he was away and attended school in New Hampshire.

He had not been forthcoming at supper, answering her and Fletcher's questions in *yes* or *no* responses. Julia still felt awful that she hadn't written to him more often during their time apart. It was just so difficult for all three of them to be together at the same time, especially now that Fletcher was at Harvard. Their father's aspirations and resulting successes first as a lawyer and then as a senator had unfortunately spelled separation for the family, though they had been able to all live under the same roof when their mother was alive even as their father's travels back and forth to Washington increased. Now, it was a miracle if the three of them were able to spend part of the summer together.

As she watched Edward's eyes settle on his hands folded in his lap and stay fixated there, she turned to Fletcher helplessly and only got a shrug of the shoulders in response. Thankfully, Doris came in then and asked if any of them wanted something more to drink. Doris had been their housekeeper longer than Julia had been on this earth and though she had grown slower over the years, she remained the one the family trusted wholeheartedly with their home. Julia often imagined her standing on the other side of closed doors, waiting for the opportune moment to assert herself into potentially volatile situations, much as she was doing right now. She took the glass of cider that Doris offered, thanking her for more than just the beverage; she might have saved Fletcher from Julia administering a swift knock to his arm.

They sat in silence for a time after Doris hobbled off to the kitchen until Edward softly said he was tired and headed upstairs to his room. Fletcher massaged his forehead and sipped his scotch, looking defeated. Agitated, Julia rose from her chair and paced back and forth in front of the fireplace.

"He's worse than he was in August," Fletcher's voice carried across the room, giving voice to Julia's thoughts. The three of them had accompanied their father down to Washington for a brief week-long stay before returning up north so that Fletcher could begin his studies. Edward had been quiet and slightly aloof then but at least he had talked to them. "Why didn't Achsah write to me?"

"She doesn't know him like we do," Julia replied, crossing her arms over her chest. She didn't fully understand why she was defending Achsah. "She probably just thought he didn't want to talk. She knows he's never been an open book. Edward has always kept to himself but at least he still did things that made him happy. He just seems so distant now."

"Unreachable is more like it," Fletcher sighed, downing the remainder of the contents of his glass. It always made Julia uneasy when Fletcher was this serious. He was normally boisterous and wise-cracking and Julia knew that something was surely amiss when he failed to be either. She could tell he was truly worried about Edward and this only increased her sense of anxiety.

"Do you think I should convince him to come with me? Maybe being around Papa would make him feel more at ease," Julia said, biting her lip. She knew it was a weak suggestion, especially considering she would be attending to the arrangements of their father's marriage to another woman. The incredulous look Fletcher gave her only confirmed how detrimental that trip could be to their brother's well-being. "I know, I know. That would do more harm than good," she said hurriedly before Fletcher could say something that would make her further regret that suggestion.

"I think we should send Edward to stay with Eliza until he returns to school," Fletcher said decidedly, the firelight flashing across his features. "It will do him no good being cooped up in this house where our mother's memory is strongest. And Eliza is so caring and thoughtful she will make sure he has a proper Christmas. Fletcher stretched out his legs, bringing his feet closer to the warmth of the fire and Julia felt relief that at least one of them was thinking logically.

"Should I write to her before we leave tomorrow afternoon?" Julia asked, taking a break from pacing and sitting in the plush chair beside her brother. He nodded, rolling the empty tumbler absentmindedly between his palms. The two siblings sat in silence for some time, both lost in their own thoughts, and Julia recalled how festive the house had been when they were young and a proper family.

Fletcher eventually left the room without so much as a 'good night' and Julia could hear the creaking of the staircase as he went up to bed. The fire was now almost out, the cold beginning to seep through the exterior's cracks and causing a shiver to dance up her spine. She dutifully rose and went to the pantry where Doris kept her post, letting her know that she was going upstairs. Once in her room, Julia leaned against the closed door taking in the strangely foreign space with tired eyes. And then the tears she had been smothering all day overflowed with a vengeance, racking her body in silent sobs.

CHAPTER 2

After a breakfast of eggs, sausage, and stilted conversation the next morning, Fletcher left to visit their father's law office. Julia sat across from Edward as Doris cleared the plates and pitcher of milk, trying desperately to think of a way to help her younger brother. She and Fletcher were leaving that afternoon to begin the journey to New York and she couldn't leave knowing Edward was this distant from them.

"Would you like to go for a walk?" Julia asked tentatively, trying to keep the worry out of her voice as Edward made to get up from the table. His shrug inspired little enthusiasm and Julia hurried to fetch her cloak and Edward's coat before he escaped to his room. As they came out the rear door through the pantry, Julia noticed the cold sting that had crept into the air, a promise of the season's first snowfall in the darkening clouds overhead. They picked their way across the back lawn and she glanced over at Edward and found his face equally stormy, a profound sadness stirring in his gray eyes.

"Please, Eddy," she pleaded, stopping just outside the bare garden's periphery, reaching out her gloved hands to clasp his smaller ones. Julia hadn't called him Eddy since he was a little boy and snippets of childhood memories came back to her in a flash: snuggling up against him on the window seat to pore over a picture book, spinning him around in tight circles in the parlor until they collapsed in a dizzy, giggling heap, begging him to chase her in the yard to prove how fast she was. "You can always tell me what's wrong, you know that."

Edward wouldn't meet her gaze, his head cocked to the side as if he were enamored with the fog softened edges of the city below them. She noticed how he was losing the pudginess of youth in his profile; his cheeks seemed more angular, the set of his shoulders firmer. When he finally did look back at her, she found tears streaking silently down those cheeks and immediately pulled him into her arms, trying unsuccessfully to sooth him as he sobbed. *He's only nine and he's already been through so much,* Julia thought, rubbing his back.

"I . . . I . . ." Edward wheezed, trying to catch his breath in the cold air. Julia wordlessly hurried him back inside and into the kitchen. Doris must have been looking out the pantry window as Julia and Edward were heading back to the house as she was there almost immediately, pressing a cool cloth against Edward's reddened face as Julia worked to get his coat off and sit him down in one of the kitchen chairs against the far wall. *Mama would've known what to do,* Julia fretted as Edward continued to wheeze.

After a few moments, Edward finally began to breathe evenly, exhausted by his sudden outburst of emotion. Julia, now overheated from both exertion and the warmth radiating from the still cooling stove pipe, sank down next to him and unbuttoned the clasp of her cloak. She watched as her little brother hung his head in shame. Doris quietly exited the kitchen, nimbly averting the large hutch that jutted out a bit into the doorway that led to the rest of the house.

"I'm starting to forget what she looked like," he whispered and Julia's heart lurched, knowing this must be his deepest secret. He thought she and Fletcher would be appalled that he couldn't manage to remember their mother. "What if it keeps getting worse? What if by next year or the next I forget everything about her?"

"Oh, Eddy, that'll never happen," Julia insisted, wrapping her arm around Edward's hunched shoulders, pulling him closer to her side. "Sometimes I forget the way she wore her hair or how much lemon she took in her tea. But I'll always remember how her face would light up in the morning when she saw us or how we could make her laugh at our silly jokes. Will you ever forget how much she loved us?"

Edward shook his head bravely, clearly wanting to take solace in her words.

"Then you'll never forget her," Julia concluded firmly, hoping she could come to believe her own reassurances. The thought of never seeing their mother again frightened her too and she knew what a terrifying feeling it was to strain to remember the shade of her favorite violet dress that was woefully out of season or the beginning notes of her much-loved tune on the piano.

Later, as she hugged Edward before he stepped up into the carriage that would drop him off with Eliza, Julia looked over his tousled head at Fletcher who wouldn't meet her eyes. She hoped that she had eased Edward's fears and hated the role she had been thrust into as an unwilling conspirator in the re-shaping of their family.

* * * *

"I thought I wouldn't be seeing you again for weeks," Eliza exclaimed when the carriage door opened and three tired Websters spilled out onto the side of the busy lane. She enveloped Edward in a tight embrace as Julia leaned into her as well, her forehead plastered against Eliza's. Only Fletcher stood apart from the little conclave, clearing his throat and bouncing uncomfortably in his leather traveling boots.

"Please let us know if anything comes up," he said to Eliza when Julia broke away after a few moments.

"Of course I will, Fletcher," Eliza returned. Then, turning back to Edward, she said, "I've already told Peter to make that turkey and potato chowder you like. Let's go in, get warm, and eat every last bit of it." This elicited a small grin from Edward and Julia felt some of the weight lift from her shoulders.

"See, you're in good hands, Ed," Fletcher said a little gruffly, patting his brother's shoulder in what was supposed to be a reassuring gesture. Fletcher and Julia watched as Eliza and Edward climbed the stairs and went into the house and out of the cold.

"Not so comfortable with all of those emotions, eh, Fletch?" Julia turned to her brother, put out that he couldn't squash his sense of pride long enough to give their little brother the affection he desperately needed. Her older brother at least had the decency to look ashamed and couldn't seem to lift his eyes from the sidewalk.

"Julia, I . . . he . . . it kills me just looking at him," Fletcher responded in a low voice. "To think of him losing our mother so young . . ." Julia saw the clench of Fletcher's jaw as he looked up the street and felt guilty for snapping at him. She knew Fletcher didn't wear his emotions on his sleeve as she tended to do; he kept everything bottled up inside. She went to reach for his arm but he turned back toward the carriage. The empty air that her hand did meet before it fell to her side felt oddly colder than it had a moment ago.

"We need to get to the stop on the stagecoach line," Fletcher asserted, calm and collected once more. He opened the carriage door and frowned. "Dammit, I left my gloves at the house." Julia looked down at Fletcher's blotchy red hands and knew how unpleasant their journey to New York would be without something to keep out the cold.

"I'm sure Thomas has an extra pair," Julia said, looking back at the Lee home.

"I'll be right back," Fletcher countered. "You get back in the carriage and out of the wind. I won't be long."

Julia watched him knock on the front door and went to step up into the carriage when her foot snagged on her petticoat. She caught herself on the handle of the door before her face met the cobblestones, her heart leaping into her throat and blood whooshing in her ears as she righted herself again. "Are you alright, Miss Julia?" James came rushing from where he had been tending the horses, a concerned expression on his meaty face.

"Yes James, I'm fine. Thank you," Julia answered, hoping no one else had seen her inelegant cobblestone dive.

"My, my, how graceful you are, Miss Webster," a voice sneered from behind her. Julia's shoulders sagged as she turned reluctantly to see Christine Perry and Laurel Baker standing before the Lee home, each sporting intricately embroidered hooded capes that extenuated their dainty frames. Christine's pretty face was marred by her disdain and Laurel giggled at her friend's entirely uninspired jab while Julia's face turned pink with anger. *Isn't it going to be torture enough worrying about Edward and having to be sweet as pie to Caroline for the next couple of weeks? Now I have to deal with these two!*

Though Christine and Laurel came from the same affluent end of Boston from which Julia hailed, she thought of them as a pair of ducks attempting to pass themselves off as swans. These two were the daughters of up and coming merchants and were entitled beyond belief, using their good looks and pockets of money to claw their way to the top of Boston's young society.

Not that I would want *to take their place,* Julia thought righteously, gritting her teeth as she listened to the cackling of her peers, trying to formulate a far more cutting insult. She was far too emotionally drained to even pretend to take Christine and Laurel seriously.

"Thank you for your concern, ladies," Julia countered mockingly, dipping into a flouncy curtsy. "What foresight you have! I must remember my manners when I make my next trip to Washington to converse with heads of state and you are wedged in Boston with drunken sailors!"

Both girls ceased their tittering and scowled at Julia. At that moment, Fletcher opened the Lees' front gate, placing his hat on his tousled head of hair. Christine's keen eyes immediately snapped to this unanticipated interruption, her full lips curving into a winning smile in an instant. Julia begrudgingly had to give her points for her quick-wittedness when it came to eligible young men.

"Oh and who is this, Julia?" Christine's voice purred, her arm looping through Laurel's. *They probably practice any move they can think of in front of a mirror,* Julia thought, fighting not to roll her eyes.

"Miss Perry, Miss Baker, this is my brother, Fletcher Webster," Julia replied tightly. "Fletcher, this is Christine and Laurel. They live only two streets over from us on the Hill." Julia prayed that her flirtatious brother wouldn't feel compelled to work his magic on Christine for longer than was necessary.

"It is a pleasure to meet you, ladies," Fletcher boomed warmly, causing an uncharacteristic blush to creep over Laurel's cheeks. "Are you friends of Julia's? If so, we must call on you soon." The other girls did not seem to know how to respond to this invitation and Julia could see the warring emotions in the involuntary twitching of Christine's mouth and Laurel's bulging eyes.

"Well I . . . we. . ." Christine faltered, seeming to give Fletcher all the information he had asked for in three choppy syllables. Immediately, his eyes lost that sparkle, though he waited politely for Christine to finally say she didn't think that would be the best idea. He tipped his hat and the other girls curtsied as Julia nearly yanked her brother into their carriage to begin the short journey to the stagecoach stop.

As she waited for Fletcher to settle himself, she watched from the window as the two ducks took up their skirts, turned expertly on their heels, and sauntered in the opposite direction, still arm in arm. "She doesn't stand a chance of finding a husband," Laurel said loudly, glancing momentarily over her shoulder at Julia before snapping her head back into an aristocratic tilt.

I don't even know if I want a husband, Julia thought to herself, sinking back into the plush upholstery and closing her eyes for a moment as the carriage's wheels jolted to life beneath her. *How are they so sure of themselves? How do they know what they want? I certainly haven't figured it out.* That seemed to be the primary difference between her and those flouncing wisps of fancy. Julia was far more concerned about what her father was doing down in Washington than crocheting doilies, dancing waltzes, or painting a pretty scene. She wanted to stay informed regarding issues that would affect more than her affluent neighborhood.

No wonder I don't fit in, she thought glumly. *Oh well, at least I have Eliza and Louisa here. And Miss Searle will be back from visiting her family when I return after Christmas. It will be so nice to be with Fletcher for a couple of days, if I don't kill him first.*

"That was a rather short meeting. The rate I was going, I could have arranged myself a very profitable marriage," Fletcher teased as he straightened his waistcoat, causing Julia's eyes to snap open.

"Trust me, you're better off. It's far better for your health if you don't pay either one of them any mind," Julia shot back, pinching the bridge of her nose between her fingers, feeling a headache coming on.

"Ah well, at least we had a momentary distraction," Fletcher shrugged with a cock-eyed grin, making Julia's irritation ebb away slightly. Edward was taken care of for the moment and while Fletcher may have had his faults, he also had the uncanny ability to put Julia in a better mood no matter the circumstances. And she was going to need a touch of Fletcher's bravado if she was going to make it through their father's impending nuptials.

CHAPTER 3

The dress, high-waisted and in a deep evergreen hue, pushed the bottom edge of the corset into Julia's hips and she had to struggle to keep still as she stood in front of the unfamiliar faces of Caroline's family in the hotel's banquet hall. It was hard to believe it had been two weeks since she had arrived on the front veranda of the Eastern Hotel, Fletcher struggling with her trunk and cursing the cold as she had pulled on the brass handle of the large timber and glass door, dreading for the first time in her life a reunion with her father.

Her stay so far hadn't been a complete travesty. The harbor, with its rows of docked ships of varying sizes, was quickly being taken over by a crystalline sheet of new ice and was stunning to behold. She had of course been to New York before but never for more than a couple of days at a time. The constant hustle and bustle proved to be invigorating and she was looking forward to traveling to the theatre district in a few short days. Until then, she was content to read in the hotel's front window seat in the lazy afternoons, her entertainment the passersby who seemed to forget the hotel's patrons could see everything they were doing outside. At the rate she was going, she could finish her second Jane Austen novel before Christmas. She had even gotten to spend two evenings alone with her father since he had come up from Washington a week after she had arrived.

Not surprisingly, though, the actual planning of the ceremony had gone just as she had expected. Caroline, however polite, was meticulous and very much in tune with the latest trends, which was the reason why Julia's ill-fitting dress was such a problem now. The corset was tighter than usual due to Caroline's insistence that Julia look the part of a fashionable coquette. Julia had also witnessed more than one heated argument between Caroline and her sister over flowers and meal choices and had barely made it through the great wine or champagne debate. She had just sat back much of the time and watched the two sisters bicker as her head spun, becoming increasingly thankful that she had only brothers to contend with.

Perhaps the fact that exasperated her the most was that the daily recurrence of hurt feelings and sulky expressions had all been over a ceremony that only eight people were attending. She told herself that this was probably Caroline's only opportunity to shine, that at her age she had been fortunate Papa had rescued her from the lonely life of spinsterhood. Yet, even now as she stood in front of the huge bay window waiting for the bride to enter, Julia was still fighting to keep her eyes from rolling heavenward. *Mama never would have been this ostentatious. What can Papa be thinking, marrying a woman so different from her?*

With these thoughts, she glanced at her father standing like a statue by her side and tried to guess what was going through his mind. He had wanted to hear all about how everything was going with Eliza, what she was learning from Miss Searle, did she still like those peppermint candies from the market. However, when she had asked him about anything to do with Caroline, he had become elusive and changed the subject. It seemed to her that Papa wore the stoic expression of one attending a funeral rather than someone embarking on a joyous union with someone he loved.

What do I know? Julia thought as Caroline swept into the parlor, clearly in her glory, cheeks rosy with excitement. She forced a smile as the Reverend began the ceremony and Papa finally came to life, reaching out his hand to squeeze Caroline's. I *thought he would've waited longer.*

*　　　*　　　*　　　*

She entered the hushed room quietly, easing the door shut behind her. There was really no need for secrecy; this was her father's room at the hotel, after all, and she wasn't sure why her heart seemed to be trying to beat its way out of her chest. Perhaps it was because her motives weren't entirely pure and she was under a time constraint of sorts. Papa and Caroline would be returning in about an hour or so that the three of them could go to the theatre several blocks north of the hotel for an early Christmas celebration. All she wanted was a peek into her father's world, of a domain far removed from silk dresses and china place settings.

Taking a calming breath, Julia turned to face the room, which was considerably larger than her own just across the narrow hall. *Well, it is meant for two*, Julia reasoned as she crossed the hardwood floor to the tilted desk wedged in the far corner facing the expansive bed. She began to sift through the newspaper clippings, letters from concerned constituents, and notes on proposed legislation as quickly as she dared, careful to put everything back in its proper place. After years of performing this familiar dance, she knew how to cover her tracks expertly.

Her curiosity over what her father did while he was away had begun long before he was elected to the Senate. When he would leave for long days at his law practice or to argue cases in the courtroom, Julia would sneak into his upstairs study at home, curl up in his plush chair that stood before the window that overlooked the back garden, and attempt to read the books that lined the shelves. Almost all of them revolved around the debate between states' rights and a strong central government or the intricacies of constitutional law or countless other subjects that she couldn't begin to understand at that age. She had even touched and skimmed an essay written by Alexander Hamilton on the importance of a centralized, federal bank, though she hadn't realized its importance until her father had gone off on a Hamilton centered tangent one night at supper.

What she did know was how much she loved the feel of the yellowed pages beneath her fingertips and the copious notes her father had scrawled in the margins had made her feel strangely closer to him. As she had gotten older and understood more of what her father did, she had graduated from solely books to journals and correspondence her father had seemed to care little for. She knew he kept the most significant material at his law firm. Now it was stored in his chambers in Washington.

She had never lingered too long in that room, either. Her fear had been that if someone discovered her there, the doors would be bolted the next time she attempted a venture inside. There had been a number of occurrences when the doors would not budge, her heart had leapt into her throat, and she was convinced she would be on the receiving end of a stern lecture regarding one's privacy at the supper table. Fortunately, these lectures had never come and she grew to know that if she was patient and could steal herself for a few days, the wealth of information that was beyond those doors would be at her disposal again.

Of course, the opportunities were now few and far between to gain such insight into just what her father did down in the capital for months on end. This was why she was here now, rifling through pages of her father's loopy script. She was looking for some cause to believe in, anything that she could converse with her father about, yet couldn't begin to imagine what that could be. All she could decipher from her father's notes now were concerns about tariffs which made her head spin and many choice words directed toward President Jackson which accompanied several crude caricatures of the man.

Giving a small huff of frustration, Julia was just about to abandon her mission and ready herself for an evening out when her eyes locked onto a folded page with a black, wide *W* carefully penned on its envelope. The letter was haphazardly thrown off to the far corner of the desk closest to the window. She picked it up tentatively and found another below it, written in a much more refined hand than even her father's.

A spark of recognition ignited in her and Julia suddenly remembered where she had seen the first letter before. She, Fletcher, and Edward had gone down to Washington that past August to visit their father for a week before Fletcher was set to begin at Harvard. They had accompanied him the last evening of their stay to a gathering of a spattering of senators and their families in a chamber of the Capitol building. Julia remembered being taken by the portraits of the founding fathers, particularly the one of President Washington in his stately general's uniform, in the circuitous, high ceilinged room. The voices around her had bounced off the marble floor, echoing above her in a strangely comforting din of good-natured debate.

She had gone back to her father just as he was finishing up a conversation with a man he had introduced as Mr. Bedford Brown, the senator from North Carolina. Her father had seemed slightly agitated when Mr. Brown bowed to her and soon took his leave after an awkward silence; she remembered her father slipping this letter into his waistcoat pocket. The *W* was unmistakable. Her eyes widened now as she opened and finally read it. A well of indignation grew as she perused the second piece of parchment. She was reminded of another encounter when she was much younger, with a man whose melodic voice and assertiveness for the plight of his people had captured her utmost attention. Carefully slipping both letters into the pocket of her dress, she scurried out the door, across the hall, and into her room, the threat of bile beginning to rise in her throat.

Quickly sitting on the edge of the bed, she tilted her head upward and closed her eyes, willing her stomach to settle. Once she felt steady enough on her feet, she walked gingerly over to the washbasin and splashed the refreshingly cool water on her hot cheeks. She was just patting her face dry with a thick cloth when there was an abrupt knock on her door and, without so much as a courteous pause, Caroline came sailing in. She gave Julia a cursory once-over and, seeing that she was still wearing the dress she had on at breakfast, let out a marked sigh and came to rest before the wardrobe.

"Julia," Caroline said, clearly exasperated. She began to thumb through her new stepdaughter's attire impatiently, searching for something suitable. "Why aren't you ready? We can't be late and you've had the better part of the afternoon to yourself!"

Caroline turned, the frock Julia had donned at the wedding in her hand and only seemed to notice then that the younger woman was in some distress. Concern flickered in her eyes and she set the dress carefully on the bed, taking a step closer to Julia.

"You don't look well, my dear. Is something the matter?" Caroline made to take Julia's hand but she pulled away abruptly, facing her reflection in the washbasin rather than accept concern from a near stranger. Julia took another deep breath and faced Caroline once more, managing to pull her mouth up into a small smile.

"I'm sorry, Caroline. I fell asleep by the fire downstairs and woke up overheated. I just came back up to my room a few minutes ago," Julia answered, the lies tumbling out of her mouth without a second thought. "You're right, I should've been ready before you returned. I'll get changed right away."

"Well, I appreciate the apology. Just don't be so careless next time. And don't ruin your hair when you get your dress on." Caroline eyed Julia with an air of suspicion for a moment then gave a small shrug of her shoulders and left her alone again. Julia undressed and changed with surprising ease, her hands barely shaking as she buttoned the back of her fancier dress with the aid of the looking glass. It was only after she had bundled herself up in the foyer of the hotel and was snug in the corner of the carriage beside her father that she shuddered a bit over how easy it had been to be so deceitful.

* * * *

The lobby of the Park Theatre was rich with color and light, the gilded mirrors lining the walls reflecting the patrons in their fine clothes. They boisterously greeted one another about the enormous tree stationed in the center of the expanse of gold and burgundy carpet. Hundreds of tiny candles sat in brass holders on the tree's countless boughs, the flickering flames reflected in the mirrors. Julia had been to her fair share of theatre productions in the past but there was something exhilarating about attending a play with Christmas so close at hand. The festive scene almost made her forget about the discoveries of the day. Almost.

She followed her father and Caroline through the throng of people in the atrium and began to ascend the sweeping staircase, her hand skating over the gold plated railing. They alighted on the second level where the crowd was not as thick and began to make their way to the private box on the third level that her father had reserved. It was only then that Caroline gave a tut of dismay.

"My dear, I think I left my opera glasses in the carriage," Caroline said to Julia's father, her brows knitted in consternation. "I know they sell them downstairs. Do you have any money for a new pair? It would be a shame to miss anything on stage." Her father patted his cream-colored vest until he found the notes tucked neatly in his breast pocket and handed them to his new wife without question.

"Would you like a pair, Julia? It is simply the best way to enjoy the experience," Caroline offered, turning to Julia with a welcoming smile tugging at her lips. Julia eyed Caroline a little warily, put out that already she was asking of things so freely from her father. It seemed that forgotten opera glasses weren't of much importance or worth the money they were charged for in the lobby.

"No thank you, Caroline. Unlike you, I have young eyes," Julia replied, her voice crisp. She could feel her father's gaze boring into the side of her face but refused to look at him as Caroline murmured something incoherent and turned to go back down the staircase.

"That wasn't very polite, Julia," her father admonished when they were alone together, stepping in front of his daughter so that she was forced to acknowledge him. "I would expect you to show Caroline the same respect you would show me. She is a big part of your life now."

"And whose decision was that, Papa?" Julia countered, her frustration and slightly frayed nerves making her bold. "You never asked me if I was fine with you marrying someone who would spend all of your money at the drop of a hat!" Julia felt a stirring of guilt at her harsh words. She knew her frustration wasn't about the money or the opera glasses. It was the fact that her mother had done the same thing more times than she could count, that Caroline was trying to fill a hole in her father's life that Julia selfishly wished would remain open.

"Julia, if you were upset with my marrying Caroline, you should have spoken up before I did so," her father growled, his voice going down a threatening octave. Julia was well aware of her father's legendary temper and she knew she was venturing into dangerous waters. Now that she had begun, though, she couldn't seem to quell the urge to make her true feelings known. She only wished she wasn't boiling over in such a public place; though they weren't shouting obscenities at one another, passersby were beginning to look at them with quizzical expressions.

"You wouldn't have listened, anyway." Julia averted her eyes, letting the words fall between them, the threat of tears suddenly scratching at her throat. *This night was supposed to take me away from my problems, if only for a little while,* she thought, sensing her father taking a step closer to her. *Now I've only gotten myself into more trouble.*

"Julia-" her father's exasperated voice was interrupted by a booming male one in close proximity to them. Julia looked up just in time to see a large hand clap her father on the shoulder, causing him to buck forward slightly. She put out her arms to steady her father and tried to place the cause of this new hubbub.

The younger man her father was now turning to and glaring at didn't seem to notice he had done anything amiss. Dressed just as finely as her father, though the burgundy cravat around his neck was a little askew and his dark hair ruffled, he held out his hand invitingly. After a moment, her father shook it rather reluctantly. Even from behind her father, Julia could detect the powerful scent of whiskey on the newcomer's breath.

"Webster as I live and breathe! What brings ya to New York?" The man's voice was slurred and, with a thick Southern drawl, he succeeded in butchering the city's name.

"Enjoying the city's pleasures. Though I think you're enjoying many more pleasures than I am, Henry," her father countered, his voice taking on a chilly air. Henry guffawed loudly at her father's observation, attracting even more attention than the Websters had garnered on their own. Julia stepped out from behind her father cautiously, wanting to get a proper look at her rescuer; he might have been lacking in decorum but at least he had saved her from a full-blown argument with her father.

"Yer right there, Webster. An' who's this?" Henry had just seemed to realize that Julia's father wasn't alone. He also appeared to be thrown off by her presence, his brows knit as he tried to formulate a theory. Julia could almost see the wheels of his mind turning and she realized with a sudden sickening feeling that Henry must think she was Caroline. Her father seemed to come to the same conclusion almost simultaneously and his eyes widened as he hastily informed Henry that Julia was his daughter. He then introduced Julia to the President's recently appointed Secretary of War, John Henry Eaton.

"My wife, Caroline, should be joining us soon, as well," her father added for good measure. The tension had disappeared between father and daughter for the time being as her father's eyes flitted toward the staircase, distracted by the wholly unwelcome prospect of exchanging pleasantries with Henry.

"Of course. Happy to meet ya, dear." A light went on in Henry's eyes and his smile broadened as he took Julia's gloved hand with surprising dexterity for someone so inebriated and kissed it. She saw the clench of her father's jaw tighten out of the corner of her eye. Julia was slightly taken aback by Henry's forwardness but after he released her hand, she gave a small curtsy; this man was certainly like no one she'd ever met.

Henry suddenly seemed to remember something and wheeled around unsteadily, his eyes skimming the crowd. "Peggy? Peggy! Ah, there ya are, love," he shouted. Julia heard her father give a marked sigh as he reached into his pocket for his watch. The message he was attempting to send to the oblivious Henry was ringing loud and clear to Julia: *How could you possibly waste any more of my time?*

A beautiful woman with incredibly red lips and a pile of golden curls atop her head sporting a deep violet gown with an uncommonly low-cut, lace trimmed bodice materialized out of the crowd. Seeming to float across the carpet, Peggy Eaton came to a rest beside her husband, wrapping her arm around his back. She was followed closely by a man even younger than Henry with unruly, auburn hair and striking blue eyes. Julia could feel her cheeks flame with the arrival of Henry's family and suddenly wished she had paid closer attention to her hair, two of her dark curls looping rebelliously in her peripheral vision.

"Peggy and Matthew, you remember ol' Dan Webster. This is 'is daughter," Henry turned to Julia, introducing his wife and nephew, Matthew. She bobbed her head respectfully and after this, she was all but forgotten as her father became unexpectedly warm, asking Matthew all sorts of questions about his time clerking in the law practice. *Her father's* law practice. As the volley back and forth continued, Julia's eyes darted between the two men, intrigued by this unforeseen turn of events. So her father, who believed himself to be far above Henry Eaton, was proving himself to be quite jovial around the aforementioned man's nephew.

Caroline's re-appearance and cool response to the Eatons' presence did little to quell her father's newly acquired enthusiasm and before the two families parted shortly after, he had issued an invitation for all three of them to dinner at the hotel after Christmas the following week which Henry accepted. As she turned to glance at the Eatons once more before mounting the stairs to find their seats, Julia found Matthew's inquisitive eyes locked on hers and she pulled an abrupt about-face, embarrassed. Had he been wearing glasses this entire time? They suited him.

This day just keeps getting more complicated, she thought as she took her seat at the far end of the velvet-lined theatre box beside Caroline, her thoughts flitting briefly to the purloined letters taking up residence in her hotel room.

"I don't think dinner next week is such a good idea," Caroline huffed at Julia's father once she was sure the door to their cozy little alcove was shut tight, bringing Julia back to the present. "You do know who Peggy Eaton is, don't you, dear? I shouldn't be socializing with her if you expect me to make any meaningful connections. She's a harlot who married Henry before her first husband was cold in his grave!" Caroline blanched when she saw the look of utter horror that must have passed across Julia's face and pursed her lips, making the correct decision in not casting further aspersions on Mrs. Eaton's virtue.

Julia averted her eyes, hopelessly mortified. Never had she heard her mother or Eliza talk of another woman in that way, at least not when she had been with them, and to think about what Caroline was insinuating and the discussions which went along with it made her squirm a little. She knew she had led a sheltered life and though she wished that could continue in circumstances like this, she also knew this ignorance was all but impossible. After all, Caroline had just proven herself to be less delicate about private matters than Julia was accustomed to and she doubted her stepmother would censor herself as their relationship evolved.

"I'm sorry, Julia. That was not appropriate for me to say," Caroline apologized reluctantly, clearly feeling her argument for not dining with the Eatons was justified. Julia nodded her thanks mutely as her father gave an uncomfortable cough, whispering to Caroline they would discuss this further in private.

"Yes, quite right, my dear. These things need to be discussed in the proper time and place," her father said, giving his daughter a look of sympathy. As the lamps were dimmed and the curtain parted on stage, Julia's father continued to speak in hushed tones. Julia was grateful for the semi-darkness as she leaned in toward Caroline to catch what her father was saying. "Eaton may be a drunken, unrefined fool but his nephew is showing great promise. I would like to talk with him about how things at the firm are proceeding. Of course, I trust Kinsman but it's always good to have a second set of eyes on things. The young man has the potential to be a very accomplished lawyer."

Henry Kinsman was the dedicated, if exceedingly boring, man Julia's father had instated to run his Boston law practice. Julia had only seen him once when she had met her father for lunch the prior summer and could barely remember what he looked like, though she did recall that he got exceedingly red in the face when discussing property rights. She only hoped Mr. Kinsman was expounding on parcels of land instead of the scores of individuals being carted in through the ports down south.

Caroline looked pointedly at her husband and then, clearly bored with the direction of the conversation, turned her attention to the stage. Her recently purchased opera glasses were already glued to her face. As Shakespeare's *Twelfth Night* began to whirl in front of her, Julia sat back in the plush, royal blue chair feeling as though she were spinning uncontrollably herself.

It was all she could do not to jump from her seat, find the nearest carriage in the street outside, and hightail it back to Boston. To Eliza and Louisa and the uncomplicated albeit uninteresting life she had made for herself there. She had wanted to be a part of her father's world for so long and now here she was, with an unsettling pair of letters in her possession and an imminent dinner planned with one of the President's cabinet members. *I suppose I should've been careful what I wished for*, she mused as the Bard's poetic words floated up to her ears.

CHAPTER 4

The next afternoon, Julia perched on the edge of her bed in the hotel, pouring over the letters she had discovered some twenty-four hours before. She knew this was risky with her father taking a much needed nap across the hall while Caroline was out shopping with her mother but she couldn't seem to pull herself away. This was the first time she had been able to have a moment to herself since the night before when she had thrust the pages into the depths of her bed side table upon the family's return from the theatre.

Even without the dates to mark when these had been received, Julia could tell that they had been forgotten for some time, most likely tossed about her father's quarters in Washington and now flung into hidden recesses in New York. The corners of the pages curled slightly inward and were beginning to yellow, the ink smudged at the creases. She read each over again, growing more anxious with each perusal, her mind frantically trying to formulate some plan of action:

Mr. Brown,

I'm a cotton farmer from near Wilmington, but I hear bits of what goes on in Washington. I hear that my hero, Andrew Jackson, is makin' good on his promise to get them cherry niggers off our land. I'm writin' to make sure you sign on. Them bow benders have taken our land for too long. I need to support my youngins and teach 'em how to farm. I can't do that with so many of 'em runnin' around like they own the place. Those heathens are goin' to git us yet. They've already taken my only three niggers and now my niggers is workin' for them! I want 'em off of my property and thrown some place where they won't hurt nobody else. I can sleep at night knowin' those cherry niggers won't bother me and my family no more.

Joe Picket (as told to Mr. Smith, Esq.)

Julia continued to stare at the letter in utter disbelief; the fourth time reading it only fueled her anger and sense of injustice. The words the farmer had spoken and made sure to have written down made her think of what she, Eliza, and Louisa had witnessed that past summer near Boston Common, the public park where they took many strolls together. Julia remembered the hot sun burning her cheeks, the sweat trickling down her neck and continuing its unwanted path down her back. Eliza had been worrying over a luncheon she was hosting the next week and Louisa had momentarily fallen behind them, the street being too narrow for all three to walk abreast of each other.

A commotion had materialized when two men, swaying and disheveled, suddenly seized a black carriage driver and began shouting he was an escaped slave; the carriage sat in front of a nearby tailor's shop across the street. The proprietor of the shop had rushed out along with the irate carriage owner seconds later but not before the black man had been punched in the nose, the horses whinnying and the utterance of that filthy word unleashed into the humid air. Eliza had immediately grabbed both Julia's and Louisa's arms, turning them all back toward home. Julia had heard Louisa's sharp intake of breath and felt the fear radiating off of her, as searing as the sun above them.

Julia still fretted over whether that could happen to Louisa; angry men with vitriolic words grabbing her friend as she stepped out the front door, claiming she was their property when she wasn't. The bloodied face of the carriage driver swam in front of her eyes now until it morphed into Louisa's face, her mouth gaping in a cry for help. She imagined that was akin to what the Indians must feel, the paralyzing fear that their daily life could be violently interrupted and changed forever in an instant. Julia grasped the other correspondence with its much more refined script, trying to determine how difficult it would be to contact this Kerry fellow:

Honorable Senator Webster,

We are writing to inform you of a terrible grievance being perpetrated within our southern territories. As you may know, President Jackson has been quite hostile toward our Indian brethren in the past but we have gotten word that a new piece of legislation he is rumored to be introducing before Congress will dwarf any other action he has taken against the Indians. We are speaking of the removal of five Indian nations, the Cherokee, Creek, Choctaw, Chickasaw, and Seminole tribes, from the lands they have inhabited prior even to the formation of our nation. With all our strength, we urge you not to support this legislation and work to ensure that it does not pass in the Senate.

Several members of our organization have lived alongside a tribe of Cherokee Indians for many years. We assure you that they mean no harm and present no threat to the President's evident desire for expansion. In the time that these members have known this tribe, they have come to appreciate the Cherokees' commitment to non-violence, their attempts to adopt large-scale farming, and the employment of methods of our educational system. Our missionaries are also struck by their additional attempts to honor the treaties they have already signed with the government (many have informed our group that they agreed to these treaties to keep the land they rightfully deserve and soften the blow of the hate they encounter on a daily basis) in addition to their innate respect for nature.

For these reasons, in addition to the passion we have for the rights of all Indians, we implore you not to support the President on this matter and to ensure other senators do not support this measure, either.

Humbly Yours,
Nathaniel Kerry
The American Board of Commissioners of Foreign Missions
Missions among Peoples of Primitive Cultures

Julia's frustration was only exacerbated by the fact that she was missing the envelope for this letter and therefore a means to easily contact this man. He seemed very involved with the Indian cause and would certainly be her best place to start in learning about what could be done to prevent this. She wondered if there was any way to wheedle the information out of her father without him getting suspicious about her sudden interest in missionary work. *I can't see that working out too well,* Julia frustratingly reasoned. She knew that though her father had spent increasingly less time with her as she grew older, he wasn't the type that could have the wool pulled over his eyes and would not be inclined to help her at all if she was not honest with him.

I have to tell him what I've done, Julia concluded fearfully, her stomach twisting in anxious knots at the prospect. Her father and Caroline had apparently forgiven, or at least forgotten, her biting words from the previous night as no punishment had been carried out regarding them. The prudent course of action would be to keep her mouth shut, return the letters to their rightful place, and try to forget her discovery. Trouble was she was feeling particularly rebellious as of late; she knew she couldn't forget this discovery even if she wanted to. She had found a way to carry on the work her mother had begun and if confessing her indiscretion to her father brought her one step closer to learning more about the Indian cause, then she was willing to put herself in his crosshairs.

Trying unsuccessfully to quell the turbulence inside, Julia squared her shoulders, grabbed the incriminating letters, and turned purposefully toward the door before she thought better of it. Out in the hallway, she knocked on the door to her father's room and after several minutes heard a gruff 'Come in'. She eased into the room, finding her father still in bed, the covers pulled up over the clothes he had been wearing that morning. The exasperated expression he wore vanished when he saw that it was only Julia and he disentangled himself from the sheets, bringing his bare feet down to the cold hard wood floor.

"Will you bring me my slippers, please?" he asked Julia, watching as his toes involuntarily curled in. She obediently went over to the dressing area and retrieving the slippers. The letters remained tucked between her arm and upper body as she turned to her father with a sympathetic smile.

"They really need to put rugs by the beds," Julia said as she helped her father slip the comfortable footwear on his heavily veined feet. No matter how much she disagreed with him at times, it was frightening to see him aging before her eyes at such an alarming rate. Dark circles stained the sunken skin underneath his eyes and his jet black hair was beginning to gray at his temples. He seemed to grow more haggard each time she saw him and it alarmed her now how his untucked shirt billowed around his shrinking belly. "Would you like me to call for some hot tea?"

Her father waved off her inquiry, stooping down to massage his feet as Julia sat beside him on the bed, her heart thumping. When he straightened himself back up, Julia set the letters in his empty hands, her own fingers trembling a bit.

"I'm sorry, Papa," she said quickly as she felt her face flush all the way up to the roots of her hair. "I shouldn't have been snooping around in your things. I just . . . I just thought this was important. I know I should've told you about this last night."

As her father's eyes skimmed over the pages, Julia kept her head down, waiting for the inevitable storm that she knew would break in the next few moments. To her surprise, however, her father merely scoffed, throwing the letters back into her lap.

"Is this what you couldn't tear yourself away from?" he asked incredulously, looking at his daughter with surprise. "I was afraid you'd found something more meaningful."

"You don't think this is important, Papa?" Julia gasped, taken aback by her father's ambivalence. "These people are obviously suffering; doesn't that mean anything to you?"

"Of course it does," her father said defensively. "But what can I do? I don't represent the people who this will impact and too many other important senators are going to support Mr. Jackson. If you think about it honestly, this would be good for the country, too. Imagine how much more we could expand!"

"But if this proposal passes, it would mean that these tribes wouldn't have homes anymore, wouldn't it?" Julia pressed, trying to make her father understand the backwardness of his reasoning. It just didn't seem right to displace mass amounts of people for the sake of expansion and she just couldn't bring herself to see where her father was coming from. "And you've never been concerned about a challenge. Mama always told me that you could argue your way out of anything and convince people that you were in the right."

"They would get land in the west, more land than they have now," her father reasoned. "I have enough on my plate already, Julia. I don't need the added headache of going against Jackson on another issue. He's completely convinced that this proposal will pass."

Julia felt her shoulders sag at her father's pessimistic view of the situation at hand. She hadn't thought her predicament could get any worse yet her father had just proven her wrong. It was clear that he had already washed his hands of the cause, believed that the battle against this legislation was a waste of his time and talent. If she was going to learn more about the Indians and take action to stop this bill, she was going to be doing it on her own. The task was daunting and she doubted any efforts she put forth would make much of a difference but she needed to try.

"Well, do you at least know how I can contact this Mr. Kerry?" she asked quietly. A fire had been ignited inside her and she knew if she did nothing, it would consume her. Her father had made a career of arguing his stance on his passion projects; he would just have to accept that this was going to be hers.

"Julia, this is not your place nor your fight," her father answered, shaking his head slightly. "You have no idea how these missionaries come after me with these ridiculous causes that stand no chance of gaining any backing. And you don't know how dangerous these Indians can be. Our ancestors were battling them since before the Revolution. They have a history of siding with whoever will give them the most money or trade. They're opportunistic to the core."

"How can I contact Mr. Kerry?" Julia repeated determinedly, her voice now strong and clear. She was through with being told how to think and what to feel; she was ready to come to her own conclusions about the hundreds if not thousands of people whose futures were being decided for them. "You have always stood up for what you believe in. Why can't I be given the same chance?"

"You've only just learned about this! How can say you want to fight for something you know so little of?" her father rose and stalked over to his desk, pounding his palms against the surface with considerable force. The impact made Julia jump a little but she refused to be intimidated. Her father wanted a perfectly behaved daughter who was content to stay at home and remain oblivious to what was going on in the world. However much she loved and wanted to be accepted by him, she just couldn't sit idly by anymore; she was ready to follow her own beliefs and see where they led her.

"Well then at least give me a chance to learn more, Papa," she answered calmly, rising from the bed and crossing her arms over her chest. Her father turned to look at her and she could see the warring emotions play across his worn face in the dimming light. He finally sighed tiredly and turned back to his papers, rifling through them until he found what he was looking for. Returning to where she resolutely stood, he handed Julia a worn piece of parchment folded into thirds. She opened it cautiously and was greeted by an advertisement for the missionary's cause. Upon closer inspection, her eyes widened when she saw that the group was based in Boston. *How have I never heard of them before?* Sure enough, there was the address on Beacon Street, spelled out in Mr. Kerry's neat handwriting at the bottom of the page.

"This was with the letter I received," her father explained, shifting his weight restlessly from one foot to the other. She looked back up at her father, slightly surprised and suddenly very grateful to him.

"Thank you, Papa," she said over the lump forming in her throat, her eyes traveling again to the faded page that would be her starting point to finding answers.

"I just hope you realize what you're getting yourself into," her father replied softly as the door to the room opened and Caroline came rushing in, laden with packages of various sizes. She stopped short when she saw Julia and her father there together but when one of the boxes slid from the top of her pile and went crashing to the floor, she seemed to forget all else. As her father rushed over to his wife to help her, Julia departed quietly, closing the door behind her as if the encounter with him had been of no importance.

* * * *

Henry's laughter seemed to fill the entire parlor of the hotel as he finished telling the entire table of a boyhood adventure with a run-away turkey which had gone terribly awry in the North Carolina backwoods. As he pulled out his handkerchief to mop his brow, Julia couldn't help smiling herself. Mr. Eaton had proven himself to be an entertaining distraction for the evening, chattering on so much that Julia had an excuse for her silence. She had had much on her mind other than brightly colored bows and boughs of festively decorated spruce.

It had been over a week since she had penned her letter to Nathaniel Kerry and, though she knew it could be some time before she got a response, had not stopped worrying over it. Her father had surprised her by informing her that she was traveling with Caroline and himself to Washington the following week. She was hoping that her return to Boston after the New Year would provide new resources and answers for her. Until then, she was playing a waiting game.

Julia was pulled back into the present by the arrival of their food and as she picked at her trout with little interest, she noticed her father and Matthew conversing quietly while Henry continued to regale his less than captive audience. *What could they be talking about?* Julia thought, taken aback by the twinge of jealousy she felt. Matthew had seemed to have her father's ear from the moment the Eatons had arrived and she couldn't say she was pleased with this development. She knew her father took his law practice very seriously even though he was no longer involved in any of its cases but did he really have to be so chummy with Matthew?

As if he could hear her thoughts, Matthew looked across the table at her with that piercing gaze of his as if challenging her to speak. She averted her eyes quickly, feigning interest in her vegetables as she felt her face catch fire. *Why do I keep doing that? This is so ridiculous!* Julia scolded herself. Waiting a few more minutes before daring to look up again, she felt relief at being utterly ignored once more. Though she wouldn't consider herself outgoing in the presence of near strangers, she could at least converse with them normally. Yet here she was, stuttering and turning red in the face in the presence of an attractive young man like some kind of uncultured dunce.

The remainder of the meal passed by uneventfully and Julia was looking forward to the Eatons' imminent departure when a quartet of musicians filed into the dining space and began to play. Her heart sank as her father took Caroline by the hand and led her toward the expanse of floor before the roaring fireplace. Henry and Peggy joined soon after and before long, half a dozen couples twirled gracefully, their shadows traipsing along the bar on the opposite side of the dining room. Julia sat rigid in her seat, avoiding eye contact and unable to decide on what she should do or say now that she and Matthew were alone at the table, though on opposite sides. *I can't possibly dance with him*, she thought frantically as she heard the scraping of Matthew's chair against the floor and, a moment later, felt his warmth as he seated himself in the recently vacated chair next to hers.

When he didn't make a move to speak, she turned toward him tentatively, finding it difficult to avoid his presence when he was so close to her. The firelight that danced over his unreadable face further added to the air of mystery that he exuded and despite her misgivings, she wanted to know more about him and how he had ended up in Boston.

"So, you . . . you work in the law office, then?" she began lamely when it became clear that Matthew was content to just sit there silently, simultaneously tapping his foot to the music while making her increasingly uncomfortable. He nodded in response, seeming to be caught up in the scene before them. Julia turned back toward the dancers as well, twisting the chain of the locket she wore around her neck absentmindedly. She was beginning to feel uncommonly hot and was about to excuse herself in order to get some fresh, albeit cold, air when Matthew seemed to find his voice.

"He's a good man, your father," Matthew stated, his voice carrying the warm hint of a Southern accent. She turned her face back toward his and was greeted by a small though friendly smile and could feel herself beginning to soften. "We studied his cases from top to bottom at Harvard and I was grateful when I ended up in his office. Where in Boston do you live?" he asked.

"We live in, um, Beacon Hill," Julia answered, her curiosity over Matthew's backstory increasing. She had only just become aware of him two weeks earlier but now she wondered if she had passed him on the street before and hoped she hadn't been doing anything embarrassing if that was the case.

"Ah, the Hill. I've heard that's where only the best families live," Matthew replied without an undercurrent of bitterness. Julia could feel her face becoming the shade of a tomato again but held Matthew's friendly gaze, her heart clip clopping in her chest.

"I see our reputation proceeds us," Julia quipped, enjoying the chance to be carefree if only for the moment. "Only the best homes and parks will do there." That produced his most genuine smile yet, crinkling the corners of his eyes and exposing his slightly crooked teeth. *Am I actually being charming right now?* she wondered, not wanting the jolt of confidence that gave her to fade away.

"I'm renting a room not far from there," he continued, looking her straight in eyes now. "I hope to see you out and about."

Julia was in the process of crafting another witty response when she glanced away and saw Caroline lead her father away from the other dancers. She could hear his coughing fit over the piano and violin as Caroline eased him into a chair.

"Yes, that would be lovely," Julia answered distractedly. "Please excuse me, Mr. Eaton. I think my father needs me." As Julia rose from her chair, Matthew stayed her hand, his touch a whisper on her skin. She glanced down at his strong fingers that were slightly darker than her own pale complexion.

"Let me help you," he said firmly and without hesitation, he crossed the room and helped Caroline raise her father up out of the chair. Julia fell into step with Caroline as Matthew supported her father and was able to get him away from the little crowd and onto the first step on the staircase leading to their rooms upstairs. As Julia sat next to her father and rubbed his back as he continued to splutter, she watched as Matthew walked back into the dining hall to speak with the hotel's proprietor about the closest doctor. *These Eatons are certainly a surprise,* she thought as she met Caroline's worried eyes.

CHAPTER 5

"You tell the damn doctor I'm fine. I don't need to see him when he comes later," Julia's father grumbled as Caroline took the serving tray which balanced a half-full soup bowl and passed it on to Julia. As she glanced up from the remnants of the hearty beef and vegetable stew and looked into her father's tired eyes, she was relieved to see that at least his color was better than the night before.

"Daniel, you gave us all a scare last night," Caroline returned gently but firmly. Julia hated to admit it but she had been impressed by Caroline's steadiness throughout this whole ordeal. While she had felt like she was whirling around all last evening and getting in everyone's way in her haste to help, Caroline had directed the flow of hotel staff with brisk efficiency. She knew just where the extra pillows needed to go so Julia's father wouldn't slide down in bed and who to ask to refill the water basin when he had gotten sick all down the front of his nightshirt and needed to be cleaned up.

They had both stayed up after the commotion had died down and it was just the three of them, the women two sentries on either side of the bed as he snored heavily. Julia had awoken in the pink tinged dawn, unaware of when exactly she had fallen asleep, her back aching from spending the night hunched over the bed. As she had blinked the sleep out of her eyes and stretched her numbed toes, she saw Caroline holding her father's hand as she dozed in the rocking chair, their joined fingers forming a bridge in the cold air.

The fire in the grate facing the bed had long since gone out and a patchwork of frost was crisscrossing the corners of the window. Julia had risen silently, pulled the quilt up under her father's chin, and had tried to leave the room as quietly as she could. She was easing the door open when Caroline had startled awake and looked over at her first in confusion and then with sudden realization. She had sat up straighter in the chair, looking as though she had wanted to tell Julia something.

"I'll send someone up for the fire," Julia had whispered, darting out of the room before Caroline could see the tears glittering in her eyes. *It's a bout of influenza, not a death sentence,* Julia had reassured herself as she'd gone down the stairs and released a shaky breath.

"We want to make sure your illness doesn't get worse," Caroline continued now, pulling Julia back into the present. She sank down onto the side of the bed, her hand reaching for her husband's balled fist.

"Why doesn't anyone around here listen to me?" Julia's father bellowed hoarsely, a touch of his fighting spirit sparking in his eyes. He pulled his fist away from Caroline, pounding it against the mattress with an anticlimactic muffled thud. "I keep telling you I'm-" his sentence was cut off by a sudden coughing jag and he slumped back against the pillows as quickly as he'd tried to lift himself from them.

"Julia, please go check to see if Dr. Stevens is on his way," Caroline said calmly, taking her husband's shortened outburst in stride. "I'm not trusting your father's expert medical opinion at the moment."

"Of course," Julia replied, trying to suppress an incredulous smile as she watched her father and stepmother vie for control. Shuffling over to the open door with the heavy tray in her arms, she stepped out into the hallway and tried to figure out how she was going to shut the door as a couple of the hotel's patrons shot her curious glances from across the hall as they passed by. Thankfully, Dr. Stevens came striding up the staircase at that moment and, after assuring her her father's case of influenza seemed to be on the mild side, let himself into the room and closed the door.

Thank goodness he doesn't seem overly concerned, Julia thought with relief. *Now all I have to do is find someone to take this blasted tray.* She headed down the hall in the opposite direction, hoping to find one of the hotel's staff nearby. Her luck held out as she nearly ran into a harried looking maid who came rushing out of another room and only glared at her a little when Julia thrust her load into the other woman's arms. She started to apologize but the maid huffed away before she could get the words out.

I think a nap is in order, she decided as a great yawn sent her mouth gaping in a decidedly unladylike fashion. Her exhaustion was finally catching up with her. Turning back toward her room, Julia pulled up abruptly when she saw who was about to knock on her father's door.

"Mr. Eaton," she exclaimed, surprised to see Matthew. She knew she must look a sight with her rumpled clothes and sallow complexion, her wild curls barely contained in a haphazard braid slung over her shoulder. Yet, she was so grateful to see him that any thoughts of her appearance quickly slipped her mind. The sincere smile he flashed her way warmed her from the inside out and she continued back toward him. "How kind of you to come check on my father. The doctor just went in to see him."

"It's no trouble at all. Thank you for telling me about the doctor, Miss Webster," Matthew returned, taking off his woolen cap and sending a few flakes of snow floating down to the floor. "How is the patient?"

As if on cue, Julia heard her father loudly complaining that Dr. Stevens' hands were too cold. Even with the door closed, she could still pick up on the indignation dripping from his admonition.

"Beginning to improve, I'd have to say," Julia observed, shaking her head a little with a wry smile on her lips. "I wouldn't want to be Dr. Stevens in there. My father often forgets his manners when he's arguing his case."

"Yes, he's an undisputed lion," Matthew chuckled, eyeing the door to the room again. The prolonged chimes of the grandfather clock echoed from the parlor below, indicating that it was already noon. He twisted his cap absentmindedly in his hands, turning his full gaze on Julia. "Since your father is going to be preoccupied for a while, would you like to join me for a cup of tea downstairs?"

Julia's stomach rumbled and she suddenly realized she hadn't eaten anything all morning save the biscuit she'd choked down hours before. The ease she had felt a moment ago unexpectedly turned to trepidation. *What would Eliza say about this? Would she think it would be too forward to accept?* Then, Julia really considered his offer and decided that her growing interest in Matthew was worth the risk of any judgement she could face downstairs. *It's not like we're going to be* alone, *alone together,* she reasoned. *It's just tea!*

"Yes, thank you. Tea sounds wonderful," she answered. They turned and walked down the stairs, Matthew allowing her to go in front of him in the narrow passage. They passed through the foyer and entered the dining room. Weak sunlight was filtering through the hotel's front windows, making the sparse snowflakes falling outside sparkle. Julia was thankful that one of the tables in the sunlight was still open and she and Matthew settled in the comfortable chairs.

Now that they were across the table from one another and removed from what had brought them together in the first place, she wasn't sure how to break the encroaching silence. *Why do I do this to myself? I was perfectly fine earlier.* She played with the edge of the napkin, feigning a sudden interest in the crisp tablecloth between them. *I need to get out of my own head!* The tea arrived and she sipped the hot liquid, its heat a balm on her scratchy throat.

"I'm sorry, I don't think I asked where you and your family are staying," Julia said, attempting to restore the rapport they had shared upstairs. She forced herself to look up and meet Matthew's steady gaze.

"Oh, we're at the Winthrop. It's a little more uptown than you are."

"Is that the hotel by the park with all those hidden paths? We almost lost my brother in there when we came down to the city once. That was years ago, though."

"Yes, that's the park across the way. You can tell how vibrant it would be in the summer. We don't have a view like this, though," Matthew looked out at the harbor with admiration. "There was a river that ran along the outskirts of our town growing up but it was nothing like this."

"It's beautiful but the ocean scares me," Julia admitted, shivering a little at the thought of being surrounded by all that water. "I couldn't imagine not being able to get to any land." Given that she had lived on the coast her whole life, she knew how to swim but she also knew she'd quickly become disoriented if all she saw was churning, white-capped waves. She couldn't wrap her head around the fact that sailors like Quentin, Louisa's brother, endured weeks or even months at sea. Thinking about Louisa made her incredibly homesick so she decided to bring the conversation back around. "Where did you grow up? It had to be away from the coast."

"North Carolina. My father's family started off near Charlotte which is in the northern part of the state. He wanted to get out from under my grandfather as quickly as he could. Once he and my mother were married, they traveled across the state until they settled in Asheville. They liked being near the mountains, away from everyone they grew up with."

"So your uncle. . ." Julia trailed off, allowing Matthew to fill in the blanks.

"Is my father's younger brother, yes. He was indignant when my father left the fold, felt like he abandoned his duty."

"What was his duty? Did your grandfather have unrealistic expectations?"

"He expected perfection. No matter how hard my father worked to help build their business, grandfather always demanded more. Uncle Henry didn't know how taxing it all was until he was caught in the line of fire."

"What do you mean by. . ." she started to say but a faraway expression had seeped into his eyes and she stopped. He seemed to forget where he was for a moment, staring absently out the window over her shoulder. As he shook his head slightly and cleared his throat, she wondered if something had happened to his family.

She was mulling over whether she should attempt to ask him again about his family when she saw Dr. Stevens come into the room over Matthew's shoulder. The doctor scanned the guests until his eyes finally landed on her.

"He's resting comfortably now, Miss Webster," Dr. Stevens said after he arrived at their table and Julia had introduced the two men. "What he needs most over the next few days is rest. Make sure he doesn't overexert himself. I understand you're planning on leaving for Washington soon."

"Yes we're set to arrive the day before New Year's Eve. Do we need to change our plans?"

"As long as he rests and doesn't become . . . overexcited, you shouldn't need to postpone your trip. I'll be back tomorrow around this time to make sure your father continues to be on the mend."

After she had thanked the doctor and he left the dining room, Julia turned back to Matthew. Any hint of the discomfort she had seen before they were interrupted was long gone and he was his stoic self once more.

"If it's alright with you, Miss Webster, I'd like to go up and see your father for a bit," he told her, rising from the table.

"Of course. I'm sure he'll be very happy to see you. I think I'll stay down here for a bit, anyway."

He was about to walk away from the table when a thought seemed to occur to him. Turning back to her, he adjusted his glasses and said, a bit shyly, "I'm looking forward to seeing you down in Washington."

With that unexpected admission, he briskly walked out of the dining room, leaving her to process this new development. All she could do was look out the window so that no one could see the light burning in her eyes.

She was suddenly very much looking forward to her family's return to the capitol.

*   *   *   *

Three days later, Julia was struggling to comprehend how she had managed to fit all of her belongings into her traveling trunk before she'd arrived in New York. She was beginning to sweat as she attempted to stuff her dresses into the now conspicuously smaller trunk. After another five minutes of trying to unsuccessfully buckle the straps, she was on the verge of going out in the hallway and pleading with someone to sit on its top while she closed it up or vice versa. When a knock sounded on her door, she decided she would be grateful to anyone who had come to rescue her.

"Come in," Julia gasped, wiping at the strands of hair now plastered to her forehead. Her heart sank a bit when Caroline came through the door with her typical brisk air. *Well, some help with a sprinkling of condescension is better than no help at all, I suppose.*

"I'm about to send for a carriage to take us on to Washington," her stepmother informed her, taking in her disarray with a slightly raised eyebrow. "You don't look like you're ready, though. Do you need some help?"

"Yes, I'd appreciate it, Caroline," she said, biting back the sarcasm that threatened to worm its way into her answer. She was tired, sweaty, and worried about how her father would do going down to Washington. He had looked well at breakfast, if slightly pale, but she still wasn't completely convinced.

A part of her wanted to hold back her reservations from Caroline, to simply bury her concerns and keep the woman at a safe distance. Yet Julia had witnessed how adept she was in caring for her father and so she asked the question that she had been mulling over incessantly for the past few days.

"Do you think he's strong enough to travel?" Her voice was uncharacteristically soft as Caroline threw open the lid of the trunk and started rearranging her belongings.

"Your father is determined to go so I think he'll be fine," Caroline said, folding Julia's dresses into a neat pile as she spoke. "He's not completely recovered but his stubbornness will work to his advantage in this case."

The sureness of her words eased Julia's nerves more than even the doctor's assurances had. He had only seen snippets of her father's recovery, after all, and Caroline had witnessed the whole of it.

"How do you know so much about healing?" she asked as she went around the room, checking to make sure she wasn't leaving anything behind. Her hairbrush still lay on the bedside table and she quickly snatched it and threw it in the trunk when Caroline reached for a shawl on the bed. She was curious as to what Caroline had experienced that gave her such a sense of calm under pressure.

"Well, my father was never a healthy man and sometimes it was too much for my mother to handle by herself. You've met my sister so you know that she's headstrong. But she couldn't handle seeing him bedridden, much less getting sick all over the place. It became my responsibility to be his nursemaid and I quickly learned what it took to ease his discomfort and keep him calm while we were waiting for the doctor to arrive."

Julia watched as a faraway look shadowed Caroline's face for a moment before she continued on. "I was there with him for the entirety of his last bout of pneumonia. His poor heart wasn't strong enough to see him through. God rest his soul."

Caroline told her all of this in her straightforward way but Julia could see the grief tinging the corners of her steel gray eyes. It must have been dreadful to watch her father waste away. She knew because, at the end, she had witnessed her own mother go from a vibrant philanthropist to a ghostly figure with hollowed out cheeks and icy hands. The ghastly transformation had taken only a matter of months, the tumor winning out in the end.

"I'm very sorry, Caroline," was all that she could whisper. It was too painful to talk about her mother's swift deterioration and she wasn't fully comfortable discussing it with her father's new wife.

Her stepmother opened her mouth as if she to ask Julia a question then clamped it shut, instead reaching out and giving her hand a brief squeeze. After a weighted silence that dragged on through a few ticks of the clock, she went back to her work and the lid of the trunk closed easily. Caroline expertly strapped everything into place, all business once more.

"See. All you needed to do was slow down. You'll waste more time rushing to try to make everything fit than taking your time from the beginning."

Clearly, their moment of bonding had come to an abrupt end. But as Julia followed her out of the room, she had to acknowledge that this was the most connected she had felt to her stepmother in their brief relationship. Perhaps there was hope for the two of them yet.

CHAPTER 6

"Have you been to one of the Wolfson gatherings before? I always find them to be a great diversion before all of the pressures of the New Year take hold," Dr. Lindsley boomed in his warm baritone, which was unexpectedly deep for someone so young.

The Websters had been staying with the newly minted physician for since their arrival in Washington a two days ago and would continue to rely on his hospitality until Julia and Caroline went back up to Boston the following week. He was some sort of relation to Caroline but the days since their arrival had been such a whirlwind that Julia couldn't recall if he was a cousin twice removed or a long lost half nephew or something else entirely. All she knew was that they were now pulling on their coats in the doctor's elegant foyer to go to a fancy soiree across town to celebrate the beginning of another year.

"No, I can't say that I have. I've only talked with Ted a handful of times about his practice. He's a fine lawyer and I hear he's a hell of a shot," her father answered. As the two men engaged in an animated discussion of premiere hunting grounds, she immediately tuned them out. How anyone could think of riding through the woods on a sticky, sweltering day trying to catch a poor, defenseless fox as a form of entertainment was beyond her. Even the braying of their neighbor's three beagles back at home set her teeth on edge.

"Oh, Daniel, enough talk of hunting rifles and hounds. If we don't hurry up, we'll be late," Caroline interjected. Her father's face fell a bit but a quick glance at his pocket watch confirmed what his wife had said. Julia was grateful that she had been the one to speak up and the quartet made their out into the dank evening.

Though Dr. Lindsley's residence was in the middle of several other houses, sizable expanses of unadulterated land spread out from either side of the small sub-plot with trees acting as a natural periphery in the back. The dirt roads that snaked in between the clusters of houses were incredibly muddy as it had rained heavily that afternoon. The air had turned unexpectedly cold that evening and she had to watch the puddles pocketing the edge of the lane as some were beginning to freeze over. She had not even caught a glimpse of the White House or the Capitol and she wasn't sure if this was because they were so far away or due to the dense fog which had descended upon the city. No matter, though, there was a party to attend.

The ride over to the Wolfson house was relatively short but the deep grooves in the road made it seem to go on for ages. Julia's teeth knocked together painfully on more than one occasion and she had to make an effort not to slam into Dr. Lindsley, who was sitting beside her and taking up more space than he required. When they finally pulled up in front of the huge house on a rolling hill blazing with lamp and candlelight, she knew the doctor hadn't been exaggerating about this couple's lavish gatherings.

Carriages of various size lined both sides of one of the few cobbled streets in the city and it was difficult for the driver to find a space for their own. They had to walk quite a distance once they'd piled out of the carriage and she could hear her father breathing heavily the farther they walked. She slipped her arm into the crook of his unoccupied elbow, wondering if he'd been telling the whole truth when he'd insisted he was fully recovered earlier that afternoon. Caroline was on his other side and looked at him with a concerned expression but he didn't seem to notice.

The mansion's full splendor came into focus the closer they came to it and by the time her father was pulling back the gold knocker on the front door, Julia was completely taken in by the sheer three story size of it. The brick façade was as wide as it was tall, stretching out on both sides of the main house. Around the east corner, she could make out one side of a glass paned greenhouse, the bright faces of tropical flowers sagging against its wall. Intricately carved spindles marched along the perimeter of the covered porch where they stood, their order interrupted by the stately columns holding the whole front of the home up. They looked as if they were the home's newest addition, the enticing aroma of freshly hewn wood permeating the air.

A smartly dressed butler answered the door and, after taking their coats, passed them on to another servant who led the party down a plush carpeted hallway adorned with family portraits which led to the ballroom in the center of the house. *And I thought Mrs. Whittle had a grand ballroom*, Julia thought as they entered the brightly lit space which was teeming with Washington's elite. The circular room was painted white from domed ceiling to hardwood floor, enhancing its clean elegance. A chandelier dripping with innumerable crystals hung from the pinnacle of the dome, reflecting a few stars in the visible night sky and shaking a little precariously as the party below swelled with music, laughter, and dancing.

At the center of it all stood Mr. and Mrs. Wolfson, he a handsome man with graying hair and impeccable posture and she at least fifteen years his junior, resplendent in a violet hued velvet dress with a high, laced collar and puffed sleeves. Her perfectly placed string of pearls wrapped around her dainty neck and rested where the tight bodice of her gown flowed seamlessly into a full skirt. Though she was wearing her best gown, Julia felt supremely underdressed next to the hostess.

After her father had made the introductions and Julia had managed a stiff curtsy, they found an empty table stationed on the periphery of the dance floor. Dr. Lindsley spotted a colleague of his and excused himself with a merry salute. While Caroline went to find some warm brandy for her father, she looked around the room and marveled at the thought of so many powerful men sharing the same space. *What must it feel like knowing you hold the power to make real change? What will they decide to do with it?* And then, a more treasonous thought crossed her mind as she caught the words of a nearby congressman reprimanding his teenage daughter for giving two dances in a row to the same young man. *Shouldn't these wives, mothers, and daughters be afforded the same advantage?*

She pushed that treasonous notion down as Caroline returned and they made small talk. When her father was finished methodically drinking his brandy, he rose and took Caroline's arm. Julia wondered if she'd be left to her own devices and was considering whether she could find the entrance to the greenhouse when her father nudged her.

"Do you see the man two tables over? The one with the long, white hair?

Julia nodded, trying to place the trim man her father was referencing. He had a stately nose and was dressed in a brown waistcoat.

"That is Mr. Henry Clay, a very influential member of our party. I'm going to introduce you. He may have some interesting insight into the cause you've decided to take up."

Her mouth went dry as she followed her father and Caroline over to Mr. Clay and his wife. From the snippets she had heard, Mr. Clay had a wealth of experience under his belt in both houses of Congress and had even served as Secretary of State. This was all entirely unexpected and she felt suddenly conscious of every move she made.

Trying desperately to project an air of maturity, she nearly collided with a chair someone had left in the middle of the aisle. Caroline, who was in step next to her, put out a hand to steady her and gave her a quizzical look. Evidently, she hadn't an inkling of what Julia's father had up his sleeve either. When the three of them were finally before the renowned politician, they were greeted with a tight-lipped smile that could've been mistaken for a grimace.

"Henry, how are you my good man?" her father began. "Haven't seen you in ages. How is everything back home in Kentucky?"

"Never a dull moment, Webster," Mr. Clay replied, his accent dull yet not fully extinguished. "Especially with the fool in the White House thwarting all my best laid plans. I'm thinking of coming back to Washington to do more than just spite him."

"You're thinking of running for the office again?" Her father raised his eyebrows in surprise at what Mr. Clay was inferring.

"Well, it's too early to say. The next election isn't until '32. But I'm weighing my options." An awkward silence followed this admission. For being members of the same political party, the relationship between them seemed more than a little strained. She wondered if that was a side effect of ambition, the fact that one could never fully trust the other.

Mr. Clay then turned his perceptive eyes to Caroline and herself. Julia felt as if she was being scrutinized by a curious bird who was debating whether to engage or fly away.

"This is my wife, Caroline and my daughter, Julia," her father said, picking up on his former colleague's shifting focus. They were quickly introduced to Mr. Clay's wife, Lucretia, who at least exuded more warmth than her husband. She and Caroline seemed to hit it off straightaway and soon excused themselves, sashaying away to watch the dancers. Her father then turned to Mr. Clay, taking Julia's arm gently and bringing her back into his line of vision.

"My daughter has recently taken a keen interest in the Indian Removal Act that the president is bringing before Congress next month," her father said. "I've been too engaged with other issues to pay it much attention, though that will need to change soon enough. I know that you're deeply opposed to it. Perhaps you can give her some more insight into its status?"

An unexpected light went on in Mr. Clay's eyes and he seemed to look on her with new esteem. His evident interest transformed his face completely, a congenial smile making him seem much more welcoming. She was taken aback when her father excused himself and joined Caroline and Lucretia, feeling emboldened that he had faith enough in her to allow for this private conversation. Shifting her focus to Mr. Clay, she found that she had the gentleman's undivided attention.

"It appears that I've underestimated you, miss," he said. "For that, I apologize. I don't often encounter young people who have taken such an interest in the well-being of the southern tribes. How did you learn of the president's plans?"

"My father doesn't keep everything under lock and key, sir. And I've witnessed enough of my father's passion for politics that I fear it's ignited my own."

The knowing nod he gave her heightened her courage to continue. She didn't want to press her luck by appearing too straightforward but this would likely be the only time she'd have Mr. Clay's ear. She chose her next words carefully, hoping to confirm what she already assumed.

"If I may be so bold, you seem to give President Jackson the same treatment my father does. He's not very fond of him or his way of governing the country."

"You are a perceptive young woman and are correct, I'm afraid. While your father doesn't approach some issues like I would, it's nothing compared to the rift between myself and the president. To be frank, he and I don't agree on a great many things, my dear. Chief among our many disagreements is his insistence on removing natives from their ancestral lands. I find the whole idea morally repugnant. Who does this cruelty serve? The answer is Jackson and his land squatter supporters. He's allowed his biases to cloud his humanity and good sense."

Though his tone was slightly condescending, Julia had to admit she agreed with his broad statements concerning both the Indians and President Jackson. She listed intently as Mr. Clay plowed on.

"You cannot separate his military service from the wars he waged against the Creek Indians. I don't know if you were aware but between 1814 and 1824, before he took office, Jackson was involved with *nine* out of the eleven treaties that took away land from the five southern tribes and simply gave them land farther west. He sees no problem with pushing them to the breaking point and dishonoring the treaties they've signed. The legislation he's touting needs to be given a swift kick out of Congress, if you ask me."

What Mr. Clay revealed astounded her. She had inferred that the president's record concerning the tribes was suspect but the way Mr. Clay lined up the facts, Jackson's actions seemed like more than a desire to expand the country's reach. No, this was a vendetta with which the president had a deep personal connection. The thought of his stalwart prejudice sent a shiver up Julia's spine.

"And that Henry Eaton. He cannot wait to be the president's strong arm in uprooting the tribes," Mr. Clay continued, so worked up himself that he didn't seem to notice her widening eyes.

"What did you say?" Julia whipped her head around to face him so quickly that her neck popped a bit in protest. This was completely unexpected. She knew Mr. Eaton was the Secretary of War but his charm had disarmed her, made her believe that he could be one of the sympathetic members of Jackson's cabinet. Instead, he was the president's right hand man in all of this. And where did Matthew align with his uncle? Had she misjudged him so completely that his seemingly kind nature was simply all an act?

"You seem surprised. I'm sorry to inform you but Mr. Eaton is only too willing to debase the treaties that've been hammered out. I've heard rumors that he'll gladly implement the removal of the southern tribes and use military force to make it happen."

She must not have hidden her emotions very well because Mr. Clay lowered his voice, sympathy lining his once intimidating features.

"I'm grieved if I've upset you, my dear. My feelings on this issue often overtake the conversation and, by extension, my perceptiveness."

"Oh, no. I cannot thank you enough, Mr. Clay. You've been incredibly informative. It seems I've much to consider."

He opened his mouth again as if to continue the conversation but then shut it, seeming to pick up on storm of emotions now welling inside her. He clearly wasn't convinced of her well-being but he gripped her hand warmly and slipped away to rejoin his wife who was now talking with another couple, shooting her a final backwards glance as he wrapped an arm around Lucretia. She watched him go, feeling guilty over the fact that she'd lied to him. As she searched for her father and Caroline, Julia didn't know if she'd ever feel settled again.

CHAPTER 7

She hadn't returned to her father and Caroline for more than five minutes when a sudden hush overtook the ballroom and Julia turned toward the entryway, brushing against her father's shoulder. Still reeling from all that Mr. Clay had imparted to her, she didn't know what to make of the jumble of emotions that boiled up to the surface when she saw whose arrival had caused such a stir. Despite her fury, she also felt a strange current of electrifying anticipation snake its way to her fingertips.

But she also knew her feelings didn't mean a whit in this scenario and her stomach dropped involuntarily. She tucked her chin down into her chest, praying that the inevitable confrontation wouldn't be too bombastic. The group of musicians in the corner, picking up on the abrupt change in the room, ceased playing the gay reel that had set toes tapping and skirts swishing just a moment ago.

It seemed that the silence stretched on for at least ten minutes before she heard Mr. Wolfson clear his throat and she dared to look up. Henry Eaton stood there, taking in the room and its revelers with a steely gaze. His arm was looped protectively around Peggy who had her head held high and a fur cloak fastened at her neck. Julia felt her breath catch in her throat when she saw Matthew, his hair slicked back from his face, standing at Peggy's other side. They all looked as though they were ready for a battle.

"What the devil are you doing here, *Mr. Eaton*? You and your wife were most certainly not invited," Mr. Wolfson said incredulously, stepping forward so that only a few feet separated him from Henry. The chilly undercurrent of his words made even the nervous tittering among the party's guests cease, the already prominent tension ratcheting up another notch.

"There's no need to be exclusionary, *Mr. Wolfson*," Henry bit back. The jovial air that had lowered her guard during their previous interactions had evaporated and she was now confronted with how stalwart Henry was. "My family and I should be able to come to any gathering that we choose to."

"Not after the way you two carried on. And then tried to worm your way into good society, putting my wife and the other respectable women of Washington into an impossible bind. The president may vouch for you but we all know what you were both about."

The unspoken accusation hung in the air like a living thing, a bird of prey waiting for its next victim. Mr. Wolfson might as well have shouted it into the high-ceilinged ballroom, allowed it to echo on and on until the guests were convinced of its validity. Everyone knew that once the implications of adultery were out there, it was impossible to force them back into the darkness. Henry looked so enraged that she was sure physical blows were imminent. Matthew shifted his feet as if he was about to switch places with Peggy to hold his uncle back when a familiar and authoritative voice cut through the taut air.

"Come now, Ted. I don't think we need to bring such unsavory rumors into this," her father interjected. "It's the New Year, after all. Time to mend fences that shouldn't have been broken in the first place." She looked around and saw that all of the heads in the tense room swiveled at her father's words and she could see the derision in some of the party goers' expressions. She sensed Caroline stiffen at her husband's defense of the Eatons and felt some of the sympathy she had gained for her stepmother slipping away.

Julia also felt a wave of shame wash over her. In situations like this one, she wished she could be more like her father, not afraid to speak up for what was justified. She could talk all she wanted about taking the honorable road when she was with someone she knew but in affairs like this, she felt paralyzed by the fear of what others would think of her. Her father always seemed to have the most indelible words in public situations like this. It was as if the persona he had crafted for the Senate floor took over, allowing him to fill the room with his voice.

Though she was enraged by what Mr. Clay had told her about Henry, she knew deep down that the way he and Peggy were being ostracized wasn't right. Only they knew how their relationship began and if they said it was after her first husband had passed, then others should believe them.

"This is my home, Daniel, and I can dismiss any morally bankrupt characters I see fit to." Mr. Wolfson looked as though he was going to spit fire and his haughty wife came to his side, a smug sneer marring her pretty face. The host turned to Henry, his expression turning to stone. "Leave with your party, Mr. Eaton. Now, before I have you thrown out." If this was the Washington society Caroline wanted so desperately to be a part of, Julia wanted nothing to do with it after this performance.

Julia noticed that Matthew shook his head slightly as he practically pushed Henry out of the room and back toward the front door of the mansion. In the confusion the trio had created with their surprising arrival and abrupt departure, she was able to get away from her father and stepmother and slip out of the ballroom with no notice. She dashed down the hall but by the time she entered the foyer it was already empty and her heart sank, hoping she could still catch Matthew outside.

The frigid night air bit at the bare skin of her arms as Julia stepped out onto the front porch. At the sight of Matthew gesticulating at Henry by the carriage across the road, a mixture of trepidation and relief flooded her and she slunk down the stairs as quietly as possible. In the short time that she'd known him, Julia had never seen Matthew so visibly upset and she didn't want to get involved in the familial argument. Not yet, anyway.

"What were you thinking?" Matthew shouted at his uncle as Julia approached, still unseen.

"I want those bastards to accept Peggy!" Henry returned, his cheeks rosy with anger. "Why should we be excluded from any celebrations? We've done nothing wrong."

"You're only going to make it worse for her if you continue to think you can change these peoples' minds," Matthew said, his voice losing some of its indignation. "You need to wait for this whole affair to blow over."

"What if it doesn't, Matthew?"

"Well, you can't think like that. Peggy is beautiful and incredibly persuasive. It'll be no time before she's won everyone over, even the high and mighty prigs in there."

Henry looked so forlorn at that moment that Julia could almost forget Mr. Clay's admission that he was one of the removal bill's most ardent supporters. She could only see a man wanting he and his family to be accepted. Then, Henry's expression turned cold when he spotted her coming across the lawn over Matthew's shoulder.

"Would you look at that? A Webster is approaching," Henry spat out. She was taken aback by the venom punctuating his words. Matthew turned around and his eyes widened slightly at the sight of her before he regained his composure.

"You can tell your saintly father that I don't need him to defend me," Henry continued.

What right does he have? If Papa hadn't stepped in when he did, the whole thing would've gotten out of hand. He should be thanking our family, not deriding us.

Julia's moment of empathy was wiped out by the churlish tongue of a newly realized political opponent, replaced by a renewed fury that nearly took her breath away. Any warmth that had existed between the Eatons and the Websters in New York had been snuffed out.

"How dare you-" she began, sounding braver than she actually felt. But Henry turned away disgustedly and heaved himself into the carriage to comfort his wife, not even giving her the satisfaction of chastising him.

"You can find your way back to the hotel, can't you Matthew?" he yelled out the carriage window. "I'm going to take Peggy back." Without waiting for a reply, Henry directed the driver to depart, leaving his nephew to walk who knew how many blocks back to where they were lodging.

"Why did you let him come?" she hissed at Matthew, stunned by Henry's unceremonious abandonment. Henry's coldness toward his nephew was beyond words and she wanted to see if he was as shaken as she was. How could she have entertained any pity for Henry Eaton?

"Why are you inserting yourself where you don't belong?" he snapped back, the edge in his voice bringing the doubts that had been planted earlier that evening to the surface. Apparently, the New Year couldn't wait a few more hours to knock her over the head with all the firsts she was experiencing tonight.

"Forgive me for wanting to make sure you were alright," she said, trying in vain to keep the anger and hurt out of her voice. "The way they treated you in there was awful. But, clearly, I'm not wanted here."

She turned to leave, a sudden heaviness making her feel like she'd been left to tread water in an icy stream and she was slowly losing the battle. Why had she been taken in by his family? Why had she allowed herself to believe she and Matthew had anything in common besides a deep respect for her father?

"I'm sorry, Julia," he said from behind her. She glanced over her shoulder cautiously and noted the strain in his jaw, the unmistakable tension of the evening carved into the rigid lines of his cheekbones. But there was also regret there in the slight sagging of his shoulders and his inability to meet her gaze. Despite her better judgement, she waivered in her plan to stomp back up the hill to the mansion.

"I tried my best to convince him that this was a fool's errand," he continued softly, taking advantage of her renewed attention. "He refused to listen to me and Peggy herself. Now it's turned into a humiliating mess for them."

Julia could feel herself softening but kept her arms tightly crossed over her chest. Matthew didn't need to know her seemingly defensive stance was all to try to dispel the goosebumps marching up her arms and prevent her teeth from chattering. It seemed she wasn't fooling anyone, though, as he shrugged out of his overcoat and, closing the distance between them, draped it over her shoulders. She could still feel his warmth in its wool lining and the slight tang of his cologne nipped at her nose. After she murmured a quiet 'thank you,' he continued.

"And I can't explain why he just lashed out at you. Your father did him a service by standing up for him and Peggy. The only pardon I can make is how taxing this evening has turned out to be for him."

"For you, as well," she said, finally finding her voice. She knew that Matthew's earlier irritation toward her must have been his breaking point. "Why aren't you more upset that he dragged you into this? That he left you here to find your own way back?"

"It's not an excuse but this isn't the first time his temper has gotten the better of him. He can be a good man when he wants to be, and he has been to me. He's the reason I'm able to be here in the first place. But . . ." he trailed off then and she was reminded of their time in New York, when he had seemed to drift off to another place at the mention of the past. And again he pulled himself back into the present so quickly that she questioned whether he'd even paused at all.

"I may be in my uncle's sphere but that doesn't mean I agree with him on every matter. I have my own thoughts about how some things should be handled."

Before she had a chance to press him on just what he and Henry felt differently about, a familiar voice broached the otherwise still air.

"Julia!" She started, turning to find that her father was walking purposefully across the lawn toward them, any hint that he'd been suffering from the remnants of his illness gone. As he drew closer, she could tell that he'd been looking for her for some time, his expression a mixture of aggravated annoyance and fatherly concern. Luckily for her, Caroline had remained indoors.

"Why didn't you tell me you were coming out here? You can't just run off and expect that no one will notice," her father said sternly, seemingly oblivious to the private conversation he'd interrupted.

Julia felt her face grow prickly from embarrassment and quickly slipped the coat off and handed it back to Matthew. The way her father was chiding her, it sounded as if she was still in grammar school. She was chagrined by the further reminder that while Matthew was out on his own, she was still under the watchful eye of her parents.

"I only wanted to make sure that the Eatons were alright, Papa," she muttered, averting her eyes as her father joined the pair. She would never get a word in edgewise now as her father wrapped his own coat around her and then pulled Matthew aside. *How can he trust me to hold my own with Mr. Clay but is practically barring me from even looking at Matthew?*

The men spoke in hushed voices and she tuned out their muffled conversation, wanting instead to reflect on all that had transpired that night. It would take the remainder of her days in Washington to mull over all she had learned. She was convinced now more than ever that she was in the right to be very concerned about the Indian issue. And to know with certainty who she was up against had been an unexpected gift.

"It seems that I've lost my ride home," she heard Matthew tell her father and turned her focus back to what was happening on the Wolfsons' front lawn.

"Well, I'm sure I can convince our driver to take you the rest of the way," her father replied. "Caroline is so taken with the connections she's made in there that I doubt she'll miss us if we take some time to ourselves. Julia, will you join us?"

"Yes, Papa," she answered and before she knew it, he had summoned the driver and all three of them were trailing behind him in search of Dr. Lindsley's carriage. Once she was snuggly inside, she could hear Matthew giving the driver the directions and a few moments later, he and her father climbed in and they departed.

"I'll call on you when I get back to Boston," Matthew whispered from beside her, the tickle of his breath sending feather-light tingles down her neck. She only nodded, not trusting her voice enough to respond as well as not wanting to draw her father's attention. Her return to Boston beckoned and, with it, the opportunity to reunite with the other half of her family and see where her journey would take her next.

CHAPTER 8

"I missed you so much," Julia said, embracing her brother a week later. With Eliza's arm snug across her shoulders, she watched over Edward's head as Caroline shifted ever so slightly from one foot to the other, clearly nervous to meet the last of her step-children. This was the first time Julia had seen her lose even the semblance of control. They had just arrived at Eliza's after the lengthy ride back from Washington and she was desperate for a wash basin and comfortable sheets. But nothing would get in the way of her making sure Edward had improved under Eliza's care.

He already seemed more animated as she peppered him with questions about how his Christmas had been. The light that shone in his eyes as he told her about his new sled and how beautiful the church had looked warmed her heart and she knew she'd always be grateful for Fletcher's decision to keep him in Boston. Once she had let him get out all that he wanted to tell her, she turned him toward Caroline and the air in the entryway grew strained.

"Hello, Edward. I've heard a lot about you. I'm Caroline," she said, looking him straight in the eye. Julia was grateful that she was taking her first meeting with Edward seriously.

"It's nice to meet you, mam," he returned, stepping forward to shake her hand as he'd been taught to. Caroline looked a bit taken aback but grasped his smaller palm firmly, as if they were making an unspoken pact to give one another a chance.

"Well, now that the introductions have been made, I think we should let these ladies sit," Eliza suggested as Caroline released Edward's hand. "They've been on the road and need some rest."

They made their way to the front sitting room, Thomas neatly stacking their traveling trunks in the hallway before he joined the rest of the party. Julia sank gratefully into one of the plush chairs, her skirts pooling over her traveling boots. Though she had been sitting for the majority of the past three days, it felt refreshing to sit in a seat that wasn't jostling constantly underneath her and didn't smell of molding cheese. Cold late afternoon sunshine filtered through the gauzy curtains, creating fading, elongated rectangles on the hardwood, the roaring fire that was already in the grate a welcome relief to her cramped toes.

"You both must be famished. Would you like me to see if Peter can whip something up quickly?" Eliza asked after an awkward silence stretched on for a few minutes. Now that they'd been introduced, Edward couldn't seem to stop shooting wayward glances at Caroline and Julia wondered what must be going through his mind.

"Thank you, Eliza, that's very kind of you to offer. But we must be getting back to the estate. I fear there'll be much to do since we've been away for so long," Caroline replied, causing Julia's head to whip around from her brother.

"I thought Edward and I would stay with Eliza until he goes back to Connecticut for school," she said in a clipped voice, trying to prevent her exhaustion from heightening her irritation. She had planned on catching up with the family she hadn't seen in weeks and if Caroline was going to interfere with that, she wasn't sure if she could let that stand.

"No, I think it's best if you both come home with me. I'd like to iron out our routine before Edward leaves us." She looked stalwart and Julia was afraid she wouldn't be able to get her to budge on her decision. Her brother could only take Caroline in small doses right now and she couldn't let him retreat into himself again. The progress he'd made was too important to be wiped out. Spending too much time around Caroline right at the onset would likely do just that. And, if she was being honest with herself, it would be nice to have a break from her stepmother, no matter how short it was.

"I don't know, Caroline. I think it's best if Edward isn't moved around again before he goes back with the cousins."

Caroline regarded her coolly and she was afraid she'd overstepped her bounds when Edward's quiet though clear voice cut through the silence.

"I'd rather stay here if I can. Peter is teaching me how to make soup and bread and all sorts of other things. I wanted to stay until I have to go back to school to see if I can get it right."

"Edward is becoming quite the cook," Eliza confirmed. "He helped with the dinner last night and makes a very hearty beef stew. We would be happy if both Edward and Julia stayed. It would give you some time to straighten everything out, Caroline." Thomas nodded his agreement, effectively siding with the others against Caroline.

Julia couldn't believe it. Edward wasn't known to be so forward, especially around adults and particularly with someone he barely knew. He must have been resolved to stay before she and Caroline had arrived and she was pleased that he was beginning to find his voice.

She glanced over at Caroline to gauge her reaction and saw that she did look taken aback. However, the consensus in the room was against her and Julia wondered if she would yield in the face of it or continue with the fight.

"It seems I'm outnumbered," she said tersely, though Julia thought she saw relief flicker in her eyes before the polished mask of indifference came down again. "Both Julia and Edward may stay here for the next week. But, if any problems arise, they must come home right away."

She tried to remain as stoic as Caroline but she couldn't help but grin when she saw Edward's satisfied expression. It was encouraging to think about her brother gaining some of the trademark Webster fortitude.

*   *   *   *

Every day at Eliza's after her return felt like a respite from the storm and Julia was trying to savor every remaining moment she had until her return to the Webster estate and Caroline the following Monday. She told Eliza about all she had seen in her travels, regaling her with tales of the bustling streets of New York and glossing over the tense exchange at the Wolfson party. She intentionally downplayed her exchanges with Matthew Eaton when she talked with Eliza, not wanting her guardian to get too many ideas about the fledgling relationship.

However, she dissected every detail with Louisa as they sat side by side on her bed the evening after Edward left for Connecticut with Thomas. The familiar slate tablet lay between them unmarked while the sun dipped below the horizon and bathed the room in a honey hued sweetness, making Julia think of summer despite the snow on the eves. Louisa had stayed after her shift and got up to light the lamp, listening as Julia told her of her and Matthew's unexpected first meeting and how she had initially resented him for taking up so much of her father's attention.

"But once I started to see who he really was, how he cared about Papa, he began to win me over," she said, a shy smile lighting up her face.
"Look at you grinnin'. Oh, he must be handsome. He is, isn't he?" Louisa plopped back down on the bed, curling her legs underneath her. Any inkling either of them had of continuing with the alphabet had been forgotten.

"He is, in a bookish sort of way. His eyes are the clearest blue I've ever seen. And the way he looks at you. It's like he knows what you're thinking without you having to say a word."

Louisa giggled behind her hand, a dreamy expression softening her face. Her reaction made Julia a bit lightheaded and giddy herself. She then went on to tell her friend about her and Matthew's encounter in Washington and how it hadn't gone as she'd planned at all. They'd parted on civil terms all things considered but she wasn't convinced he'd pay her a visit once they were both back in Boston.

"There's no doubt in my mind you're gonna see him again. It sounds as if he likes you very much."

"I don't know if he likes me the way you think he does. He was interested in what I had to say and learning more about me, of course. But I'd be surprised if he saw me as anything more than a new acquaintance."

"But Julia, he said he'd come a callin'. A gentleman doesn't just say that to anybody, much less to every lady he meets."

"All I can do is hope, Louisa. Hope that he's really the gentleman he seems to be and hope that he doesn't agree with his uncle about everything." They fell into silence then, each lost in her own thoughts for a time.

"Well, I have a bit of news, too," Louisa said, her cheeks turning rosy. Julia was instantly intrigued and turned her full attention on her friend. Taking a deep breath, Louisa's next words tumbled out one on top of the other. "Peter kissed me on the cheek on Christmas Eve."

Julia didn't know how to react for a moment and she tried to come up with an articulate response. Instead, all she could come up with was, "Peter? As in strong but silent Peter?"

Louisa bobbed her head hurriedly, as if she couldn't believe it herself. "Someone had hung mistletoe in the kitchen doorway. I was gettin' ready for my uncle to walk me home and he gave me a warm biscuit to take with me. He says 'Have a blessed Christmas' and then kisses my cheek, light as you please."

"Oh, Louisa. I can tell he's a good man. He can't be much older than twenty but he works hard at everything he does. I've seen him helping our James more than once and I know he goes above his duties for Tom and Eliza. But he's . . ."

Julia snapped her mouth shut, the words she was about to say turning bitter on her tongue. *He's white.* It shouldn't matter that Louisa was black and Peter was white but it did. The two of them could be thrown in prison if they decided to take things further than a simple peck on the cheek. All it would take was the wrong person seeing them together to report it. This was so much different than Louisa being sweet on Fletcher because that could never happen. Fletcher had never given Louisa a second glance. But Louisa and Peter were of the same social class and they worked alongside each other. There were far fewer obstacles in the way of them growing closer.

"What did he say when you saw him again?" she asked hesitantly, afraid to hear what the answer might be.

"He acted like nothin' happened. Asked me how my Christmas was and that was it."

Before Julia could interject that this was probably for the best, Louisa pushed forward. It seemed that now that someone knew her secret, she needed to say everything she'd been holding back. "It surely was a surprise. But I felt it down in my belly, Julia. Men don't pay me much mind and, I don't know, he made me feel . . ." she trailed off.

"I do catch him lookin' at me sometimes and his eyes look soft, like he's thinkin' bout that night, too."

This was the last straw for Julia. She knew she couldn't let Louisa go any further down this road without telling her how she felt.

"You need to tell him this can never happen, Louisa. You mean so much to me and I couldn't bear if something horrible happened to you. Or Peter, for that matter." She hated being so blunt, of trying to cut down her friend's hope. But she knew this was the only way to keep both her and Peter safe.

Louisa looked over at her silently from the other side of the bed, the hurt in her eyes making Julia wish she had the power to take it all back. She was right but it didn't make her feel better. Even when Louisa's hand snuck into her lap and clasped hers, she couldn't bring herself to look into the other girl's face.

"You're right, Julia. I don't know what I was thinkin'. It's not going to go beyond friendship for me and Peter. I promise you."

Julia finally looked up and reached out to tuck Louisa's head against her shoulder in the crook of her neck. The two stayed like that for a long time until Louisa glanced at the clock on the wall and told her she was going to meet her uncle at the livery so they could walk home together. The sky was now impenetrably dark as Louisa bundled up and left to go down the back stairs. As Julia sat looking at the flickering flame in the kerosene lamp, she felt powerless against a system she had no control over and guilty that she could pursue a relationship with Matthew if she wanted to. Her friend didn't have that luxury.

CHAPTER 9

Over the course of the next few days, Julia fell into a new noontime routine which involved sitting and fidgeting for a half hour before the mail was slid through the slot in the front door. Any sewing project had been abandoned during that time as she had pricked her index finger more than once during the first day after her return; her normally smooth skin looked as if it had gotten in a fight with the beak of a chicken.

She would then bolt for the pile on the floor and hurriedly fly through the envelopes, searching for the distinct curve of Mr. Kerry's writing. When she couldn't find a trace of it, she would huff unceremoniously back into her chair, plopping the envelopes down on the end table. She could tell she was beginning to frustrate even Eliza's calm demeanor by the third day of this nerve fraying dance.

"Why don't the two of us go to the indoor market? It would be good to stretch our legs and find something different for tomorrow's dinner." When Julia opened her mouth to decline the suggestion, Eliza rushed on. "We could take Louisa with us. I don't know what's going on with her but she could use a bit of cheering up. We've all been cooped up long enough."

While poor Louisa had been completing her tasks with her usual efficiency, she had also been quiet and withdrawn and Eliza was too perceptive not to pick up on this sudden shift. Julia could only pray that her cousin wouldn't start digging around to find out why Louisa's shoulders drooped when she didn't seem to think anyone was watching her.

"Oh, alright," she agreed and a half hour later, the three of them trekked down the lane toward the city's center, the snow muffling their footfalls. The sun caught the light of the flakes falling lightly onto Julia's dark brown woolen cape, making it seem that crystals were interwoven in the fabric. A bitter squall had blown itself out the night before and the light wind traipsing over the rooftops was a welcome change.

The cold seemed to loosen their lips and once they had arrived at the market several blocks away, Julia was overjoyed to see Louisa acting more like her normal self. As Eliza combed through the wares and enlisted their help in picking a pheasant for supper the next night, she pushed the absence of the much-anticipated letter from her mind. She was more than happy to debate the best way to boil potatoes or which sauce would go best with the prize bird. After they had picked out the food, they went up to the second level to examine the new fabrics from France, get lost in a cascade of brightly colored ribbons, and stare at the ornate bonnets that would adorn the heads of only the most fashionable ladies come springtime.

The two hours they were there flew and by the time they crunched their way back to the house, the mood amongst them was considerably lighter. They came through the front door each with rosy cheeks and noses, in the midst of a lively conversation, to find Peter waiting for Eliza in the foyer. Louisa's eyes widened and, curtsying hastily, she said she needed to get back to the laundry. Julia watched as she walked purposefully further into the house, taking off her cape and cap as she went. It wasn't lost on her that her friend made a beeline in the opposite direction of the kitchen. Thankfully, Eliza was hanging up her own things and headed directly into the parlor after telling Peter what needed to be done for the bird and vegetables.

"A letter came for you, Miss Julia," Peter said in his deep voice, nodding toward the roll top desk in the main hallway. "It was hand delivered 'bout ten minutes ago." He was already on his way to the kitchen at the back of the house with the food Eliza had purchased at the market.

"Thank you, Peter," Julia called after him, pulling her cap off impatiently in her rush to see what had come for her. The sight of Mr. Kerry's now unmistakable handwriting adorned the envelope and set her heart racing. It took all of her strength not to yell out in excitement and she dove into the parlor, practically bowling Eliza over in her haste to share the good news.

"Eliza, you're a genius! I just needed to get out of the house. It came, it finally came!"

If Eliza was rattled by her sudden presence, she didn't let that on. "See, I told you all you needed was to take your mind off of it for a bit. What does it say, Julia?

Julia tore open the envelope a little sheepishly and removed the two pieces of parchment within. She'd been so preoccupied with actually receiving the response that she didn't know if Mr. Kerry would even be willing to meet with her or not. Clearing her throat for dramatic effect, she began to read:

Miss Webster,

I was delighted to receive your unexpected but very welcome response to our call for assistance. Our primary mission is to bring awareness to the plight the native populations in the South are currently facing. The impending introduction of the Indian Removal Act before Congress has caused great alarm in our ranks and we are doing all we can to educate the public on the devastation this would cause if the bill were to pass both houses. Your enthusiasm for our cause is much appreciated, especially from a well-connected person such as yourself.

To answer your query, yes, I would be most happy to meet with you and discuss the opportunities we have available. We have missions that travel down South on a regular basis, especially with the onset of warmer weather in a couple of months' time. There are also many ways to get involved right here at our headquarters in Boston. You will find the list of available dates on the additional sheet of parchment. Once you mark the date that would

work the best for you, please return this sheet in the envelope I've enclosed. I look forward to your response and to our eventual meeting.

Humbly Yours,
Mr. Nathaniel Kerry

She looked up from the letter into Eliza's bright yet concerned eyes. This was more than she could've hoped for. "He wants to meet with me," she squeaked out, surprised she could get anything out around the sudden lump in her throat. "I could go and actually meet with those I want to help. Wouldn't that be remarkable?" Her last question was meant more for herself than for her cousin, grand plans of her standing up to injustice already beginning to form in her mind. She was just imagining herself storming into the Senate chamber with an impenetrable case against President Jackson's proposal when Eliza's response pulled her back down to earth.

"Don't get ahead of yourself, dear," she said, the worried look that Julia had initially dismissed now very difficult to ignore. "This is a decision you can't make on your own. Your father is going to need to give his consent. Do you think Caroline would let you go to the meeting with Mr. Kerry by yourself?"

She looked at Eliza in silence, trying to come up with a response that didn't reveal how little thought she'd given all of these details. Convincing Caroline to let her do anything on her own was going to be an uphill battle. Her father would probably be the lighter touch given his efforts to help her but how would he feel about her going on a mission trip down South? She'd undeniably need some sort of escort for that leg of it. *Would Fletcher travel down with me? I'd probably need to do some serious begging. And pick a time when he can get away from his studies.*

Composing herself, Julia was able to meet Eliza's gaze. "Would you go with me to meet Mr. Kerry? I'm sure Caroline wouldn't object if she knew you would be there." Her cousin bit her lip, looking torn. Julia spoke before she could turn her down outright. "Please? I just want to hear what opportunities Mr. Kerry has to offer. This is so important to me."

She felt guilty for taking advantage of Eliza's soft spot for her. But this would make her path to making a difference so much easier if Caroline wasn't the one to accompany her on her first meeting with the missionary society. Her stepmother would likely insert her opinions into the conversation and Julia didn't want to risk alienating the people who could pave the way for her getting to go on a mission. Nothing was more important than actually interacting with those whose world could be turned upside down by this.

"Let me talk with Caroline about going with you for the first meeting," Eliza conceded after what felt like hours. Julia threw her arms around her in exuberant relief, thankful to have someone who supported her no matter the circumstances. Eliza gave a quick squeeze but after she pulled away, her cousin refused to let her off the hook. "I want you to know what you're getting yourself into and have realistic expectations. You could be facing barriers you can't foresee right now."

Julia nodded, only half listening to Eliza's advice. She wouldn't be brought down by her apprehension. Mr. Kerry was willing to take her interest seriously and she was sure she was on her way to making a difference.

* * * *

Louisa proved to be right that Friday when Julia heard a knock sound on the front door in the early afternoon. She was up in her room, taking advantage of the burst of adrenaline she felt after sending her response back to Mr. Kerry. She was surprised that Caroline hadn't put up more of a stink but she was prepared to hear her stepmother's undoubtedly stern advice when she came back under her wing in a few days. Even this knowledge couldn't dampen her spirits. Her meeting was now set in stone and when Eliza had recommended she start packing her things up before she had left to call on one of her friends, Julia had leapt at the chance to work off some of her excess energy.

She heard Louisa's soft footsteps padding against the floor and didn't think much of who could be downstairs until she heard a familiar voice wafting up to her through her open door.

"Is Miss Julia Webster at home? I apologize for not giving any notice that I was coming," she could hear Matthew say from below. For a moment, she was stunned into inaction, the shawl she was folding hanging limp between her fingers. Then, she put the shawl on top of her trunk and was out the door, fighting the urge to go barreling down the stairs.

"She is at home, sir. May I ask why you'd like to speak with her?" she heard Louisa say, her tone taking on the practiced formality that Julia would never get used to after spending so much time laughing and talking together. By now, she was at the foot of the stairs and she crossed the hall to the front doorway. Matthew's form was silhouetted against the backdrop of the bustling carriages in the lane beyond, his face still in shadow.

"Louisa, this is Mr. Eaton. Please show him in," she said. Her unexpected voice made her friend start a little but Louisa composed herself quickly and whisked Matthew out of the weather and into the warmth of Eliza's home. After she had taken his overcoat, she passed by Julia to hang it in the closet, giving her the briefest hint of a knowing smile as she passed.

She and Matthew were alone, then, and she looked up into the face she hadn't seen in nearly two weeks. He hadn't changed much, of course, but her heart still leapt into her throat as if she was meeting him for the first time. His kind eyes met hers and she felt a wide smile bloom on her lips.

"Mr. Eaton, I'm so glad you came to call. I wasn't sure if you'd catch me before I went back to my father's estate. May I show you into the sitting room?" she said, trying to remember the correct protocol for unexpected, though not unwelcome, visitors.

"Yes, that would be lovely. And please call me Matthew from now on. I think we've been through enough together to be on a first name basis." He fell into step beside her and she could see the twinkle in his eye as she snuck a sideways glance at him.

"You can call me Julia, too," she said, trying to keep her head pointed straight ahead. She didn't want to reveal how pleased she was by this new development.

She stepped aside to let him pass into the front sitting room, keeping the door open to listen for Eliza. She had said she'd be gone until the late afternoon but Julia didn't want to be caught doing anything that even nominally bent the rules.

"I can ask Louisa about getting some tea," she continued, turning to see if she could find her friend but his words stopped her.

"I'm in between appointments so I can't stay very long. I just wanted to see how you were since we'd last spoke. I hope that night in Washington didn't leave you with an unfavorable opinion of me or my family."

"Of course not," she said too quickly, turning back to face him. *It's not a complete lie,* she told herself, going to sit in the overstuffed chair opposite his. *I don't have a mean opinion of him. His insufferable uncle on the other hand. . .* "That evening was as unpredictable for you as it was for me."

"Well, I hope we can put it behind us," he said with a sudden seriousness that spoke to his sincerity.

"Yes, I'd like that. It wouldn't be right of me to hold your uncle's actions against you," she answered. There was no point in quibbling over what had already been hashed out. This was the second time he'd apologized and it was evident that he wanted to continue their budding friendship. On that, she was happy to oblige him. "When did you return to the city?"

"Right after the holiday. I had a great deal of work to catch up on and haven't had the chance to be very social. I was fortunate to get this break today and come see you. How have you been?"

She wanted to tell him her exciting news but she wasn't sure how he would react. Though it was possible that he would be sympathetic toward her stance of the forthcoming legislation, it was just as likely that this was one of the issues he fell into step with his uncle on. Treading carefully was of the utmost importance.

"Oh, I'm glad to be back. My cousin Eliza was gracious enough to let me stay with her while Caroline outfits our home to her liking." Pausing for a moment, she decided to continue. "I've been lucky enough to be considered for an incredible opportunity."

"Really? That's wonderful, Julia. What is it?"

She took a deep breath and told him about the missionary society and the work they were known for. As she did, she gauged his reaction, trying to determine if she could share her true motivation for becoming involved. He didn't scoff but rather gave her his full attention. The intensity in his eyes gave her the courage to continue.

"I'm meeting Mr. Kerry within the next week. My hope is to go on a mission myself eventually. I have a particular interest in an issue that's occurring in the South right now. It could even effect the area where you grew up."

"That's very ambitious and good of you. What has you so inspired to consider traveling down there?"

Giving him one last glance, Julia plunged head long into her plan. She tried to not blurt it all out at once but she also didn't want to give him too much time to dissect her reasoning if it didn't align with his own.

"Well, I'm not sure if you've heard but President Jackson is bringing a proposal before Congress that would remove the Indians of five different tribes from their lands. From what I've heard, he's willing to use force if it comes to it. And . . . I can't and won't agree with it. I'm hoping that by seeing what the Indians are actually experiencing, I can make some sort of difference."

She had been fixated on her hands in her lap as she'd explained herself to Matthew. Now, she dared to look up at him through the canopy of her eyelashes. He looked as if he were turning her words over to glean their full impact and her heart began to beat more rapidly. Had she just committed an irreversible error?

"Of course, this isn't more than a fancy at this point," she hurried on, wishing she hadn't allowed her excitement to cloud her judgement. "You must think me too bold for mentioning it."

"No, I don't. Forgive me for making you question yourself. It's not what I was expecting you to say, that's all."

Despite his assurances, she could feel her anxiety continue to climb. What could he think of her, taking on a mission that was so much larger than herself, which his uncle would vehemently be opposed to?

"I think what you want to do is ambitious," he continued thoughtfully. "But I also think that you're right to be concerned. Though my uncle hasn't talked with me about the president's plans extensively, I know he's willing to pull out the stops to make sure it passes. And my uncle is only too happy to indulge him. That's why he avoids the subject when we're together."

"You disagree with him, then?" The wave of relief that overtook her when he nodded his affirmation made her giddy enough to nearly laugh out loud. She bit the inside of her lip to prevent just that as he went on.

"I've only really known him for the past few years. My parents were insulated from the rest of the family and my uncle didn't want to rock the boat further with my grandfather by coming to visit. That all changed when my parents . . ." he cut himself off and she didn't know if he was going to continue. She had suspected that whatever had befallen them, it hadn't been good.

"They died in a house fire," he whispered, the somber look in his eyes making her throat constrict with unshed tears. "I was in town closing up the store that they owned. The fire in the wood burning stove threw sparks and by the time I got out to the house, the whole thing had gone up. They were trapped inside and I couldn't get in. It all happened in less than half an hour."

"My goodness. That's awful, Matthew. I'm so sorry," she said, knowing her sentiments weren't nearly enough. She knew how devastating it was to lose a parent and she couldn't wrap her head around the thought of her father not being here either.

On instinct, she reached over and took his hand, the sweat of his palm and shakiness of his fingers giving her the motivation to squeeze it in what she hoped was a reassuring way. His fingers stilled and he squeezed her fingertips back and she knew she'd done the right thing. She hadn't expected their reunion to take such a tragic turn. It was some time before Matthew spoke again, his voice gaining strength.

"I want you to understand how much influence my father still has over me. He would take me on hunting trips pretty frequently when I was growing up. We almost always encountered Indian hunting parties and he taught me to defer to them. It was their land, after all. Some would even allow us to join them. I've seen firsthand how they treat one another, the respect that's infused in their interactions. And the way they treat the animals they hunt. It's sacred to them. After witnessing that, I could never support my uncle in his ideas no matter how much he's done for me."

Julia swallowed the lump that had formed in her throat. How could it be that his father and uncle were brothers and yet had been so different? He truly understood where she was coming from. She told him about meeting Wohali and the impact that his story had on her. He listened attentively and only when she was finished did she realize that their hands were still joined together. After reluctantly easing herself out of his grasp, the air seemed much colder against where her fingertips had overlapped with his. The unexpected chiming of the clock in the corner made them both look up.

"My god, is it really three o'clock?" Matthew exclaimed, getting quickly to his feet. He'd already been there for half an hour. "I apologize for my abruptness but I need to leave. They're expecting me back at the law office."

"Of course. I'm sorry to have kept you so long," she returned, standing up to show him out. She had learned a great deal during their conversation and she wouldn't have minded if he could've stayed longer.

When he got to the door, he turned back and gave her a brilliant smile. "Thank you for trusting me with your plans. And for giving me such a sympathetic ear. I look forward to hearing how your meeting goes with Mr. Kerry."

"You're too kind, Matthew," she managed before he was out the door and quickly swallowed up by the jumbled crowd zipping back and forth along the sidewalk. She shut the door, shaking her head incredulously and walking into the parlor to find Louisa conspicuously dusting the furniture.

"So, that was Mr. Eaton?" she said, looking up from her task. "How was your visit?"

"Heart breaking and strangely wonderful," Julia replied, not quite knowing which of her warring emotions took precedence at the moment.

"Well, I have the feeling that I'll be seein' him again."

"Yes, you can be sure of that, my dear," was all she could reply.

CHAPTER 10

"So, where exactly is this missionary society?" Caroline asked the following week as Julia hurriedly gathered the journal and pen she'd set on the window seat in her room at her father's house. Eliza would be there in a few minutes to fetch her and Caroline hadn't ceased with her questioning all morning.

"Boston's chapter is on State Street, near the wharves," she answered, trying to keep the impatience from creeping into her voice. She had already told Caroline this last night at supper. What she wouldn't give to have Fletcher in town now, to be a charming, sarcastic buffer between their stepmother and herself. "The society has different branches all over the state but the one in Boston is the largest. It's a very reputable organization."

"I don't doubt it is, Julia," Caroline said, pursing her lips. Evidently, she hadn't done a very stealthy job of masking her annoyance. "I would just feel better if you'd allow me to accompany you, that's all. Eliza is a lovely person but she's much more likely to . . ."

To give into me, Julia thought, finishing the sentiment Caroline had left up to the imagination. Deep down, she knew that if anything happened to her, Caroline would need to answer to her father and that she should have more sympathy for the possible predicament she'd put the other woman in. But she was still put out that Caroline didn't think she'd done her due diligence in looking into the missionary society.

"I know what I'm doing," she answered half under her breath, flipping through the pages of her journal as if they contained the most fascinating sentiments in the world. She chanced a sideways glance at Caroline, worried that she'd gone too far.

"Well, I expect a full report when you get back," she said briskly. "Don't agree to anything until you've talked with me first. And I plan on speaking with Eliza, as well."

I wouldn't expect anything less, she thought meanly as Doris came into her room to let them know Eliza had just arrived and was waiting downstairs. Caroline turned smartly on her heel and brushed past Doris who sent Julia a sympathetic look as she sulked by. *It's not like I'm discussing a state secret! If Fletcher was the one going to this meeting, he wouldn't even be questioned.*

Julia felt her mood brightening once she saw Eliza, though. After not talking with her for a week, it was all she could do not to leap into her arms and beg her to take her back to the Lee home. She restrained herself to a relieved smile, though, as Caroline gave Eliza the same instructions before they escaped out the front door.

Once they were settled and on their way, Eliza turned to Julia. "She seems . . . invested in what you're doing, at least. If she didn't care, she wouldn't show that much interest in what you're about."

"I think she cares more about what my father will say if I trip up and embarrass the family in some way," Julia answered, the feeling of stepping on eggshells when she was around Caroline already beginning to dissipate. She felt like she could finally speak her mind without being silently assessed for social miscues.

"I'm only asking you to think about things from her perspective. She's suddenly in charge of a headstrong teenager and an introverted boy who is still grieving his mother. It's a lot to take on, especially without your father here."

Eliza's ability to look past her current situation and think of how other people fit into the larger picture was one of the things Julia typically most admired about her. But she wasn't feeling particularly charitable toward Caroline after the grilling she'd had to endure.

"She had to know what she was signing up for," Julia returned, sounding petulant even to her own ears. "I'm not a child she can simply order around. I'm only trying to follow what I know is the right thing to do."

"I'm not siding with her completely, I promise," Eliza insisted as the carriage bounced along the rutty lane curving down the sloped hill toward the always bustling wharves. "Her way of giving orders isn't exactly winning me over, either. But I think she really has your and the family's best interest at heart."

"Let's not talk about this anymore. I won't let anything dampen my excitement, including Caroline's lack of faith in me."

"She doesn't know you like I do, Julia. You need to give her some time to see that when you're passionate about something, you put all of your effort behind it. She'll learn that very quickly, I'd imagine. Remember the woolen cap project?"

Eliza gave her a conspiratorial wink and she shot her a sheepish smile in return. What she said was uncomfortably true.

Late last autumn, Louisa had come to her in tears when she'd learned that Quentin and the other poor sailors on his ship wouldn't be provided with warm hats for the long winter months. Her friend had been worried about frost bitten ears and frozen hair crusted with ice. The outrage Julia felt had been blinding and she'd taken Louisa in her arms and assured her they would remedy the situation. Eliza had taught her how to knit two winters previous to that and Louisa had years of experience under her belt already. In the span of a week, the three of them had gotten all the material, patched together 50 woolen caps, and delivered them to the ship before it left the harbor to deliver supplies to another port. Julia had even secured Doris's help and Peter had gone to fetch her to work with them for the too short afternoons.

She'd stayed up that last night until the wee hours and she could still hear the rhythmic clicking of her needles as she'd tried desperately to stay awake and finish the last cap. It was as if her ambition had possessed her and her vision had tunneled down to focus only on the task at hand.

"Well, that was for a good cause, too, wasn't it?" Julia insisted. "Louisa didn't have to worry about Quentin and his companions catching frostbite because of what we did."

"That's very true. I just want you to keep an open mind about this meeting. I'm interested to see what Mr. Kerry has to say but don't let too much on, my dear. It's better to be cautious until after you have all the facts laid out."

On that note of advice, the carriage stopped in front of their destination, skidding ever so slightly on a patch of ice poking through the snow. Looking up through the carriage window, she observed that the building that housed the mission's city headquarters was innocuous enough. It was a sturdy brick building that stretched up three stories and was utterly unadorned with architectural flourishes. It was clearly there for function, though the candles that burned in all the windows gave it a welcoming air. Still, with Eliza's advice buzzing in her ears, Julia felt some of her excitement turn to a bit of trepidation. This was going to be her chance to prove herself and she knew she had to take advantage of it.

A middle-aged man with graying sandy hair and dressed all in black answered the door when she knocked and, after hearing who she was there to meet, led them through several corridors and up the main flight of stairs to the second floor. Mr. Kerry's door was just a few feet down the main hall and already stood open. Having deposited them safely in his office, the older man bid them good day and plodded back down the stairs with purposeful steps.

"Welcome, Miss Webster," Mr. Kerry said in a deep, steady voice. "I was very glad to receive your letter of interest. Who have you brought with you today?"

As she introduced him to Eliza, she tried to hide the fact that she was already taken aback by him. She hadn't known what to expect when she turned to shake Mr. Kerry's hand for the first time but she did know she hadn't expected someone so young. He couldn't have been much older than Fletcher or Matthew, his dark hair parted smartly to the side and just brushing the fold of his cravat. Though he was dressed simply in a subdued brown waistcoat and breeches, he carried himself in a stately way that seemed more in keeping with men her father's age.

After he had them settled in the two chairs facing his pine desk, he sat in the chair on the other side and turned his full gaze on her. The conviction she felt even in the one motion confirmed that she'd chosen the right person to seek this opportunity from.

"Well, I have to say I was pleasantly surprised by your interest," he began after a short, though not strained, silence. "We don't get very many Bostonians, regardless of age, who are very informed or enthusiastic about helping with the Native cause. It's a point of pride for us that we've been able to maintain such lasting relationships with many of the tribes in the Carolinas and beyond. What, would you say, is the main reason the Lord brought you to us?"

"From what I've learned during my recent trips to New York and Washington, the situation is very concerning, sir. The legislation is being brought before Congress next month and I know for a fact that there's at least one influential politician who is very troubled by what the consequences could be."

"My father was good enough to get me the address for your organization," she continued, trying in vain to decipher Mr. Kerry's placid expression and what could be brewing beneath the surface. "I thought you would be a good person to talk with and see how I could help. I also know that you've organized mission trips down south and, if possible, I feel like I could make a difference there."

She could feel Eliza shift in the chair beside her at the mention of traveling down south but Julia never found out what her cousin was going to say as Mr. Kerry finally expressed his thoughts.

"You do realize we're a religious organization, miss," he interjected. "This would factor into any mission trip you wish to take part in." Though he didn't say it sharply, it made her re-think her approach. She and her family, though categorizing themselves as Christian, weren't devout in any faith and she had to be careful she didn't trip herself up and offend Mr. Kerry.

"Of course, sir. My apologies for overlooking that important point. My father is always concerned with what the political implications are. I'm afraid my pre-occupation with the consequences of such a bill overtook me."

She held her breath as Mr. Kerry considered her explanation and she could see Eliza open her mouth out of the corner of her eye, ready to come to the rescue if need be. However, the warm smile that transformed his face, however brief it was, again put her at ease.

"I'm sorry if I implied your motives weren't sincere. I like to prepare those seeking us out of how seriously we take the faith and the conversion of souls here."

Julia made sure she gave an understanding and respectful nod but she could feel a spark of anger light inside her. The idea of conversion was all well and good when there wasn't a crisis coming down the pike but there was one. This was larger than what Mr. Kerry seemed most concerned about; it could mean that entire nations of people would be forced to leave the only land they'd ever known. She was desperate to understand more about them and determine what she could do.

"I can see how much you want to help, Miss Webster," he said. "If you're willing to put in some time and work with our missionaries who already have established relationships with some of the tribes, then I would recommend you go on a mission to North Carolina."

Julia nodded vigorously, her acceptance of this arrangement on the tip of her tongue before Eliza brought the whole thing crashing down with her response.

"My young cousin is indeed very eager to help, sir. She has a good heart. However, I'm not sure that it's wise to talk of a missionary trip so soon. Her parents would need to be consulted about this. And arrangements for an escort would need to be made if it's decided she can go. I couldn't see that happening until at least the summertime."

Julia could see how much it pained Eliza to link Caroline to her father in that way. It conjured a lump in her own throat that she couldn't quite swallow down. To think that Grace Webster could be replaced in both of their lives with such a woman was decidedly unfair. That she even needed to pursue these permissions was an affront all in itself. An uncomfortable mix of sadness over her mother and frustration that she wasn't able to pursue what she desperately wanted silenced her when she would have typically countered with a passionate flourish.

Mr. Kerry, for his part, seemed just as disappointed with Eliza's pragmatic outlook on the situation. Though he covered it swiftly with a quiet "Of course, Mrs. Lee" it was evident that his own plans had hit a snag. The daughter of Senator Webster being actively associated with his society could have untapped benefits to it, though she knew that was not the only reason for his discouragement. She could tell how dedicated he was to his work just from this one interaction.

He must not get very many young, unwed women who are interested in going on mission trips, she thought with a slight shake of her head and acknowledgement that Eliza was sadly speaking the truth. *If Fletcher wanted to take part in this, there wouldn't be any complications to consider. He could just do what he wanted.*

She shook off her bitterness, though, as she made plans to come back the next week with Eliza's approval and took satisfaction in the fact the Mr. Kerry perked up at the probability of her return. After they were snug in the carriage, Eliza also insisted that she would talk with Caroline about making this arrangement permanent as they bounced back to the Webster estate.

The cloud that had settled after her set back lifted even more as she listened to Eliza's wholly positive assessment of Mr. Kerry.

"This is clearly a reputable organization, Julia," she said. "Mr. Kerry may have been a little hasty with his enthusiasm but I was impressed with his dedication. I promise I'll do what I can to convince Caroline of this, too."

"Thank you. I'm so happy you were the one who went with me, Eliza," she returned, feeling ever more grateful to have an ally like her. Eliza reached over and squeezed her hand reassuringly, warming her heart. By the time they pulled up in front of the house, Julia vowed to focus on the positive strides she had made that afternoon. She had proven herself to Mr. Kerry and was a step closer to accomplishing what she was setting out to do.

CHAPTER 11

Eliza must have worked her powers of persuasion because the next week, Julia was again pulling up in front of the brick façade of the missionary society's building. She tried to ignore the fact that Caroline was the one accompanying her this time around and strove to be grateful that her stepmother was showing an interest in what she was doing. But she also couldn't help but hope that after Caroline was satisfied, she would leave her to her own devices.

"You're only going to talk with Mr. Kerry for a moment, right?" she asked, turning to look at Caroline. She was constantly trying to keep her cards close to her chest but never felt like she was successful, especially when it came to her stepmother. Her ability to see through Julia's bluster and discern her true motivations was uncanny given how brief their relationship had been.

"Yes, that's my plan," Caroline said, meeting Julia's anxiety with a passivity that could be mistaken for actual boredom. Julia knew better than to let her guard down, though. That passivity could turn to a sharp inquisitiveness on the turn of a coin.

As she opened the carriage door and James helped her down to the street, the tang of nearby saltwater nipped at her lips, reminding her that an uncustomary warm spell had thawed the ice on the edges of the waterfront. It made her suddenly long for spring which was, regrettably, still a long way off. There was so much to be hopeful about in the season of new beginnings that she had to force herself to remain in the present.

It was Mr. Kerry himself that met them in the already open front doorway and Julia was relieved that Caroline didn't immediately begin questioning the poor man after they'd been introduced. The three of them went a different way than she and Eliza had during their previous visit, instead venturing deeper into the mission's first floor. They went past several rooms where others were working diligently on various tasks until they finally came to a small room whose perimeter was lined with shelves. The shelves were stacked with navy blankets neatly folded into bundles and tied with thick yarn.

There was an open doorway in the far corner that allowed access to another of the small rooms they'd just passed, giving the whole level a labyrinthine feel. A woman came hurrying in with several of the blankets stacked on top of each other and she was followed by another woman who carried what looked like wooden stethoscopes in one hand and dental forceps in her other hand. Julia could hear the whirring of an industrial loom in the distance but she couldn't tell where it was located.

These supplies were placed on a table before an innocuous looking couple who looked to be in their mid-forties. The man sported close-clipped dark hair and a bushy beard that was slowly losing its battle to remain as dark as the hair atop his head. The woman beside him was petite in relation to his tall frame with kind green eyes which shone behind half-moon spectacles that seemed incapable of staying on the bridge of her button nose. Mr. Kerry addressed them with warm familiarity.

"Abigail, Jacob, this is Miss Webster. She is interested in helping with the Native cause, particularly down south. I know our focus has shifted somewhat during the cold months but I thought it would be good to pair her with you as you could tell her of your numerous experiences. Miss Webster, this is Mr. and Mrs. O'Connor. They've been part of our mission trips for the last ten years and can help get you better acquainted with how our society runs."

He then turned to Caroline and politely invited her to join him in his office to discuss the particulars of his expectations for Julia. She seemed placated by Mr. Kerry's offer and followed him without a fuss, simply shooting a backward glance whose message was clear. *Behave.* Once the two of them were gone, Julia breathed an audible sigh of relief. At least her orientation to her work would go smoothly for the time being.

"Miss Webster, are you alright?" Abigail O'Connor had come up behind her on silent feet and seemed concerned by her reaction to her stepmother's departure. She looked over at the other woman and was surprised when she needed to tilt her head down a bit; she wasn't used to anyone being shorter than she was.

"Oh yes, Mrs. O'Connor. I didn't mean to worry you. I'm just . . . a little anxious about all of this." Julia didn't want to get into the particulars with someone she'd only met a few minutes before. It was best to downplay her worries about Caroline and instead put all of her energy into the task at hand.

"I can understand. This can be overwhelming when you first start here. But we're here to help you and answer any questions you have." She tilted her head toward the table and turned back to where she and her husband had been working before Julia had interrupted them. She followed Mrs. O'Connor, taking in the procession of bundles in various stages of completion. In between the blankets and medical supplies, there was a stack of neatly folded cotton shirts. After Abigail had tasked her with untangling the stethoscopes from one another and then placing one alongside a set of pliers on the shirt within the blanket, she continued to talk even as her hands flew with her own duties in this little assembly line.

"My husband and I have been involved with the society . . . what, ten years? Is that right, dear?"

"I believe it's closer to fifteen," he answered quietly, the adoration in his eyes when he looked over Julia's head at his wife giving her the early impression that these two were inseparable.

"Oh, that's right. It doesn't seem possible that we've been involved for so long but here we are. We've seen quite a bit of change since those first years. Why, when we joined, there wasn't any talk of going overseas to speak with different groups. Now, these bundles are for our missionaries who will be traveling to various countries in the summer months."

"Have you been on any of the mission trips that travel overseas?" Julia asked, wondering if Mr. Kerry had made a mistake. She had intended to stay in the country and didn't feel comfortable being paired with a couple who would be braving the stormy seas to reach those in far flung places.

"Oh, heavens no," Mrs. O'Connor said, her eyes widening behind her glasses. The prospect of traveling to another country seemed to have never crossed her mind and Julia felt her growing sense of panic dissipate. "God bless the missionaries who feel a calling to do that sort of work, of course. But Jacob and I have been working with the same group of Indian tribes for at least the past ten years. I'm sure that's why Nathaniel . . . err, Mr. Kerry paired you with us."

"We're simply helping with the preparations that go into those missions. It's still such a new endeavor for us and from what I've heard from the others, there's a great deal of poverty over in places like Singapore or the Congo. It's so important to not only spread the Word but to help the downtrodden our missionaries meet in the process."

Julia had never even heard of the places Mrs. O'Connor was referencing, much less be able to locate them on the globe in her father's study. She had prided herself on staying informed about what was happening in her own country but felt suddenly very self-conscious about her lack of education in circumstances and matters in other countries.

"It's a lot to process in one afternoon," Mrs. O'Connor said sympathetically and Julia knew that her face must have given her away. "I think we should focus instead on where your own interest lies. Why were you drawn to the Native cause in the first place?"

I might as well start from the beginning, she thought taken in by Mrs.

O'Connor's infectious curiosity.

"Well, I suppose it started when I was younger. My mother was very invested in philanthropy and I met a Cherokee man during one of the events we went to."

"How wonderful that you had that experience so early in your life! We hadn't met an Indian until our first mission trip. Your mother must have been very dedicated to expanding your worldview."

"She was. The importance she placed on other peoples' well-being was very inspiring to me. And it helped that my father became involved in politics as I grew up. He was always passionate about what was going on in the country."

"So it's true." Mrs. O'Connor turned to her conspiratorially, pushing her spectacles back up her nose. She wore the air of a woman who secretly devoured gossip but didn't want to let it on. "I heard that you were the daughter of a senator but wasn't sure if I should believe that or not. I'm so thrilled the Lord has called you here to help us."

Julia gave her a strained smile, uncomfortable with Mrs. O'Connor's vocal reverence for her religion. She knew she should've expected it, given that she'd chosen a missionary society to educate herself but she'd need to get used to it. Her father would have scoffed at putting so much faith in a higher power, being the pragmatist that he was. She couldn't very well blurt that out to Abigail, though.

"What you've heard is true, mam." She had to concentrate very hard on keeping her hands busy and not let Mrs. O'Connor see how uncomfortable she was making her all of a sudden. There was no telling what the older woman would expect of her now that she knew Julia's parentage.

"Wouldn't it be wonderful if your involvement brought more exposure to our cause. Does your father know anyone at one of the newspapers? It would be splendid if the press were to write a piece on all of the good we're doing."

Julia stammered a bit, not sure what to say. To be used for her connections with her father was something that she'd encountered often enough to know the signs. That this was coming from Mrs. O'Connor was a little bit shocking and she wasn't sure how to handle it. It was Abigail's husband that unexpectedly came to her rescue.

"My love, I don't think that's the main reason Miss Webster is here," his quiet voice cut into the conversation. Julia said a silent *thank you* and hoped Mr. O'Connor realized how grateful she was. Though Abigail's intentions seemed to come from a good place, her plans for Julia had definitely put her in a position she shied away from. She was here to make some sort of difference, not to be the conduit to Daniel Webster.

"Like us, she wants to help others," Mr. O'Connor continued.

Recognition dawned on Mrs. O'Connor's face and she looked so chagrined that any annoyance Julia had felt washed away. "How unfair of me to put that kind of pressure on you, my dear. That's one of the many reasons I love my Jacob-he brings me down from my lofty ideas and settles me in the here and now again. The very fact that you're here with us is cause for joy. And I've many stories that I could tell you to help you know that you're getting involved with."

There; that was what Julia had been looking for. Her understanding of what the Indians were facing was murky at best and she would appreciate having it more fleshed out. The idea of submitting some sort of appeal to her father had been rolling around in her head for the last couple of weeks. With Abigail's knowledge and an experience involving her own interaction with an Indian tribe, that idea seemed much more realistic.

She was just about to ask Abigail what kind of stories she could tell her when Caroline entered the room and her questions died on her lips. Mr. Kerry wasn't with her now and she wore a placid enough expression to convince Julia that she'd heard all the right things from the director.

"Time to go, Julia," Caroline instructed all but glancing at her bare wrist to indicate her stepdaughter was wasting her time. She looked at the ticking grandfather clock in the corner and was surprised to see she'd been helping the O'Connors for more than an hour.

"We hope to you again soon, dear," Abigail said as Julia ducked out of her place on the assembly line and thanked the couple for their kindness. She followed Caroline through the maze of passageways to get back to the front door and they were on the way back home when her stepmother finally turned to her.

"You may give two afternoons a week to this cause as long as you have someone to take you. I'm satisfied that Mr. Kerry is running a reputable establishment and the service you can provide would be helpful. But I don't want to hear of you causing any trouble."

"Of course, Caroline," she answered, trying to batt down a triumphant smile. Now, she only needed to find out how to contact Abigail to see if she and Jacob would be willing to transport her down to the missionary. But her own two feet were just as good if worse came to worse; she was always hearing how important exercise was for a young lady.

*   *   *   *

January 20th, 1830

Dear Fletcher,

I hope Harvard is treating you well; it's unfortunate you had to go back before the holidays came and we weren't able to see each other then. Edward looked much improved the last time I saw him so there's one less thing for you to fret about. Eliza and Thomas were a godsend to him-you were correct in keeping him with them. I'm sure you heard about Papa's bout of influenza in New York but he looked so much like his old self when Caroline and I left Washington.

Caroline and I are learning to live with each other. I cannot say how the next few months (or year or a lifetime) will unfold but at least there's been no blood split. I will say that a new philanthropic opportunity has come my way that is keeping me very preoccupied and out of trouble. You remember how Mama loved the work that she did and it seems I do, as well. Being with the fellow missionaries at the society I'm devoting my time to has been an eye-opening experience to say the least. I'm particularly fond of a woman named Abigail O'Connor and her quiet husband. I've learned so much from them. They've thoroughly convinced me that a missionary trip is the best way to know the people we're working to help and will give me a better understanding of how I can be of even more service.

I think you'd make an ideal chaperone for this, don't you? It would certainly be the ideal way to make up missing my 17th birthday. Perhaps this could be arranged during your Easter break from the university?

I hope to see you soon. All my love,

Julia

CHAPTER 12

The doldrums of January and February had typically been Julia's least favorite time of the year. Time seemed to move at half the normal speed in her anticipation of spring, which brought the prospect of tilling new flower gardens and resuming her daily walks with Louisa and Eliza. However, this year was refreshingly different as she settled into a busy pattern of calling at the Lee home at least twice a week and taking the carriage to the missionary society about as often.

She barely contained her surprise the first time Caroline allowed her to travel with Abigail unaccompanied. Caroline was sure to be relieved to have her out of her hair for some part of their time together in that big house that oftentimes felt like a finely furnished, echoing cavern. Her taste in the finer things was slowly but surely replacing Grace's simpler yet functional style and Julia often caught herself thinking things like: *Why do we need new China teacups?* or *What's the purpose of having a silk tablecloth for the old dining table?*

The purchases were all nice, of course, but Julia thought they were hardly necessary. It was only when Caroline's friends began calling that she realized her stepmother's underlying motivations. It was all about keeping up appearances and she was taking full advantage of her new position as the wife of a respected senator.

It was a shame that she was living beyond their means. Julia had to feign ignorance and pretend that she hadn't seen the ledger book, that the

.mily's finances could absorb Caroline's increasingly extravagant purchases. Even as she had spent more time over at Eliza's home after her mother's death, Doris had been faithful in reviewing their financial status with she and Fletcher every month. She had no control over what was spent nor could she control what her father spent down in Washington, of course, but she had tried to keep Fletcher informed of what was happening when he was away at Harvard so he could communicate with their father. She knew she was fortunate to even have an inkling of that information and even more so to have a brother who was willing to allow that to continue for as long as it had.

Now that Caroline was in charge of the household, it was more difficult to see what was actually occurring behind the scenes. It was fortunate that Doris, however attentive she was to her new mistress's needs, was still very loyal to Julia and would discreetly leave the book open whenever she was able to. This knowledge only made the way Caroline looked down her nose at Abigail that much more grating, though.

The most expensive item that Abigail and Jacob owned had to be that small and slightly dilapidated carriage they carried her to and from the missionary society in. It only required one horse and Jacob served as the driver but the ride was always smooth and the conversation enlightening in the confines of its box. Julia was embarrassed for her stepmother that she would put so much weight in the approval and gossip of others. If that practice was what allowed her to get out of house with minimal trouble, though, then she chose to be grateful for it.

She hadn't known what to make of Abigail after their first meeting but she had found her to be an invaluable resource as well as a unexpectedly spunky companion. Behind those half moon spectacles was a mind that looked at the world in a larger, philosophical way and Abigail challenged Julia to see their situation in a way she wouldn't have thought of before. She still wasn't convinced that a higher power was calling them to this work but over the course of those weeks, she grew to respect that Abigail certainly thought so.

Jacob deposited her on one snowy afternoon that was on the cusp of turning over to evening. She went through the pantry and spoke with Doris as she knocked the clods from her boots and watched as the housekeeper directed their new cook, Philip, on where everything was in the kitchen. Julia passed through to the front of the house in her stocking feet, barely making a sound as she went to hang up her coat on the rack in the foyer. As she was coming back, she was surprised to hear muffled voices coming from the parlor. She hadn't noticed an idling carriage in the semi-circle of a driveway out front and wondered who was still visiting past the usual time for calls.

Easing herself over to the closed door, Julia tried to make out who Caroline could be talking to. She had to scurry across the main hallway and up the stairs only moments later when Caroline and her companion unexpectedly exited. Hidden on the landing of the carpeted and shadowy staircase, she now recognized Mrs. Oldach, the wife of the city's Treasurer. She and Caroline had become fast friends.

"You will come next week, won't you? It's been so delightful having everyone over for tea during these dreary times," Caroline's voice floated up to her ears as the two women planted themselves in the hallway.

"Oh, yes of course. Why, your teas are all that anyone is talking about nowadays. It's always good to get fresh blood in our circle. It becomes so dull after awhile when it's all the same ladies. If I had to hear Millie bring up her daughter's new imported chaise lounge one more time, I was considering throwing myself into the bay. And yes, I know it's frozen right now!"

"You mustn't be too hard on Millie. You know she only brings up her daughter every five minutes because she doesn't want the subject of what a scoundrel her husband is to come up. I heard he took his mistress to The Lacewings in broad daylight! It's one thing to have a whore in secret but it's entirely different when you take her out for refreshments with expensive pearls around her neck."

Mrs. Oldach gave a concessionary nod and Julia rolled her eyes, gulping down an exasperated sigh. There were many reasons why her mother hadn't been comfortable socializing with these women; their uncanny ability to tear down members of their own circle was one of them. She was about to try to make a break for her bedroom when the mention of her name caught her attention.

"How are things going with Julia? I know you've mentioned before that it hasn't been an easy adjustment for you. Her mother never brought her up properly, if you ask me. I always saw her galivanting around with that handsome brother of hers where a well-bred young lady shouldn't be. A girl her age has no business knowing how her father makes a living."

Outrage snaked through Julia until she was full to brim with it and she worked hard not to give herself away. She'd begun to grind her jaw and she pressed her lips together to keep from being discovered. How could this woman, who she'd exchanged no more than ten words with in her life, judge her and her family like this? It was inexcusable and she wished she could tell Mrs. Oldach that to her pinched, haughty face. The only thing that stopped her was her desire to hear Caroline's response to this. She wasn't holding her breath that her stepmother would even pretend to defend her.

"She is headstrong, yes. I hadn't expected that when Daniel entrusted me with our estate here. But at least she's putting some of her energy toward helping others, I suppose."

"Hmph," came Mrs. Oldach's muffled reply. Julia wished she could have one of her headstrong moments right then but she stayed rooted to her spot as Caroline continued.

"I just don't know what to do with her sometimes," Caroline conceded in whisper, as if ashamed to admit she didn't have control over every part of her life. "I try to reach her and relate to her. But I often feel like I can't say the right things. And the way she looks at me sometimes, as if I don't have any idea how to run my own house. She makes me feel so small, like I'm not worthy of trying to take her mother's place."

"What an insolent child. She sounds like a troublemaker to me. I would advise you put her in her place and soon. Goodness knows what damage she could bring to the family name if she's allowed to run amok. I know that her work might seem innocent enough but be careful, my dear. A girl like her will take advantage of her freedom, mark my words. I'm just grateful my girls always knew their place."

"Well, I. . ." Caroline's voice grew faint as the two women began to walk toward the foyer and away from the staircase.

Julia eased her way up the remainder of the stairs as silently as she could, shutting the door behind her and padding over to her bed. She couldn't sit down for her agitation, though, so she began to pace the width of the room. To say that Caroline had surprised her was an understatement. She'd been so wrapped up in her own thoughts and wants that she hadn't considered what effect she had on Caroline. It made her feel unexpectedly ill at ease to know this was all boiling under the surface between them.

How naïve she is to confide in that awful woman, she thought indignantly as she went back to thinking of the other person in that exchange. She could envision Mrs. Oldach airing Caroline's fears to another woman in their group without a second thought. Her stepmother was useful to her now because she was willing to play the hostess to their horrible get togethers. Once she had served her purpose, Mrs. Oldach and her society matrons would surely abandon her if Julia did indeed "stain" the family name.

A firm knock on her door made her stop in mid-stride and take a deep breath to center herself. When she opened the door to Caroline's unreadable face, she fought to keep her own features just as placid.

"I didn't realize you'd come home, Julia. I wanted to let you know that dinner will be ready in a few minutes. We'll be fortunate to try the new cook's salmon tonight."

"I'll be down in a minute, thank you," Julia answered, wondering if the waver in her voice was as obvious as she thought it was. When Caroline turned and went downstairs without a second glace, she sagged against the doorframe, wondering how she'd gotten herself into such a complicated place.

*　　　　*　　　　*　　　　*

Julia was home when the post was delivered the next day. She almost missed the letter from Achsah as she turned over Caroline's secrets with dogged single-mindedness. When she tore open the envelope, she found that the letter was brief but it contained some of the best unexpected news she could hope for. Edward was coming home for a week in a fortnight.

CHAPTER 13

Edward's unexpected presence was a most welcome respite and Julia set about trying to make his brief visit with them as unbothered as possible. She arranged a visit with Eliza and the three of them spent the next afternoon cozy in her sitting room as their cousin peppered him with questions. Julia tried to get Louisa to sit with them for a bit, as well, but her friend claimed that there was too much work to be done around the house. She had insisted that Eliza would understand but Louisa had become vehement in her refusal and she had let it go. There had been something evasive in Louisa's expression that she couldn't quite place and she worried that her friend was keeping something under wraps. But then Edward's laugh made her grin from ear to ear and she reluctantly put Louisa's odd behavior out of her mind.

When they left Eliza's to walk back home, the sun was beginning to peak out from behind the clouds as it set. The sky had come alight with its brilliance and Julia watched as wispy clouds traveled across the emerging blue expanse at a fast clip in the breeze that had begun to blow. It was as if a fire had been doused but the embers refused to be extinguished.

The next morning brought a radiant sun that had begun to show its face the previous day and suggested that spring was in the offing. Julia was recruited to help Doris with a reassessment of supplies in the kitchen but she didn't mind the monotony as she bustled around in the warm pool of light coming in through the window. It gave her an excuse not to mull over the awkwardness that had intensified between her and Caroline.

When she came out to check on Edward, he was writing away in his journal in the front sitting room, his brows knit in abject concentration. It was such a relief to see him involved in any activity that she just smiled softly and tiptoed back to the kitchen to continue her work. The post came and brought an unexpected letter from their father, which made the day even brighter. They sat together on the small sofa, Julia's arm around Edward's shoulder, and pored over the six pages that recounted various happenings in the capital, his insistence that he was doing well, and his hope that they were all in good spirits. She wondered if Fletcher had somehow gotten word to him that Edward was again in Boston and was grateful for his thoughtfulness if he had.

Caroline was out making calls and the day passed in quiet ease through the mid-afternoon. Even after their stepmother's return and perusal of the exciting correspondence, there was a tentative peace as the three of them gathered together in the sitting room in the early evening. Julia was just about to pick up her book when a knock sounded at the front door.

"Were you expecting anyone?" Caroline asked her and she shook her head silently. They heard Doris bustling out of the back of the house to answer the door and, moments later, she entered the room with Matthew Eaton behind her.

"Mr. Eaton it's good to see you. An unexpected surprise to be sure." Caroline said. Her eyebrows arched as she glanced over at Julia quickly and then turned her attention to their guest. For her part, Julia kept her eyes downcast, embarrassed that her affection for Matthew hadn't gone as unnoticed as she'd hoped. Why did he have a habit of dropping in when she least expected it?

"I apologize if I'm intruding, Mrs. Webster. We received a notice at the law office from your husband earlier today and it reminded me that I've neglected my duty to call on all of you." He was still standing in the doorway, waiting for an invitation to sit. Julia was reluctant to step on Caroline's toes but she was beginning to squirm in discomfort at the rudeness of not allowing him in.

"Do you work at the law office?" Edward asked, unexpectedly breaking the building tension. Julia started a bit, suddenly remembering that her brother hadn't met Matthew before.

While Caroline regarded Matthew with off-handed politeness from her matron's chair, Edward seemed completely taken in by their unexpected guest. As Doris went off to fetch him something to drink, Matthew gave his full attention to her younger brother, fielding all of the questions he had about life in the country and what animals he'd encountered in the forests that surrounded the town he'd grown up in.

She was pleasantly surprised by how easy it was for Edward to talk with Matthew. It was typically difficult for her shy brother to open up to anyone and Matthew had found an instant connection with him. It helped that he'd peaked Edward's interest with his tales of tire swings suspended over ponds, seeing wayward packs of coyotes lurking at the edge of their land, and the harrowing hunting excursions he'd gone on with his father.

"You got to hunt with real Indian braves?" Edward asked excitedly. "What was that like?"

"Edward, one shouldn't ask too many questions. You don't want to pry into Mr. Eaton's affairs," Caroline said. The crestfallen look on Edward's face made Julia want to get up off the settee that she was perched on and shake the other woman for being so dense. It was fortunate that Matthew took it all in stride.

"It's no trouble, Mrs. Webster. I'll admit I'm starved for a captive audience and Edward has given me more attention than I might deserve." He winked at her now grinning brother before diving back into telling him of the first time he'd seen a true Cherokee hunting party.

Caroline looked vaguely annoyed but didn't press the issue, choosing instead to pick up their copy of the *Boston Courier* and thumb to the society pages. Julia tried to smooth her own ruffled feathers and turned her attention to the animated pair facing her on the other side of the sitting room table.

As Doris whisked back in with Matthew's drink and departed just as quickly, she found herself being sucked into Matthew's story right along with her brother.

"Did they really take down a bear?" Edward said. His eyes were wide with wonder after their guest had described the technique the Cherokee leader had used to corner a black bear against a rock outcropping.

"Yes, they certainly did. The leader even allowed my father to help. I was in the woods on the other side of the clearing and got to watch the whole thing."

"What was that like? You seem like you remember it all like it happened yesterday."

"I do. It's one of the most remarkable experiences I've had and that's why I can picture it so clearly." When Edward made to say something, Matthew gently went on before he could ask more questions.

"But there's something you need to understand about the Cherokee, Edward. They only hunt what they need to survive. There wasn't any baiting or unnecessary violence done to the creature. It's for food, of course, but every other part has some use to the tribe. And I think that's the most important lesson I learned. That, and a bear is much bigger up close than you think it's going to be."

"I wouldn't know. My father's never taken me out hunting," Edward said, his sullen expression dampening Julia's amusement over his earlier excitement. "And now my brother is off at college so he can't take me, either."

"You still have plenty of time to try it," Matthew said. Caroline seemed about to object to this as her newspaper came down to reveal her shocked expression but Edward beat her out with the speed of his reply.

"Do you still go with your father? Maybe I could go with the two of you."

Poor Edward seemed to realize almost instantly that he'd made a weighty miscalculation as all the air in the room became charged and an uneasy silence descended. Julia tried to catch Matthew's eye but he was suddenly very fascinated with the contents of his still steaming teacup. No one spoke for what felt like hours until Matthew broke the silence with only the hint of a quaver in his voice.

"I'm sorry that won't be possible. My father passed on a couple of years ago."

Edward's eyes sparkled with tears and Julia was just about to get up and go to him when he replied in a remarkably steady voice, "My mama passed away, too. I miss her very much but Julia says I'll always have my memories of her. And you'll always have those memories of your papa, too. I'm sorry about what happened to him."

Julia could feel her eyes widen as she tried to process this shift in her brother. When had he developed this insight and strength? She wanted to believe that what she had said to him before Christmas was impactful, that his choice to open up to her about his feelings had helped him come to terms with the struggles he was still going through. To hear him try to comfort Matthew now was confirmation that she'd made the right decision and she had to blink a few times to keep her own tears at bay.

She chanced a glance over at Caroline who had gone still and slightly rigid at the edge of her chair, her hand at her temple as if she were coming down with a headache. It was a rare instance that her stepmother didn't have some opinion to offer and she wondered what must be going through her head as she took in the discussion of the woman who had come before her. Caroline may have been in the process of making their home her own but it must have been difficult to face two flesh and blood reminders that she'd been their father's second choice. And after she'd overheard that conversation with Mrs. Oldach, Julia couldn't help but feel some sympathy for her and her situation.

"Thank you, Edward," Matthew said. She hadn't wanted to look at him after the conversation had taken such a fraught turn but the look of esteem he bestowed on her brother made her heart soar. "Would you like to tell me a story about your mother?"

"I think I'll make sure Doris has the correct number of hens for our supper," Caroline said, her feet meeting the floor with a decided *thunk* as she stood. "Will you be joining us, Mr. Eaton?"

"I'm sorry, Mrs. Webster, but I must get back into town soon," he answered. His gaze was a little wary as she nodded and left the room without another word. Julia decided to stay put and listen to her brother. It would have been impolite if they'd both abandoned their guest.

"I didn't mean to offend Mrs. Webster," he said to her as she accompanied him to the foyer some twenty minutes later. "I should've realized that it would be hard for her to hear Edward talk about your mother."

"It's alright. I'll try to speak with her later," she said. "But I'm so grateful you brought Edward out of his shell. He doesn't normally open up so willingly."

"He's very impressive. And I think much of that is a credit to you, Julia."

She looked up at him with surprise, trying to will the blush coloring her cheeks away. His kind eyes held more than they usually did and it took her a moment to realize what that emotion was. Admiration. He admired her.

"Oh, I don't know how much I've helped him. Eliza should be credited with much of that. She's been such a blessing to all of us."

"I heard what he said about how you reassured him. He needed to hear that, especially from someone he loves so dearly. Someone who continues to love your mother like he does. I can tell how hard you've tried to be a solace to him."

"I'm his sister. Of course I'm doing all I can to be there for him."

"Not all siblings would be as dedicated as you've been," he said. The expression that overtook his face made her think that he was thinking of his uncle and father, about the tension that had split his family apart. She wanted to say something about Henry but his face told her it wasn't the right time. He was rarely as guarded around her as he was now and she could sense he didn't want to go down that road.

"Well, I appreciate you saying that I'm making some kind of difference for Edward. I feel guilty every time he leaves to go back to our relatives in Connecticut. I know that it's important for him to finish school there but I hope he's back with us later this year. It seems you've gained him as a friend."

"I hope that's the case, Julia. I think it would do him much good if you were all together again. I'm happy to be his friend. As well as yours." He tipped his hat to her as he went out the front door and she watched him stride toward the stable to fetch his horse for longer than was necessary. Turning away, she chastised herself for lingering so long; she needed to be careful that she didn't come to expect the presence of those warm blue eyes and the feelings that were beginning to rise up inside her.

* * * *

March 7th, 1830

Dear Julia,

I'm sorry that this letter is such a late response to the one you sent me in January. The semester has been particularly busy. Caroline sent me a letter just last week letting me know of Edward's impromptu visit. I'm glad you were able to spend some time together and wish I could've gotten away from Professor Hits-me-over-the-head to see him too. That's the professor's real name, I give you my word! He teaches Latin, ironically enough.

While you trying to cajole me into being your chaperone down south strokes my ego nicely, I need more details before I'll agree to anything. Do you really think this is the best use of your (and my) time? I know what an impression Mother had on you regarding her charitable work but this seems excessive. What has prompted this sudden need to crisscross the country and not just stay in Boston, continuing to serve in your current duties?

You're a persuasive girl, I'll give you that. But I need more of a reason to potentially miss some of the semester than 'I've been called to do this' or whichever force is motivating you. We can discuss this more when I'm home for Easter.

Your brother always,

Fletcher

CHAPTER 14

Julia could feel the color rising in her cheeks as she read Fletcher's letter again. She'd gone up to her room as soon as she'd recognized her brother's uneven scrawl on the front of the envelope. His arrogance had always set off a wave of annoyance within her, a feeling so familiar that she couldn't stop the involuntary rolling of her eyes after she took in his words. But what she was feeling now, this was so much more. She couldn't remember the last time he had infuriated her to this extent. Even as her eyes took in the crown molding around the edge of the ceiling, she had to press her lips together to keep from yelling out in exasperation.

Of course, she hadn't expected him to drop everything to help her. She knew how important college was and that she was asking for a lot, maybe too much. When she'd put pen to paper, she'd known this would take an aggressive appeasement campaign on her part and she'd been prepared to swallow her pride and stroke his ego. But she hadn't been prepared for the way he would patronize her, as if she hadn't done her research and knew what she was getting into.

You're a persuasive girl. Those words were particularly hard to swallow and burned against her eyelids as she closed her eyes and tried to collect herself. Had they fallen so far apart that he couldn't acknowledge that she was seventeen now and capable of weighing her options in a thoughtful way? This wasn't some fanciful trip to the gallery or orchestra that she was planning with some society girls. This was incredibly important to her and he'd essentially dismissed her before she'd even gotten the chance to prove herself.

A knock sounded and she had to will herself to get up and open the door to Caroline whose perpetual raised eyebrow of suspicion was working Julia's last nerve. Was everyone in her family resigned to the belief that she was thinking of ways to destroy their reputation when all she needed was some privacy?

"Did you see the letter from your brother?" her stepmother asked, trying to look past Julia's strategically placed shoulder and into her room.

"Yes, I did," she replied tightly, fighting not to give anything away.

"Good, I wanted to make sure. Do you . . . how confident are you about your missionary trip? I'm assuming that's what he was writing to you about." If Caroline sensed that she was distressed, it could give her the wrong idea that she was giving up on her plan. Which she wasn't; Fletcher's apathy had only made her realize she needed to ramp up her campaign of persuasion. She was her father's daughter, after all, and could bring anyone over to her side if she really tried.

She wanted to stay as close to the truth as she could, though. Lying wouldn't do her any favors if she was too pre-occupied in trying to keep her story straight.

"He's a little apprehensive about the whole thing but I think I can get him to come round. We're set to leave for the mission in early May so I still have time."

"Well, you know him better than I do, of course." Caroline gave her a skeptical look, seeming to want to continue but stopping herself from doing so. Instead, she changed the subject when she saw the clock on Julia's chest of drawers. "Look at the time. The O'Connors will be by to pick you up soon and I need to speak with Doris about what I'll be taking to the Gibbons soiree this Sunday. You need to start thinking about what you're going to wear to that."

"I didn't realize you wanted me to go," she answered as she turned around and began rummaging around for her wrap. She was able to slip Fletcher's letter under her pillow as she came around to her closet on the other side of the bed. A corner of the envelope was left exposed so that way she'd know if Caroline was sneaking a peek at it while she was down at the missionary.

"I thought it was obvious, Julia. You haven't attended so much as a tea since the New Year's party in the Capitol and you need to get out there and form connections with people your age. It's one of the best ways to stay relevant in society."

You really mean connections with people that you don't consider beneath us, Julia thought as she swung her wool wrap around her shoulders. The thought of going to the Gibbons sprawling estate on the edge of the city and thinking of things to say made her feel slightly queasy. So much of her childhood had been spent in the company of adults and she found it difficult to relate to these girls who had grown up in Boston society attending balls, teas, and concerts together and who knew each other so well. She'd spent much of her time moving around as her father forwarded his career and she and her brothers had bumped along with him.

Philanthropy was all well and good as long as you also kept up appearances which she'd been neglecting for months now, not that she'd established a very consistent streak prior to this. She was sure to get some raised eyebrows from the girls there if she began an impassioned speech about congressional proceedings and the rights of Indians.

"I'll think about it, Caroline," she said, though she already knew what her answer would be. The two women walked down the stairs together silently and from the droop in Caroline's shoulders, Julia could tell her stepmother already knew what her answer would be, too.

*   *   *   *

"I've finally heard from my brother," Julia said to Abigail as they worked side by side, kneading the dough for the biscuits that were being delivered to a poor house several blocks over the next morning. She had been pleasantly surprised when she discovered that the missionary society wasn't just committed to helping those outside the city; it was part of a network that assisted those who couldn't get by in Boston, as well.

The air in the cavernous kitchen was close and humid, a small army of volunteers dedicated to various tasks working in well-orchestrated conjunction with one another. There was a joy to the hard work that she fed off of as she listened to the women talking and laughing together, the clatter of mixing bowls, the thud of rolling pins, and the crank of the scorching oven adding to the cacophony. She practically had to shout for Abigail to hear her and they were barely three feet apart.

"That is good news indeed," Abigail said, wiping a bead of sweat from her brow with her forearm before it trickled under the rim of her glasses. "What did he say? Do you think you'll be able to go with Jacob and I?

"He still needs convincing but I'm certain I can get him to serve as chaperone."

This conversation was eerily similar to the one she'd just had with Caroline and she suddenly wanted to change the subject and not dwell on what a difficult task it would really be to convince Fletcher to come with her. So she decided to dive into a subject she'd been thinking of bringing up with Abigail but had been too timid to until now.

"Now that this all seems to be moving forward, could you tell me what it's like when you go down there? It's all very exciting but I'm starting to feel a bit overwhelmed that I don't know how it all works."

"You're right, we haven't gotten a chance to talk all that out. I'm sorry, my dear. I've just made this journey so many times that I sometimes forget what it's like for someone who hasn't. It can be intimidating the first time you go, to be sure. Ask me anything."

Encouraged by Abigail's eagerness, Julia decided to start with a simple question. She hoped she wasn't going to sound too uninformed but that was the only way she'd have an idea of what to expect.

"How is a village set up? I know they don't have large buildings like we do here. Or big cities like Boston or New York, for that matter."

"Yes, the villages are much smaller than what you're used to here. But they're all interconnected and there's much communication between the prominent families. I have to say I admire the sense of community they've managed to hold on to. We have that within these walls, undoubtedly, but it seems we're beginning to lose it in our city, don't you think? So many people are only concerned for their own well-being and can't be bothered with others."

Julia nodded but wasn't entirely sure if she agreed with Abigail's stance. All she'd known growing up with her mother and brothers was security and how much community meant to her family, especially her mother. She was beginning to realize how sheltered a life she'd led and was doing all she could to remedy that.

"What other things are different? Are there any customs that I need to know about before I go down?"

"The men likely won't look directly at you or acknowledge a curtsy. They don't think of it as rude, that's just how they are. There's much discussion and thought that goes into their decision making and they value consensus before any actions are taken.

"Many of them go out in hunting parties and their villages are often near rivers or streams so fishing is a very common, as well," Abigail continued. "The gardens the women keep are large and plentiful; they really know how to get everything they can from the land. And, speaking of the women, they have much influence in the way villages are run. They're involved in decision making and even hold influence over how their children are raised and who they're married off to."

Abigail recounted this last bit of information in a whisper, as if anything could be overheard in the din surrounding them. But Julia felt it was more than a fear of eavesdropping. The other woman seemed to be scandalized by the fact that Cherokee women held such high positions in their villages. She couldn't say that she shared Abigail's view but she couldn't deny that she was a bit taken aback by that fact, as well.

What would that look like? she thought as one of the other women came up behind them and fell into conversation with Abigail. Julia kneaded her dough distractedly as the other two women talked, her gaze wandering to the large half-moon shaped window above the oven. Dust danced in the streams of sunlight shining through but all she could think about was how different it must be to live with that level of equality.

She couldn't help but recall flashes of memory of a little girl she'd played with when they were both five or six. Her name had been Rose and all she could really remember was her full head of perfect curls and the fierce hugs she would give Julia when she would leave. The girl's mother had been elegant and tall but she'd always seemed smaller when both she and her husband had come to pick Rose up after they'd been on an outing. Rose had said that she was scared of her papa, that he hit her mama but Julia had thought she was making up stories because she'd never seen that with her own parents.

Then, the last day she'd seen Rose, her father had come to pick her up and said she wouldn't be coming over anymore, that her mother had left and wasn't coming back. Rose had looked back at Julia with tears in her eyes as her father had practically dragged her out the front door. She'd looked up at her own mother in confusion and was surprised to see how troubled she looked. Julia had eventually learned that Rose's parents had gotten divorced and that he'd taken her and her two sisters with him to New York, leaving Rose's mother behind and in disgrace. No money, no prospects, and no family.

Divorce was scandalous and rarely if ever happened in her sphere. But she knew that when it did happen, most women never saw their children again. It was as if they were wiped clean from a slate, never to be spoken of in polite society. Did that happen in the Cherokee villages, too, or were women protected and allowed to stay with their children no matter what? From the picture Abigail had painted, that seemed highly unlikely and Julia already had to admire them for that fact alone. It was certainly a lot to mull over.

Abigail eventually turned back to her, looking a little sheepish. She'd obviously completely forgotten about what their conversation had been about.

"I'm sorry, Julia; I got distracted. Mary Louise was telling me that her son is going on one of the missions to India in a couple of months. How exhilarating, don't you think? Now, what were we talking about again?"

"It's alright, Abigail. You've given me a lot to think about." Julia glanced over at the grandfather clock in the corner of the kitchen and blanched. It was later than she'd thought it was and she began undoing the bow of her apron. "My stepmother has likely already sent the carriage to pick me up since she knew you and Jacob were going to be here through the evening today. I better get cleaned up before it comes."

"Oh, yes. Safe travels, my dear." Abigail had already focused her attention back on Mary Louise and the tales of her saintly son. Julia went to the washroom to clean the flour from her cheeks and made her way to the front of the building, grabbing her wrap off one of the many hooks that lined the entrance hallway.

The month that loomed in front of her before she would see her brother again seemed almost too much to bear. It wouldn't do any good to write to him, especially since he didn't seem to feel the urgency that she did. She didn't think she'd ever looked more forward to Easter.

CHAPTER 15

"Oh Lottie, I cannot thank you enough for bringing these extra eggs. Mrs. Webster would've had a fit if we didn't have enough of them deviled for Easter."

"Of course, mam. I can't believe Mrs. Webster asked you to take this on so close to Easter. Why, it's Good Friday, for heaven's sake!"

"Well, you know how it goes. You can never count on them having a quiet moment with their own family, now can you? It always has to be a production."

Julia hesitated in the hallway that led to the kitchen, feeling a little guilty that she was eavesdropping on such a candid conversation. A letter had come from Doris' son who was a fisherman up in Maine and she'd wanted to deliver it straightaway since she knew how much their housekeeper worried about him.

She rounded the corner and found that Doris was speaking with one of Mrs. Oldach's servants from up the hill who she had seen more than once scurrying down the lane to run errands for her very particular mistress. Lottie's dark, lined face turned crimson when she saw Julia and she ducked her head in deference. While she was younger than Doris, she looked old enough to be Julia's mother and her shoulders sagged a little in exhaustion, though they'd grown rigid when Julia had entered the kitchen. She immediately wanted to assure the poor woman she didn't take any offense to her very true statements.

"There's no need to worry. I'm not going to tell my stepmother what I overheard," Julia said nonchalantly, trying to put Lottie at ease. "Honestly, I think she's a bit ridiculous for deciding to have such a large gathering myself."

"Miss Julia," Doris clucked good-naturedly, turning to set the eggs down on the table. "Your impertinence is going to get you in trouble. Make sure you mind your tongue."

"Don't fret, Doris. Caroline is out on calls while you slave away in here. She's probably trying to find more people to invite." Julia grimaced and hoisted herself up onto the table beside the eggs, trying not to dwell on how much feigned smiling was going to be in her near future.

"She's just returned," Doris said dryly, inclining her head toward the front of the house. Julia immediately dropped from her perch where she'd been absentmindedly swinging her legs, hoping that this wouldn't be the precise moment that Caroline would come bustling in. When she heard her stepmother's footfalls on the stairs, she breathed a sigh of relief.

"Why didn't you warn me earlier, Doris? I thought we were closer than that," Julia winked, still feeling impish despite Caroline's return. Lottie let out a strangled cough but Julia liked to think she was actually trying to suppress a laugh.

Doris gave her a warning look and then glanced down at Julia's hand where the letter was still clutched. "Is that. . .," she began.

"Oh, yes. That's why I came back here. I'm so sorry I forgot. It's from George."

"No need to apologize. Thank you, Miss Julia. If you would excuse me, Lottie. It's a letter from my boy," Doris said, her eyes misting a bit. Julia handed her the letter and she swept out of the kitchen, likely headed to her small room down the hall to read it.

An uneasy silence settled between Lottie and Julia and she wished the other woman wasn't so ill at ease in her presence. Then again, the environment she was used to over at the Oldach estate was likely much more stringent than it was in the Webster household. At least Caroline treated Doris with the respect she deserved; Lottie was likely only an afterthought in that awful woman's home.

"Well, I should be off, miss," Lottie said, dipping into a low curtsy.

"You can stay for a bit, can't you? You look like you could use a minute to put your feet up."

"Oh, I don't think that would be wise, miss. Mrs. Lofton, our cook, would be wondering where I'd gotten to."

"Will you at least let me walk with you back up there? I could use the fresh air and it would make me feel better that you'd gotten back safely." Their neighborhood was quiet to be sure but Julia didn't want to risk the poor woman being accosted by some errant, drunken bounty hunter from the South. There seemed to be more of that happening in the city, unfortunately.

"I. . .well, if you'd like. It would be nice to have some company."

Lottie looked grateful and Julia wondered if her thoughts had turned to those stories in the papers, too. After Julia had run to tell Doris that she was accompanying Lottie, the pair set out up the hill. It was chilly for April despite the sun and Julia was grateful she'd brought her wrap with her. Lottie's empty basket thumped against the edge of her own woolen shawl as they walked.

"How long have you worked for Mrs. Oldach?" Julia asked after a couple of moments, trying to catch her breath on the hill's incline. Lottie didn't seem to be bothered by the elevation change in the slightest.

"Since I was sixteen. . .no, eighteen, I believe," Lottie furrowed her brow in concentration as if trying to remember the exact timeline. "My mother had worked for Mrs. Oldach's sister who lives closer to the harbor. The late Mrs. Peters was kind and recommended me when my mother asked for her help in finding me work. I was the youngest of six and my mother needed to get me out of Mrs. Peters' house, you see."

"Your mother lived with Mrs. Peters just like you live at Mrs. Oldach's, then?"

"Yes, that's right."

Julia had gotten Lottie to open up and now was treated to a glimpse into her story as they crested the hill and she stopped for a moment to catch her breath, chest heaving a little.

"Mrs. Peters allowed all of us to stay in that great big house. We took over her attic and made it our own, helping out wherever we were needed. Poor Papa, God rest his soul, was in a horrible carriage accident when we were babies that took him from us. We'd have starved if Mama hadn't answered Mrs. Peters' advertisement for a seamstress.

She fretted so much after Mrs. Peters passed away, didn't know where she was going to stay. All of us made sure that she could still live close to the shoreline in a little cottage that we all put her up in. She worked her entire life to support us so we all wanted to make sure she was comfortable after she couldn't work anymore. She's seventy-two now and can still sew circles around anyone, just like my grandmother."

Lottie seemed to realize how long she'd been talking and made to pick up the hem of her skirts and continue on toward the Oldach estate. But Julia didn't want the story to end quite yet. The soothing cadence of Lottie's voice had entranced her and she tried to grab onto what the older woman had last said to gain some more time with her.

"What about your grandmother? Your mother must have learned much from her."

"Oh, my grandmother was one of the most endearing people you'd ever meet. She was a sewer and storyteller both."

Well, that explains why Lottie is keeping me at the edge of my seat, Julia thought, smiling as Lottie swished her skirts back into place and began to tell her about her grandmother.

"When we'd go to visit, we'd sit in front of the fireplace on one of her old blankets and listen to stories of when she was a little girl growing up down south. Her memories were so vivid of her early years yet she never wanted to tell us how she got up to Boston, would always shy away from it. Until, one night, I finally wheedled it out of her. She was sold to some farmer with acres upon acres and brought up here."

Lottie said this last bit so matter-of-factly that Julia thought she hadn't heard her correctly. She blinked and looked at Lottie again. The other woman's expression remained unchanged.

"She. . .was a slave?" Julia croaked out, her heart quickening its tempo and her mouth drying out. Of course she should have considered that possibility but the prospect of it still unsettled her. She was ashamed to think about how, not that long ago, slavery would've been commonplace in their own neighborhood.

"Yes, miss." Lottie finally seemed to realize that she may have shared too much and she shifted from one foot to the other, her face turned toward the bay below. Julia suddenly didn't know what to do with her hands. The chill in the air now seemed to have teeth and she pulled her shawl tighter against her body.

"Please go on. I didn't mean to. . ."

"She was a young, captured girl from a powerful Seminole tribe," Lottie continued quietly, seeming to forget Julia was even there as her eyes turned to the horizon. "A farmer up here needed someone to be the kitchen girl and then a seamstress and that's what she was for far too many years. She didn't want to talk about that part of her life, as you can imagine, only the life she had before she was sold. The mother, father, and sisters she never laid eyes on again. Thankfully, her owner wasn't a complete brute and she was able to gain her freedom, to live her life as she wanted to."

"Your grandmother. . .was an Indian?"

Now Julia couldn't seem to get her vision to focus and a cold sweat broke out along her upper lip. She swayed a little and tried desperately to find her equilibrium again, not wanting to frighten Lottie even further.

"Yes, miss," came Lottie's far off reply. An unexpected roar filled Julia's ears, as if the harbor had crept up the hill without her noticing it and the waves were now beating the ground all around her. Lottie's hand on her arm was the only thing that brought her out of it. "Are you well? You look as if you've seen a ghost."

How can I possibly say how fervently I wish that your family didn't have to endure so much unnecessary pain? Julia was beside herself with helplessness so all she could say were the hollow words that followed.

"I'm just so sorry for your family, Lottie. That is all."

"Well, it was a long time ago, miss. Better to keep those terrible memories in the past and look to the future. That's what my grandmother would say."

"That still doesn't make it right," Julia replied fiercely.

Lottie looked as if she wanted to say more but a sudden shout came from behind them. They both turned to see a very disgruntled women in a flour covered apron huffing between the stone lions that flanked the drive up to the Oldach house.

"Mrs. Lofton, I. . ." Lottie began but didn't get another word in before the cook began laying into her about her incessant laziness.

"Please, don't lash out at Lottie. I'm the one who kept her from her duties. I apologize," Julia said when Mrs. Lofton took a moment to come up for air.

"And who are you, little miss?" Mrs. Lofton said, her Irish accent strong and her venomous gaze honing in on a new target.

"I'm Julia Webster, mum. My father and stepmother own that house just down the way."

Mrs. Lofton at least had the grace to look chagrined when she saw which home Julia was pointing to. With a stilted "My apologies," she practically dragged poor Lottie across the road and toward the back of the towering manor house. Lottie shot one helpless glance over her shoulder before she disappeared behind Mrs. Lofton into what Julia could only assume was a house of horrors.

She turned over Lottie's last statement before they'd been interrupted as she reluctantly turned back to walk home. *Better to keep those terrible memories in the past and look to the future. But it's not in the past. There's a pattern here and that horrid bill is another rung on the ladder,* Julia thought, feeling the color drain from her face.

Julia wanted to scream at the injustice and brutality of it all, to have her words reach the ears of the ones who could prevent more heartbreak but she couldn't. She needed to convince Fletcher to accompany her down South if it was the last thing she did. Lottie's unexpected story had compounded her sense of urgency and her will to do something, *anything,* to do what she could to stave off more suffering.

CHAPTER 16

The Monday after the holiday brought unexpected snow and the overwhelming need to talk to Fletcher alone. She'd tried and failed on the holiday as Caroline had turned what was typically a quiet day into a swirling soiree. It had taken all her composure to be polite to Mrs. Oldach and her weasel faced husband when they'd been introduced and she'd worked hard to avoid them the entire afternoon. Caroline's mother and sister had also traveled from New York and were staying with them through the end of the week. She was reminded of the odd dynamic the three women shared as she watched Caroline dote on her mother and cycle between pleasant and cold exchanges with her sister.

It was all she could do to escape that morning's breakfast after a thorough questioning from Mrs. LeRoy. The woman had wanted to know everything and Julia had felt like she was being asked to pass a test she hadn't prepared for:

"Do you still study the classics?"

"Yes, literature is very important to my tutor. And we're making nice progress with my French."

"Good. I'm so glad French is still considered an essential language. What balls have you attended this year?"

"The Wolfson party in the capitol. It was enough of an experience that I haven't attended any since."

"Just the one at New Year's? My dear, you need to get yourself out there. A lady is defined by the company she keeps."

"Have any young men caught your eye? It's important to only associate with the best families. There were a couple of strapping fellows at the celebration yesterday."

"No, ma'am. I've been preoccupied with other endeavors."

"Other endeavors? My goodness, Caroline. It seems you're helping to raise a nun."

After that comment and Caroline's stifled laugh that came out as a cough, Julia had stopped toying with the remaining sunny side up egg she'd been swishing around on her plate and asked if she could be excused. Fletcher had already left the table and was off in the house somewhere. He'd been elusive since he'd arrived late Saturday evening and she needed to find him before he jaunted back off to college on Tuesday morning.

Now she was upstairs and headed toward her father's study. It was the most likely place Fletcher would have holed up to get away from all the activity in the dining room. She pulled on the door handle, found that the door was no longer locked, and slipped into the quiet room. Her brother sat behind the large desk, his legs crossed at the ankles and resting on its glossy, though dusty, surface. He wasn't even wearing shoes and the geometric pattern on the bottom of his gray socks danced as he wiggled his toes.

"Oh, no you've found me," he quipped as she shut the door behind her. The snow was coming down heavily on the other side of the window now and she lit one of the kerosene lamps to give them some light.

"You've been avoiding me," she said, crossing her arms across her chest.

"How was I to know Caroline would invite so many people yesterday? Or that they would bring their eligible daughters? It's my duty to find a wife and continue the Webster line, Julia. I was really laboring yesterday if you think about it."

"Yes, I see how stressful that was for you. You were practically dozing when I came in here." The casual shrug he gave her only heightened her annoyance; he wasn't even trying to deny that he'd been avoiding her. "Thank you so much for leaving me to the wolves, by the way. Mrs. LeRoy practically accused me of being a spinster in the making after you got up and left."

"For that, I apologize. That woman is intimidating to say the least. You're braver than I am, Julia."

"In more ways than one, Fletcher," she said, trying to bring the conversation back to where she wanted it to be. It was only a matter of time before Caroline came looking for her and she needed to solidify where she stood with her brother. "Speaking of which, have you thought any more about my request? You haven't given me your answer."

"You're asking a lot of me, dear sister," he said, bringing his legs down off the desk and leaning forward with his elbows propped on the edge. "Why has this become so important to you? I know our mother was invested in countless causes and this was one of them but you were barely involved when you were young."

"I can't explain it. I met that Indian chief, Wohali, when I was 12 and don't quite know why he's stuck in my mind all this time. Maybe it's because that was one of the first times she took me with her or maybe what's happening now is so overtly cruel that I need to do something. Or maybe is a combination of both. Either way, I feel so connected to this trip that I can't give it up. I need to know what's out there.

"Please, Fletcher," she begged, hating the note of pleading that had wormed its way into her voice. "Father already thinks this venture is hopeless. Let me see if I can prove to him that he's mistaken, that there's hope for the people I'm trying to know more about. Maybe even help them."

Fletcher looked at her long and hard, suddenly serious, and she tried not to squirm under his gaze. He seemed to be sizing her up and she felt like a bug under a magnifying glass with the sun's rays honed in on her. She just hoped she didn't burst into flames before he answered her.

"I didn't realize you felt so strongly about this," Fletcher finally said, clarity dawning on his face. Julia's temper finally got the better of her as she exploded with the questions that had been on the tip of her tongue for weeks, if not months.

"My letter wasn't enough, Fletcher? If Edward was my age and he wanted to do this, you'd support him with no questions asked. Why don't you or Caroline take me seriously? Why do I have to fight tooth and nail to do what I feel is right?"

She tried to keep her arms folded over her heaving chest but she couldn't seem to keep still and fought the urge to pace. *I've done it now,* she thought as Fletcher moved to the windows of the office and looked out at the front lawn, his jaw a hard, clenched line. *Why did I lose my temper now, when I need him in my corner? This whole trip is up in the air now.*

"There are rules, Julia. An unaccompanied woman traveling across state lines without a chaperone? That's unthinkable and you know it."

"I never suggested I'd go alone. I was simply pointing out how different the rules are for me . . ." Julia began but Fletcher interrupted her and turned back toward her, the color rising in his own cheeks.

"It's not an issue of faith in you, Julia. You could be the most trustworthy person in our family, which sadly you're not given what Caroline's told me, and I still would need to weigh every possible outcome. It's about propriety."

"Do you think that's all I'm good for? So Papa may defend his position in front of his colleagues in the Senate and you may argue your cases in court but I'm only to sit politely with my hands in my lap and not lift a finger when I see something that needs to change? What a pitiful box you've placed me in, Fletcher."

His expression flipped from aggravation to hurt so quickly that she almost forgot how furious she was with him. She may as well have slapped him across the face with the stricken expression that had overtaken his eyes and puckered the corners of his mouth. The next words he said drained the rest of the fight right out of her.

"Of course not, Julia," he said quietly after a few moments of silence. "All I want to do is make sure you're safe. You have no idea what the world is like beyond your secure little bubble. If anything were to happen to you, you know our father would have my head."

"Then let me prove to you that I'm ready to step beyond that bubble. You'll be with me the whole time and you'll see how important this whole venture is. I know you will."

Fletcher glanced at her out of the corner of his eye and sighed with a resigned expression. In that moment, she knew she'd convinced him to go with her.

"I'll have some time in May right after my exams. We won't be able to be down there for more than a week but I will serve as your chaperone."

Julia crossed the distance that separated them and threw her arms around her brother's neck, burying her face in the fabric of his cravat and holding back the tears of gratitude that threatened to soak through to his skin. He smelled of pipe tobacco and some foreign cologne that she couldn't quite place but his solidity was so familiar that she had to bite back a fresh wave of tears.

"You won't regret this," her voice gurgled up, muffled by her proximity to him.

"God, I hope not," he said returning her embrace and resting his chin on the crown of her head.

* * * *

The rain was coming down in gray sheets when she stepped out of the missionary society's front entrance three days later. *I've lived here my whole life and I'll never get used to how quickly the weather can change in April,* she thought, remnants of snow piles still clinging to the cobblestones of the sidewalk. She'd had to beg James to take her earlier after she'd received late word that Abigail had been struck down with a nasty cold and Jacob had stayed home to take care of her.

There was, thankfully, a covered stoop to stand on and take shelter under but she couldn't stay there forever. She glanced furtively up and down the lane but didn't see the familiar silhouette of James or the carriage anywhere. *That's what I get for staying past the time we agreed on,* she berated herself, knowing now that finishing those last few care kits hadn't been her brightest idea.

She was well and stuck now and couldn't even look to see if James was on the street behind the building without risking getting soaked to the skin. He would've had to give up his spot when she didn't come out and now the side of the street was filled with other carriages waiting out the downpour. Not wanting to catch a cold herself, she turned her back to the street to go back inside and find out if it would be possible to borrow an umbrella.

"Julia," came a familiar voice. She turned and was surprised to see Matthew unexpectedly striding toward her under a very welcoming umbrella.

"Matthew! Oh, thank goodness. What are you doing out here in this weather?"

"I could ask you the same thing," he replied good-naturedly, shifting himself over toward the edge of the lane so that she could fit under the umbrella's protective canopy. "I was walking back from a meeting with one of our clients. It was a good thing Mr. Kinsman recommended taking this with me. I would've been in the same boat as you if I hadn't."

"I should've been more prepared. I'm so grateful you came along. The only problem is I haven't found James yet. I hope I'm not delaying you from returning to the law office."

"You've nothing to worry about. That meeting was my last of the day. I was actually on my way home when I spotted you."

"Oh, it is rather late in the afternoon, isn't it?" Now that the days were getting longer again, Julia had also been thrown off by the fact there was still some faint light to the overcast sky. "I hope James doesn't get into trouble due to my carelessness. I really thought I could get everything I needed to do done before I left."

They had reached the corner by then, turning left on to the next block in an attempt to find James and the elusive carriage.

"What exactly do you do when while you're there? I don't know if I've ever asked."

"Oh, it depends on the day and what's the important mission of the day or week. I've learned quite a bit. I've kneaded dough, shelled peas, helped with big vats of laundry. But today I was putting together care kits for the missions that are going out soon. We're almost fully prepared for the ones leaving in the next three months, both within the country and outside of it."

"It sounds like your work keeps you very busy. I hope you're getting something out of it."

"It's fulfilling work as long as I remember I'm doing it in service of others. Otherwise, it would be easy to feel drained by it."

He gave her a knowing smile and she blushed at her own boldness. They had now reached the next block and still no sign of James. Julia was beginning to panic a bit. What would she do if James had decided it was best to go back home to wait out the storm? How would she get back if she didn't find him within the next couple of blocks?

"I still don't see him," she said to Matthew, fiddling with her locket. "Why don't we go back to the missionary's building, then? It would be better for us to wait in one place and see if James turns up where he's supposed to be."

"Yes, I like that idea," she said, feeling relieved. At least one of them was making good sense.

Turning back the way they'd come, a comfortable silence settled between them as they maneuvered their way through the small streams that had popped up between the stones. They were almost to the missionary's massive façade when Matthew spoke up again.

"I hope it's not this sodden in Washington. My uncle and your father could be up a creek like we are now."

"Oh, please don't even put that thought in my mind. My father doesn't need another bout with anything right now. I don't think they'd be anywhere together, anyway."

"Yes, you're probably right. My uncle seems to be avoiding your father since New Year's." They had almost made it to the steps where they had started.

"Why would he be avoiding my father? He's the only one that stood up for him during that whole messy evening."

"I don't think he interpreted it as your father doing him any favors. He's a proud man who thinks he can fight all of his battles alone."

"He's certainly hankering to fight actual battles," she muttered, unable to keep her contempt under wraps.

"What did you say?"

"Your uncle. . ." she stopped herself from saying what she really thought of Henry Eaton, trying desperately to salvage this unexpected opportunity to see Matthew. She suddenly realized they'd halted in the middle of the sidewalk and there was no steady stream of people to carry them along. They could very likely have an argument in the rain and no one would intervene.

"What? You can say it if you want to," he said, his typically open face now a mask of rigid lines. He was shutting her out right before her eyes which needled her even more. How could he put so much importance in what his uncle thought?

"He's a fool. A cruel and inept one at that." The words she spoke were barely audible as the rain poured down around them. But she had said them out loud and that was what mattered. She felt his swift intake of breath, they were so close to one another under the umbrella.

"I know how important it is for you to help with the Indian cause. But you can't attack others while you're defending it. To be frank, I think you judge my uncle too harshly. I see the way your face contorts when you mention him and his involvement in all of this. I don't think you understand the pressure he's under from the president."

"And I don't think you understand how willing he is to carry out the president's orders. You're blinded by your loyalty to him because of the assistance he provides you."

The moment the angry words fell from her lips, Julia knew she'd pushed things too far. She'd only witnessed the fury that now morphed Matthew's face into a scowl once before, when she'd followed him on New Year's Eve after Henry's disastrous spectacle. He didn't show it very often but its heat could melt brass.

"I see you're not holding back today. Please, tell me what you really think, Miss Webster."

She'd gotten so used to him calling her by her name that she was stung by his formality. His words had hit their mark and she knew how angry he really was. Well, she was furious too and felt that she had every right to be. Her father wasn't there to rescue her from speaking so harshly and she'd grown tired of Matthew's compassion toward his uncle. How could he not see what a formidable adversary the man was?

"I think I already have, Mr. Eaton," she retorted. He seemed ready to tarry her blow when the clop of horseshoes sounded behind her. A moment later, James was beside them, his cheeks ruddy and his chest heaving.

"Miss Julia, I'm so sorry. One of the streets was flooded on my way here and I had to get the carriage out of a royal mess." She could now see the mud splattering his front, snaking up his burly arms, and caked under his blunt fingernails. Her heart softened at his appearance and some of her indignation dissipated.

"It's alright, James. Mr. Eaton has been kind enough to stay with me." She got the last sentence out through clenched teeth, venturing a gaze at the aforementioned Mr. Eaton whose eyes still held a steely glint. The appearance of James had seemed to take some of the fight out of him, as well, but he was keeping as much distance as he could from her under the umbrella. They had certainly had a row and were now on shaky ground.

"Thank you, sir," James said to Matthew, so frazzled by his journey here that he didn't seem to pick up on the tension in the air. "I can take it from here."

"Of course. I hope you get home safe Miss Webster," Matthew said, already turning away as James took her arm and led her to the carriage. When she was snug inside, she just watched Matthew's retreating back grow smaller and smaller, wondering what harm she had caused now.

CHAPTER 17

Two weeks later, all the hope Fletcher had gifted when he'd agreed to serve as chaperone was dangerously close to running dry. *What am I going to do?* The thought was a continuous loop in her head as she mended one of her stockings, trying hard not to stab herself with the needle again. Fletcher's words were still burned into her mind: *So sorry. My professor needs me. Cannot accompany you on your trip.*

The overnight courier had galloped in in the strengthening light of mid-morning as she was clearing out the dead leaves and weeds from around the front hedges. When she learned that the message was for her and not Caroline, her apprehension had turned to dread and she had guessed the contents of the envelope before she'd even opened it. As she had taken the rider and his heaving beast to the stable so that James could calm the poor animal and provide refreshment for her rider, she knew Caroline couldn't discover the message she held crumpled against her palm. There had to be some way, some avenue she hadn't considered for her to get down to North Carolina.

But as the day had slipped away, her anxiety had become more pronounced and it felt like the walls were closing in. Abigail and Jacob were set to pick her and Fletcher up at the estate in two days to begin their journey and it would be obvious that she couldn't go with one less person. Luckily, today was her day to call on Eliza.

"Julia, is something wrong? You seem awfully distracted," Eliza's words reached her from across the tea table. She looked up to see the concerned expression on her cousin's face and felt guilty that she didn't feel like she could confide in her. This setback was almost more than she could bear and she wasn't ready to tell even Eliza what had happened.

"It's nothing, Eliza. I'm just worried about what to pack for my trip. Have you ever been down south? I've heard it can be hot but I would hope it wouldn't be too awful in the spring."

It was good to stick close to what she would've discussed with Eliza if she was actually able to go. It would take a miracle but she couldn't give up hope; there had to a way she could still go that she hadn't thought of yet.

"No, I've never been farther south than Philadelphia, unfortunately. But I think it's a safe bet to assume that you could go through a warm spell anytime you venture south. You know who might know? Peter, our cook. He grew up south of Richmond, I believe."

"Really? He doesn't have an accent as far as I can tell," Julia said in surprise. Of course, Peter had always been soft spoken since he'd begun working in the household five years ago. But she thought that would've been something that she should've known about him.

"I honestly think he tries to hide it. Which shouldn't be; there's no need for him to be ashamed of where he comes from. He likely wants to fit in and doesn't feel like answering all the questions people seem to have for someone of the working class who isn't from around here."

Julia had never considered that before and what Eliza said only heightened her discomfort. It seemed that even your place in society defined how others treated you, to say nothing of a person's race.

"That's awful; to fear that people won't accept you because of where you come from."

"It is, indeed. I'm sorry that the older you get, the more you see the darkness in the world. It can still be a beautiful place, though, so don't lose heart. You have a good one and you're already trying your best to clear away some of that darkness."

She wished she was as confident as Eliza was in her ability to change things for the better. She may not even get the chance to try now that Fletcher was stuck in Cambridge. This time, when the needle poked through the fabric, it did stick her in the pad of her thumb and she needed to pull the pure white lace back to avoid staining it; she'd hit a vessel and it bled more freely than her previous stick. When Eliza saw, her eyes widened in concern.

"Oh, Julia, you really stuck yourself. Go to the kitchen; Peter should be able to bandage that up for you."

Julia obeyed, putting her thumb in her mouth to keep from bleeding everywhere. The taste of iron flooding her mouth was all she could concentrate on until she got to the kitchen door and heard a soft whimper on the other side, Peter's deep baritone offering words of comfort. She hesitated but even the pressure from her tongue wasn't staunching the blood.

"I'm so sorry to interrupt but my thumb-" she stopped short when she entered, forgetting her injury. She was surprised to see Louisa with tears streaking down her cheeks seated on a stool near the stove. Peter stood beside her friend but wouldn't look at her. Louisa stood up quickly, wiping at her face furiously.

"Louisa, what's the matter? Are you hurt?" Julia was more than concerned now; she was afraid. Louisa wasn't one to cry at the drop of a hat and the ferocity of her tears was something Julia hadn't experienced before.

"Don't ya worry about me; I'm fine. I just had a question for Peter and let my emotions get away from me. I need to get back."

"But, Louisa-" Julia didn't even get a chance to finish her sentence as the other woman whisked past her without a backward glance. She looked at Peter questioningly but he didn't offer much in way of a response.

"She's having some trouble with her uncle and wanted to talk. Don't take it to heart, Miss Julia. She's going through something right now."

"It's not her brother, is it?"

"No, it's not. She needs to tell you herself. I can't speak for. . .Miss Julia, you're bleeding pretty good there."

She'd been so caught up in seeing Louisa in such a tumultuous state that the throbbing pain in her thumb came roaring back after Peter's observation. Looking down, she saw that there were three red raindrops of blood on the kitchen floor, their outer pinpricks beginning to intermingle as a fourth drop joined them.

"Oh, I'm so sorry, Peter," she said as he led her over to the washbasin in the little annex off the kitchen, submerging her hand in warm water that took away much of the sting. He retrieved a cloth bandage from the cupboard in the opposite corner.

"It's no trouble. I'll get the floor cleaned up in no time. I'm just sorry you hurt yourself. You're going to have a fine bruise there," Peter said, blunt tipped fingers gentle as he wound the bandage around her thumb expertly.

"Yes, well, that will teach me to pay more attention to what I'm doing. I should get back to Eliza. Thank you, Peter."

She scurried out of the kitchen without waiting to hear Peter's response and was strangely ill at ease knowing that he shared a secret with Louisa that she hadn't been made privy to. *Well, I'll have plenty of time to talk to Louisa about it,* she reasoned as she sat back down next to Eliza and fielded her concern over her bandaged thumb. *I'm not going to North Carolina unless God himself intervenes.*

* * * *

"Would you like to accompany me, Julia? A messenger boy from the office has just rung and relayed that Mr. Kingsman received a notice from your father. He wants me to come down to take a look at it."

Julia glanced up from her book that she couldn't seem to concentrate on and found Caroline in the sitting room entrance, bonnet, wrap, and traveling boots on and ready to go. It was the day after her visit to Eliza's and she was trying her best not let full blown panic overtake her.

Caroline's wasn't the most thrilling proposition but what was she doing here? Sitting on a chaise, staring off into the distance without really seeing anything and occasionally glancing down at her book, that's what. She may as well have been perusing Italian for all the sense the words made.

"Of course, Caroline. It would be nice to pay a visit to Mr. Kinsman. Just let me get my bonnet."

The day was uncharacteristically warm with late April sunshine and though it would be a substantial trek, she knew the fresh air would do her good and give her strength for her conversation with Caroline that evening. There was no getting around it; she wouldn't be going down south and she needed to tell her stepmother.

As they made their way to the front entryway where her bonnet hung on its peg, Julia tried to put on a sense of normalcy that was just out of reach. Her attempt to act nonchalant only resulted in her tangling the ribbon of her bonnet into a hopeless knot and she could feel her cheeks filling with color as Caroline took it from her and worked the ribbon out of its crinkled mess.

"I think a walk will do us good, don't you? You seem piqued, my dear."

Julia could only nod her agreement; she didn't trust her voice.

The walk down wasn't unpleasant and she attempted to stay engaged in Caroline's gossip and then when the conversation turned to her father and his gripes about life in Washington, she was fully invested. But all the while her anxiety was lurking on the periphery, just waiting to come crashing down on her again. When they reached the imposing three story building and made their way up to the law office on the second floor, she tuned it all out when she discovered that the conversation between Caroline and Mr. Kinsman concerned the workings of the office and had nothing to do with Washington politics.

As her gaze wandered absentmindedly, she caught sight of Matthew's strawberry blonde head through Mr. Kinsman's office window. Her eyes followed him to the small office in the far corner that he shared with another of the clerks and a ludicrous idea popped into her head. It was utterly preposterous, mad even, especially after the way they'd parted after their last conversation. Her anger had subsided, though there was a bitterness there wouldn't let go. But she had no options left; she was desperate and this was going to be her one last chance to go down south.

She was anxious to get to Matthew before she lost her nerve and when there was a lull in the conversation, she turned to Caroline.

"May I say hello to Mr. Eaton? I wanted to see how he's doing since it's been some time since his last visit."

Caroline gave her a slightly pained looked but nodded her consent. Julia bobbed a quick curtsy to Mr. Kinsman and walked as slowly as she could toward Matthew's office. She could feel perspiration beginning to prickle in her palms under her gloves and her heart was racing. What she was about to ask was bordering on scandalous. She took one more deep breath and rapped lightly on Matthew's open door.

"Come in . . . oh, Julia, what are you doing here?" he said, his signature warm smile turning noticeably downward when he looked up from his documents and recognized her. He clearly hadn't been able to let everything go since their last meeting, either. Nonetheless, that leeriness turned to concern when he took in her face. She could only imagine what he saw in her expression but she couldn't seem to stop contorting her mouth into one pained twist after another. "Is something the matter? It's not your father, is it?"

"No, no Papa is well, thank goodness," she replied, trying to slow her words so that she didn't appear completely unhinged. "But I am in need of your help with something."

Wariness returned to his expression and she was afraid that her previous sharp words had created too large of a gulf between them. *If only I had held my tongue. Henry is an imposing problem but he wasn't worth alienating Matthew.* Matthew had always been reasonable in everything else they'd discussed and she shouldn't have held the gratitude he had for his uncle against him. Her Webster temper was coming back to haunt her so she was surprised and relieved at Matthew's response.

"What is it? It must be important."

"Please hear me out before you dismiss this. She paused and his quizzical yet open expression encouraged her to continue. "My brother, Fletcher, isn't able to accompany me on my missionary trip. I won't be able to go if I don't have an escort."

"That's awful, Julia. I can see why you'd be disappointed. But I can't see how I could help you with that." He seemed more at ease now that the subject of Henry hadn't been directly breached but their current conversation was going to present some new challenges.

"Well, there's one way you could help . . ." her voice trailed off and she was unable to finish the sentence, too embarrassed to say the words.

He studied her for a minute, his head angled to the side and she knew he was working through what she'd just asked of him.

"Are you suggesting *I* accompany you?" he asked, his voice barely above a whisper. As if uttering the words out loud would make her suggestion more real somehow.

"It was a thought. I wouldn't have asked you if I wasn't desperate. But I am. My father has informed me that the Senate is close to deciding on the president's proposal. If I don't go now-"

She couldn't seem to keep the words from spilling out of her, like a waterfall rushing over boulders and unable to control its trajectory. Fortunately, his next words stopped the deluge cold.

"That's impossible, Julia, and you know it. I'm not your brother and it would be inappropriate of me to travel down there with you. If that got out, it would ruin your reputation."

But not yours, of course, she felt like saying but wisely kept that thought to herself. It was all so unfair, this double standard that she'd dealt with all her life. What had been mere annoyance was now directly impacting her ability to help others and it made her so furious, she saw spots bursting in her vision and she had to talk herself down before she forged ahead into the second part of her ill-constructed plan.

"Well, the O'Connors have never met Fletcher. They've no idea what he looks like. So in that respect-"

"What, now you want me to impersonate your brother, too? To lie to these good people and convince them I'm someone I'm not? I thought you had more sense than this, Julia. What you're asking for is too much. And after our last conversation. . ."

She could feel the combination of shame and embarrassment creeping red and hot up her neck. Of course this is what his reaction would be; it was that of any self-respecting man to a young girl's misguided request. She murmured a stilted apology as she turned away from Matthew, willing herself not to cry as she saw Caroline making her way over to her.

"Hello, Mr. Eaton. I hope you're well," Caroline said above Julia's shoulder. His affirmative answer was as steady as ever but there was an edge of coldness to his tone that made Julia's heart lurch in her chest. She had pushed the boundaries of their growing attachment too far yet again and now she really didn't know if they could come back from this.

"That's very good to hear. We were just in for a short visit and should be heading back home. Are you done talking with Julia?"

"Yes, Mrs. Webster. I think we've said all we need to each other."

The note of finality in his voice made Caroline's eyebrows rise slightly but she didn't pursue it. She had taken care of her affairs with Mr. Kinsman and Julia could tell that she was ready to return home. For once, she shared her stepmother's sentiments entirely and couldn't wait to bolt out of there.

"Good day, Mr. Eaton," she got out with effort, not daring to raise her eyes to his face as she turned and bobbed her head in farewell.

"What was that all about?" Caroline asked her as they emerged from the law office and turned toward home. Storm clouds were beginning to billow on the horizon and Caroline set a brisk pace so as not to get caught in the downpour that was sure to roll in soon. "He seemed rather stand offish, don't you think?"

"Yes, he did. We had a disagreement about something, unfortunately. It may be some time before he calls again." It wasn't the truth but it wasn't exactly a lie, either.

"And what did you have a falling out about? You two seemed to be getting rather close."

Before Julia could come up with an actual fabrication, a threatening boom of thunder sounded behind their backs and raindrops began to sprinkle the air. This had all the makings of a fierce Boston squall as the wind picked up and nearly took Caroline's bonnet with it.

"Never mind; we can talk about this later. Let's hurry before we're soaked through to the skin. I can't have another cold like the one I had last month."

Julia had never been more thankful for the rain as they ran to stay ahead of the torrent.

*　　　　*　　　　*　　　　*

"Your disagreement with Mr. Eaton earlier today must not have been as detrimental as you thought. Oh really, Julia. Why would you start that now? You'll be cleaning up the kitchen until midnight."

At the sound of Caroline's voice, Julia looked up from the cake she was trying unsuccessfully to make, flour seeming to coat every flat surface of her workspace. She liked to fancy herself a baker when she was ill at ease and while her ventures turned out in the end, the process was always messy. That evening, she couldn't even manage to crack the eggs without there being shell in the batter and she had been digging the white shards out when her stepmother surprised her. If she was being honest, this went beyond nerves. It really was all an attempt to put off her conversation with Caroline until the next morning, a mere twenty-four hours before she was supposed to depart.

"I may have bitten off more than I was expecting," she admitted sheepishly. The tip of her nose itched from the flour and she couldn't do anything about that until she cleaned the egg yolk off her hands. Grabbing a cloth hanging from a peg on the wall, she cleaned herself up as best she could. "What do you mean regarding Mr. Eaton?"

It was only then that Julia saw the calling card in Caroline's outstretched hand and she turned as white as that small rectangle of paper. She came around the table and took it, her heart high in her throat.

"The currier dropped this off only a few minutes ago. Uncommonly late, if you ask me. It seems he wants to call on you tomorrow afternoon. I'll be out to Mrs. Ingram's for dinner which is an engagement I can't break. I trust you can handle entertaining him yourself."

With an uncharacteristically sly wink, Caroline sashayed out of the kitchen with an over the shoulder reminder to clean up. Julia had no idea what to think as she sank onto the stool to the right of the back door, her hands trembling as she turned the card over. A hastily scrawled message was in the bottom corner, so innocuous that she, too, almost overlooked it. *I'm in* was all it read.

CHAPTER 18

The next afternoon, Julia couldn't sit still for the life of her. She developed a pattern in the sitting room where she would sit in the chaise for a few minutes, spring up and peer out the side window, and then go back to the chaise when she saw nothing had changed out by the stables. Sewing, reading, and attempting to get a string of notes out of the piano forte had all already fallen by the wayside. *I'm sure there's a path worn into the carpet by now,* she thought as she made her way over to the window again and felt the disappointment ping inside her yet again. She was on the verge of going to see if Doris needed help with dinner when she saw a rider coming up the path to the house at a steady canter. Hurrying over to the armchair, she perched on its edge and arranged her skirts to give the air that she had simply found a calm resting place to wait for Matthew and hadn't actually been filled with a noxious mixture of elation and trepidation since the previous evening.

Of course, she was thrilled that he seemed to have changed his mind but her brain was twisting itself into knots trying to determine why he had. His unwillingness to go along with her scheme had been definite the previous day and she was concocting increasingly complex reasons as to why he would agree to it now. She had allowed herself to get to the point where she was certain that he must be plotting with his uncle to humiliate her in some way when she heard the knock at the door and the muffled sound of Doris greeting him. And then he was there in the sitting room doorway, holding his lanky frame in stiff politeness as Doris left them to hurry back to the kitchen.

The awkward silence that followed became unbearable and she finally broke it in the least tactful, but most direct, way imaginable. She was sure Caroline would've been unable to hide an embarrassed shoulder flinch if she'd been there.

"Why have you agreed to this? I know that I'm asking too much of you. *I* don't even know why I did it."

In response to her flurry of questions, he came into the room and sat in the other armchair on the opposite side of the tea table. He adjusted his glasses and fixed her with a thoughtful expression. She could see his jaw working, as if trying out different words, choosing the ones that would convey what he wanted to say.

"I saw that your intentions were in the right place. I know what it means to want to make a difference," he finally said. "Growing up with my father, I saw how he worked with people in our community and even those who didn't live in the town. He only wanted to do what was right by everyone. I saw the same look on your face that he used to get when you left yesterday."

She could see how personal this was for him and her anxiety began to abate. He didn't have ill intentions or think she was being delusional. There was no doubt she could have handled their past two conversations differently but she felt like he understood why going on this journey was so important to her.

"When you approached me yesterday, I was certainly taken aback. You certainly have a way with words. Unfortunately, there are different expectations that you face that my father never had to worry about. I could only see what other people would think and what that could do to your reputation.

"But if we can keep this quiet, I don't see much risk of it getting out. I'd been needing to go down to settle the last loose ends with my father's estate. Mr. Kinsman was aware of my plans and he was supportive. This will give me the opportunity to do just that and help you in the process. I have a vested interest in what you're working to do, as well."

"I can't tell you how grateful I am," she said, trying to keep her voice from shaking. It took all her will power not to move over to the chaise to be closer to him. "I know that passing yourself off as Fletcher isn't very honest, either."

"That's the part that bothers me the most, yes. It's disingenuous of us and I don't know how successful we're going to be in that regard. But if that's what must be done, that's what needs to happen."

"We just need to be out of Boston to make this work. I don't have much hope that I'm going to escape this without consequences." She knew that the web of lies she was weaving was tenuous at best. It wouldn't take much for her story to unravel if Fletcher came home and found out she wasn't there.

"Are you certain this is worth complicating your relationships with your family? No one, least of all me, is going to judge you if you decide the risk is too great."

"No, I need to do this now," she said almost automatically. She'd been turning over the prospect of delaying her trip until Fletcher could accompany her and she kept coming back to how the idea made her stomach churn. It felt imperative for her to not put this off, especially with the Senate voting on the legislation close at hand.

"What do you need of me tomorrow, then? I've been preparing to go to North Carolina for some time so it's all arranged on my end."

"If you can meet up with me and Mr. and Mrs. O'Connor by nine o'clock, that would be best. We're leaving from the station on King Street. Our stagecoach doesn't leave until ten but we'll need time to make sure their carriage and horse is boarded and all our belongings are secure. I already have the money for both our fares tucked into the bag I'm taking."

"How long are you going to be down there?"

"As you know, it'll take a couple of days to make the journey. We're then set to spend a week with the Cherokee tribe the society already has a close relationship with. And then there's the trip back up to Boston, of course."

"You need to know I'll break off from you the last couple of days to ride to Asheville and do what I need to there. I've been dreading it but all the loose ends concerning my parents need to be tied up and now is as good a time as any."

"Of course. I'll come up with some excuse to tell the O'Connors. I hate lying to them, too, but if this is to work, we need to be convincing. I can't remember if I've ever told them Fletcher's name. I think I've always referred to him as 'my brother'."

"Can you call me Matthew, then? I feel like we're more likely to be tripped up if I try to remember I'm supposed to answer to 'Fletcher'."

"Yes, that's a good idea."

It was, of course. But she couldn't quite swallow how wrong all this was, to deceive this couple who had shown her nothing but kindness since they'd met.

"Alright then," Matthew answered, looking resolved. He'd committed himself now and Julia felt they both knew there was no turning back.

"I will see you tomorrow morning, Matthew?" she asked as she walked him to the front door. She felt like she needed to pinch herself to make sure this wasn't a dream and wake up disappointed.

"You can count on it Julia," he said as he placed his hat over his unruly curls, took her hands in his for the briefest of moments, and then turned and strode out the door.

CHAPTER 19

"You're quite popular today, Miss Julia. There's someone else here to see you." Julia turned from the carpet bag lying open on her bed and found Doris on the threshold to her room.

"Is there, Doris? I wasn't expecting anyone for the rest of the day."

"Miss Louisa said this was going to be a surprise. It seems Mrs. Lee wanted her to drop off some pastries for you to take on your trip tomorrow. She wanted to know if you had time to speak with her."

"Of course. I'll be right down," Julia answered, abandoning her resolve to pack. She hadn't thought she'd see Louisa until after she returned and she was excited that she now had that opportunity. However, their encounter in Eliza's kitchen earlier that week dulled her excitement as she went down the stairs. She didn't know if Louisa would even address it or if she would pretend that nothing was amiss between them.

Louisa was waiting patiently for her by the front door when Julia got to the bottom of the stairs, looking serene. She quickly pulled her friend into the sitting room and shut the door, anxious to tell Louisa of her newly revised plans and to gauge how she was doing. Louisa looked a little sheepish as Julia turned to face her and any residual anger that she had felt disappeared.

"I'm so sorry for how I treated ya a couple of days ago. I was goin' through something but that doesn't mean I should've dismissed ya like I did."

"Don't fret, Louisa. I was just worried about you. Peter mentioned that it had something to do with your uncle. Do you want to talk about what's going on?"

Louisa shook her head vigorously, tight curls coming loose from the braid she had wrapped in a bun at the top of her head. Her expression wasn't as concerning as it had been a couple of days ago but Julia caught the outright fear in her friend's eyes before the curtain came back down and Louisa was calm again.

"No, not right now. I want to hear 'bout this trip that has ya all excited."

Julia knew she wouldn't push Louisa to confide her troubles today but she also knew that they needed to talk at some point about what had the other girl so spooked. Louisa suddenly pulled her into a tight hug and she wrapped her arms around her friend, trying to convey how much she wanted to understand what she was going through. Once they pulled apart and she saw Louisa's now expectant expression, she remembered that she did have news to share that was scandalous in its own right.

"I was afraid I wouldn't see ya till closer to June. Miss Eliza wanted to make sure those pastries got to ya and the O'Connors. I think Miss Doris took em to the kitchen."

"Well, you won't believe what I'm about to tell you about this trip. I . . ." She paused for a minute as a sudden thought hit her. If she told Louisa what she was planning, she would be putting her friend in a predicament where she was keeping a secret from Eliza. If it was discovered, Louisa could be reprimanded or, even worse, lose her position. Eliza was an understanding, kind employer but this secret would involve Julia and her safety. She didn't think Eliza would be able to look the other way if she learned that Louisa had been part of this scheme.

"On second thought, maybe I shouldn't tell you. I don't want to get you into any trouble. It's a big secret to keep."

"Well, now I need to know. I can handle whatever ya tell me. And keeping secrets is practically part of my job, not that Miss Eliza and Mr. Thomas have any."

"You're sure about this?" Julia asked and Louisa nodded her head emphatically, obviously wanting to be in the know.

"You were almost stuck with me until August," she said, taking Louisa's hands. "Fletcher got called back to Harvard and can't go with me."

Louisa's eyes widened at her news and she felt relieved that neither she nor Eliza had guessed what had been upsetting her the last few days. She'd needed to keep her secret under wraps and she'd been successful.

"How are ya still goin' down south, then? I thought ya couldn't unless Fletcher went with ya."

"Someone has agreed to take his place. Matthew's going down with me instead."

Louisa's mouth dropped open and she snapped it shut, the surprise on her face too pronounced to hide.

"Matthew. Matthew Eaton? How did ya ever get him to agree to it?"

"I didn't think it was going to work, to be honest, but he just agreed to go earlier today. I'd approached him a couple days ago at Papa's office. The idea just came to me and I knew I had nothing to lose, except maybe my pride. He looked at me like I was crazy at first and I can't say I blame him. Truth be told, I'm waiting for him to change his mind as we speak."

Louisa shook her head, seemingly incredulous at Julia's moxie. She couldn't say she blamed her friend; what she'd done had been uncharacteristically bold, even for her. But desperate times and all that; she'd been at the end of her rope and taken a big chance.

"Now you see why you can't tell anyone about this. I know this puts you in an incredibly hard position and it may have been selfish of me to tell you what Matthew and I are trying to do. If Eliza comes to you, you're going to have to pretend you don't know anything about it."

"No, I'm glad ya told me. Do ya really think ya can do this? It's awful risky, Julia."

"I have to, Louisa. Time, and my opportunity to do anything of significance, feels like it's slipping away. I need to see for myself what's at stake. How else am I going to help if I don't really know the people I'm concerned for?"

Louisa regarded her with warmth, her cheeks rosy and her eyes soft. "That's what I admire most about ya. Ya really care. There's so many who wouldn't do what you're about to. Not everyone would've become friends with me, neither. I'll do what I have to."

Julia pulled her into another fierce hug then, so grateful that she couldn't speak for fear that anything she attempted to say would come out as a croak. After some time she leaned back and cupped Louisa's cheek in her palm.

"It's me who should be singing your praises. You're risking everything to keep this secret. I want you to know that I don't take it lightly; I'll do whatever it takes to protect you."

Louisa grasped Julia's wrist for a moment and it was as if a deal had been struck. Her eyes then traveled to the grandfather clock behind Julia and she rose abruptly.

"I didn't realize the time. I need to get back to Miss Eliza. Just . . . be careful. I'll be thinkin' of all of ya."

"I'll see you out. Don't worry, I'm sure everything will be fine," Julia answered. As she saw her friend to the door and watched her walk down the front path to the road, the first sparks of nervousness threatened to engulf her excitement. She hoped that her reassurances to Louisa would be enough.

* * * *

"Fletcher wrote me and said he's been delayed. The O'Connors are still picking me up here but Fletcher will meet us at the station as his carriage will be coming in there from Harvard a bit before we depart."

"Why is this the first I'm hearing of this?" Caroline asked, barely looking up from her sewing. Julia was grateful for that, at least. If Caroline saw what an open book she was right now, it was all over.

"I forgot to tell you in all the excitement this last-minute change has caused. I wanted to make sure everything was arranged before I worried you."

Caroline looked up at her then and Julia tried to make her face as blank as possible, willing her gaze to meet her stepmother's without wavering. After what felt like five minutes of scrutiny, Caroline gave a nod of approval.

"Well, as long as nothing has changed with the O'Connors accompanying you, that should be acceptable. Remind me, what time are you leaving tomorrow?"

"Early, around eight o'clock."

"And you'll send me a notice when you arrive in Asheville before you go to the Indian village?"

"Yes, I promise I'll do that. You know it's going to take some time to travel down so I probably won't arrive until a couple of days after we leave Boston."

"As long as none of those details are changing, I don't see any issues. We just want you to be careful in all aspects of this, Julia. It'll be the longest you've been away from home."

"I know. I'll have Fletcher and the O'Connors there to look out for me. There's no reason to worry, Caroline."

Tiny dots were beginning to dance in Julia's vision with her effort to keep an implacable face. She needed this conversation to be over so she could retreat to her room, pack up the last of her belongings, and shove her guilt down somewhere in the vicinity of her toes. Caroline rose from her chair and Julia was afraid she'd given herself away somehow. Instead, her stepmother reached out and pulled her into a loose hug.

"Of course. I trust you, Julia," she said. Julia wrapped her arms around her and couldn't bring herself to answer her. Caroline's outlook would be completely different when she returned from North Carolina and she needed to savor this rare moment of peace between the two of them.

"Thank you," was all she could muster before she broke the embrace and turned to fly up the stairs, the guilt shooting up from her toes and clawing at her throat.

CHAPTER 20

"What a morning for our journey! I hope it's this clear the whole way down," Abigail chattered as Jacob helped Julia down from the carriage. It was a brisk morning for May but the sky above was crystal clear, the bright eastern sun promising a warm up as the day went on.

"One can hope," Julia replied as Jacob went to find a stable hand to help him store the carriage and board the horse. She and Abigail stood in the center of a flurry of orchestrated activity as porters called out, stagecoaches arrived and departed, and luggage was either thrown off of or piled on to the tops of gleaming, horse drawn vehicles.

As they waited on the platform, she kept an eye out for Matthew, a pit growing in her stomach as the minutes passed and Jacob returned to them. She was almost in full blown panic as they found their stagecoach and their bags began to be stored up top; still, he wasn't there. *He's not coming. He's changed his mind,* she realized, casting a sideways glance at Abigail to see if she'd noticed they were short one member of their party.

Luckily, Abigail was distracted by something Jacob was shouting down at her as he helped the worker secure their luggage above. She was trying to formulate some convincing story when she saw Matthew striding toward them. He was covered in dust and looked a little bedraggled but he had come.

"Matthew, there you are. I was beginning to think you wouldn't make it," she said breathlessly.

"My apologies. I started out at the wrong platform when I got back from the college. I didn't realize how big this place was." Turning to Abigail, he offered his hand and shook hers warmly. "You must be Mrs. O'Connor. Very pleased to meet you ma'am."

As she watched Abigail's cheeks grow rosy and the two of them fall into pleasant introductions, she witnessed for the first time just how charming Matthew could be. It was as if he'd studied Fletcher and mastered his easy way with people. His southern accent, though not pronounced to begin with, had been erased from his speech and he didn't seem as solemn and quiet as he'd been when she first met him. It was an astounding transformation in its simplicity and she couldn't help but be impressed by his commitment to it.

When Jacob came down from the top of the stagecoach and Matthew made him laugh, she was further convinced that this really could work. Jacob didn't show his hand very often and he was indicating that he could be comfortable around Matthew.

After the introductions were made, Abigail and Jacob turned to get into the stagecoach as their departure time was nearing. Matthew handed his small carpetbag to the worker and pulled Julia aside gently after he was sure his luggage was secure. They only had a couple of minutes to themselves before they needed to join the O'Connors again.

"That seemed to go well. What do you think?"

"Yes, I think so. You made a good first impression. Jacob doesn't open up to just anyone."

"Good." He hesitated for a moment, seeming to mull over his next words. She couldn't help but notice how much bluer his irises grew when he was concentrating and her heart was suddenly in her throat. They were going to be together for over a week without any interference from her family, which both exhilarated and terrified her. What if they fought and couldn't stand the sight of each other after this? What if he decided this was all too much and left her alone with the O'Connors? How would she answer those questions? And, the most anxiety inducing question of all, what if he uncovered how much she really thought about him, how much she wanted to be standing at his side through all of this?

But she needed to put those thoughts aside. She needed to be focused on learning all she could about the Cherokee and what they would face if they were forced out off of their land and out of their homes. So she pulled herself back from the precipice of panic and concentrated on what Matthew was saying now.

"Do you think we can really pull this off? This is incredibly precarious for both of us but especially you. I just want to make sure you know what we're getting ourselves into, how important it's going to be to stick with our story."

"We have to, Matthew. There's no other option and it's too late to abandon it all now. And I know how risky this is and how important it's going to be that everyone believes you're my brother."

Louisa's face popped into her mind then and a pit formed in her stomach. She may have been willing to risk the ire of her family but she'd brought her friend into this, too, and she hoped it wouldn't lead to any complications for her. "I haven't told anyone except a friend I know will keep this a secret and I need to keep her safe, too."

He must have seen the sincerity in her expression because he reached out and squeezed her hand briefly before pulling her around to the entrance to the stagecoach and helping her climb up the steps. As she settled in next to Abigail and across from Jacob and Matthew in the back corner, she tried to ignore the tingling in her palm where Matthew's hand had just been.

After four other gentlemen were packed into the compartment in front of theirs and already engaged in a boisterous conversation about quail hunting of all things, she felt the great wheels turn underneath them and heard the clop of horseshoes on cobblestones. They were off, for better or worse.

*   *   *   *

"We'll rest here," Abigail called three days later with the sun high in the sky. Julia looked toward the horizon that was now rimmed in by a sloping mountain range and was amazed at the fact that one country could contain so many different landscapes.

Her joints ached as Matthew helped her off of the horse's back. She'd never been so grateful to be on solid ground again and stood there for a few minutes taking in her surroundings. She had to acknowledge that it could've been much worse, though; her mother had insisted that she take riding lessons when she was younger and Julia was incredibly thankful that she had. The journey from Asheville out to the village would've been even more cumbersome if she didn't know how to ride without a side saddle.

"It's not far now," Abigail said, plopping down from her horse without any issue. She took Julia's hand and led her over to a worn path in the grass that led into the woods and hadn't been visible from the dirt road they'd just come off of. "Another two or three miles and we'll be at the village. It's an uphill climb but not too steep."

Julia looked back, concerned about how they were going to get four large horses through the tangle of underbrush. Abigail followed her gaze and waived her hand dismissively. "Don't worry about the horses. They're used to going through here and know the way. You just need to lead them with a steady hand is all. We'll reach the village before the mountains become a factor. They don't start for another ten miles or so even though they look a lot closer. There's a pretty deep valley between where we'll be and where the mountains begin."

"You know this area so well," Julia replied, imagining how much more nervous she'd be if she'd done this on her own. Having Abigail in particular as a guide had been a godsend since they'd gotten off the stagecoach in Asheville. Their two-hour ride on horseback had been made more pleasant by her near constant chatter as she'd pointed out new flowers and trees, knew where to fill up their canteens with water, and explained the shifts they were seeing in the terrain as they neared the mountains.

"Oh, it's nothing. I've been through here so many times that I've just picked up things naturally." But Julia could see how pleased Abigail was by her awe and she was happy she could help her feel that way. They headed back to where they'd left the horses and their traveling companions.

"Not much farther to go," Jacob confirmed, patting the side of his horse in a calming circle. "Do you think we should eat those biscuits now or wait until we're in the village?"

Julia's stomach rumbled at the thought of food but she didn't want to delay their progress any further. It had been an exhausting few days and she was anxious to get settled though she didn't quite know what that would look like yet.

"We're so close we might as well keep going," Abigail answered to Julia's relief. She glanced over at Matthew and he nodded in agreement. He looked a bit hardscrabble with his sun reddened skin and increasingly bristled jaw but seemed in good enough spirits.

The two of them had barely spoken since their hurried talk in Boston. The stagecoach had been much too loud and crowded to have any private conversation and they'd been understandably separated in the lodging houses they'd stayed in on the way. When they'd arrived in Asheville, she thought maybe they could have a moment to speak but Matthew had gone with Jacob to get the horses and supplies they needed. She couldn't leave Abigail alone so she'd gone with her into an open air market to stretch their legs a bit He'd seemed to have taken a liking to Jacob and the two of them had brought up the rear while she and Abigail led the way on this final leg of the journey. She could only hope they could talk once they were settled in the village.

After taking a final swig of water from her canteen, Julia positioned herself behind Abigail and fell into the single file line the path warranted.

Jacob had shown her how to firmly but gently lead her mare and her concentration was split between keeping a fist on the bridle and not twisting her ankle in the increasingly rocky terrain. She was pouring sweat after only a mile and she had to wipe her forehead every few minutes to keep the sweat from trickling down and stinging her eyes. When they'd been at it for what felt like hours and come to the crest of another ridge, she was about to suggest a rest but Abigail's words made the suggestion die on her lips.

"We're here."

The village sat in a clearing and was built into the flow of the land. About fifty small cabins constructed out of broad planks and peaked rooves were scattered around the center building which looked to be twice the size of those homes. Columns of smoke rose into the air from stone chimneys while only tendrils snuck out of the chimney of what Julia assumed was their meeting lodge. Almost immediately, a distinguished looking man came out of the entrance and walked toward them. He reminded Julia so much of her memories of Wohali that she had to study him as he was coming toward them to confirm that this wasn't the same man that had made such an impression on her all those years ago.

"Mr. and Mrs. O'Connor, welcome back," he said with warm familiarity. "The chief and shaman have gone to help one of the chiefs north of us with a burial. They've been gone three days already and will return tomorrow."

His English was flawless with a pleasant lilt that made Julia think of snuggling under a down blanket with a warm cup of chamomile tea. His dark eyes flitted over to where she and Matthew stood off to the side and she tried not to sag against her horse in exhaustion. She wanted to be alert and make a good first impression.

"I see you've brought some new faces into our fold. There are still many in our village who could benefit from the help your Good News holds."

"Oh yes, every little bit helps, Onacona," Abigail answered. "These are two young people who are willing to assist you in any way possible. May

I present Miss Julia and Mr. Matthew Webster. Their father is a senator in the capitol."

Abigail's eyebrows rose conspiratorially at her last statement and Julia squirmed a bit. She hadn't seen this side of her companion in weeks and it still made her uncomfortable to think that she could be just a way in for her, a means for Abigail to connect with her prominent father. Thankfully, Onacona didn't seem too impressed in learning this information. *They've probably heard it all, all the empty promises,* she thought as he walked over to her. She remembered that it wasn't disrespectful when he didn't quite meet her eyes or offer her his hand.

"It is good to meet both of you. I am Onacona, a member of the tribal council and overseeing the village in our chief's absence. I'll see that all of you are settled. The journey here is not easy and you must be tired."

"Thank you for your kindness," Matthew answered on their behalf when she couldn't seem to find the words to reply. She nodded her agreement and was reassured when Onacona met her gaze briefly and smiled; she hadn't offended him with her sudden inability to speak. This was so much more overwhelming that she'd expected as people began exiting their homes and greeting the O'Connors and shooting curious, though not malicious, glances toward she and Matthew.

Their whole journey had felt real enough but actually standing in the middle of a Cherokee village so full of life, delicious smells, and colorful blankets draped over clotheslines was surreal. There were snatches of both Cherokee and English as they made their way along the worn dirt path toward the center of the village. This wasn't just one of Abigail's stories or an entry in an encyclopedia or newspaper. This village was *alive* and all around her.

A small child unexpectedly ran up beside her and pulled on her dust encased skirt, looking up at her with eyes so brown they were verging on black. She instinctively crouched down and tried to get more level with the little girl whose hair was plaited in two tight braids. The girl held up a homemade doll with a sweet, upturned face and whose hair matched her own. Her thumb was firmly planted in her mouth.

"She's beautiful," Julia said, wondering if the girl knew what she was saying. A huge grin spread on either side of the little girl's thumb and she ran back to her mother who had begun walking toward Julia with an apprehensive look. She smiled at the mother, who could've have been much older than Julia herself, wanting to reassure her that it was no trouble. The other woman picked her daughter up in her arms and returned Julia's smile tentatively before turning and going back into her cabin. Abigail's appreciative squeeze of her hand as they continued on through the village confirmed that she'd done the right thing.

Onacona came to a stop in front of a handful of cabins clustered together on the outskirts of the more densely populated quadrant of the village. A young mother with a baby on her hip came out of the cabin nearest to where they stood, her hair free and blowing softly in the breeze. She made a deferential nod in Onacona's direction but kept her sparkling eyes on Julia: she could sense a fire in her that she hadn't picked up on in the other mother she'd just encountered.

"Atsila, this is Miss Webster. She'll be staying with you and Atohi for the next few days. I hope your mother said something to you about it. I told her that I would be getting ready for our visitors this morning. The O'Connors will be staying with us, of course."

"Yes, *agidoda*, she said you all would be coming in today. I am glad to meet you, Miss Webster," Atsila replied, also in perfect English.

Satisfied, Onacona turned to the O'Connors and invited them to make themselves at home in the cabin next to Atsila's. He then focused on Matthew who had been nearly silent throughout their trek through the village and the conversation that had just taken place.

"You, my son, are staying with my brother over here." Onacona pointed to the cabin across the way from where they stood. "His wife passed on some time ago and he's getting on in years. He needs some help with repairs that I've been too busy to help him with. I hope you can assist him."

"Of course; I'll do my best," Matthew said.

Onacona reached and tickled the baby's feet, making him giggle and squirm in Atsila's arms, before leading Matthew to the other cabin. A man with a hunched back and whitening hair had just appeared in the main doorway and was now watching all of the activity.

"Your brother should be on alert. My father is a very persuasive man and can wrangle others into almost anything. He may be getting in over his head with his agreement to help my uncle," Atsila said as she and Julia watched Matthew follow the other man to the cabin.

"Onacona is your father, then?" She knew she'd been picking up on something more than simply a tribal elder conversing with someone from another family. She and Atsila had turned from the main path and were heading toward the entrance to the other woman's cabin.

"Yes, he is. We've lived in this little corner of the village since before I can remember. My brothers are the only ones who've left. Gone and married other women from different villages."

"How many brothers do you have?"

"Oh, only two. They're both older than me by a bit. Their children are old enough to go out in hunting parties and help their mothers garden. My oldest brother has a son who's almost ready to sit in on the village's council gathering."

"I have two brothers, too. The one who's helping your uncle and another younger one at home. He's still going to school."

"I've wondered what it would be like to have a younger sibling, to not have to worry about two pairs of strong hands ready to throw me into the river," Atsila mused, setting Waya down in front of the hearth. By now, the pair had entered the main room of the home and Julia looked around, trying to allow her eyes to adjust to the dim light that filtered through the curtains.

"You'll have to overlook the mess; little Waya here is adventurous and beginning to get into everything."

The little one immediately began crawling toward the stone step surrounding the fireplace. A ball lay within his grasp and he pulled himself up and grabbed it with chubby fingers. He stuck it in his mouth, worked it against toothless gums, and then threw it, watching as it slipped under Julia's skirt and collided with the side of her boot. She bent down to pick it up and a joyful smile spread across his little face, softening his alert eyes and making dimples pop out in both cheeks. He began to bounce when she rolled the ball back to him, his chunky legs keeping time to music that she and Atsila couldn't hear. His little squeal as he picked up the ball and threw it to her again made her laugh with an effortlessness that she hadn't felt since Edward had visited her.

"You have a friend for life now," Atsila said, her own face beaming as Julia plopped herself down on the rug and became a willing pawn in Waya's game. She was already looking forward to what the next few days would bring.

CHAPTER 21

"How is it with Tsiyi today?" Julia asked Matthew two days later as he came up beside her in the garden in the back of the cabin. Atsila was putting Waya down for his nap inside and given how persistent his wails of protest were, that endeavor didn't seem to be going very well.

Waya had been outside with them all morning, exploring in the grass surrounding the garden that had grown wild after two days of thunderstorms that had passed through before the missionary group's arrival. He had unwittingly helped to placate it, flattening the blades under his knees as he'd crawled back and forth. When he'd found the anthill some fifteen minutes ago, everything else was forgotten and Atsila had carried him in when she suspected it was a fire ant colony. It hadn't been silent since.

"He seems to be moving around better today," Matthew answered, referring to Atsila's elderly uncle. "I don't know what it would be like to live in such pain. The salve Onacona brought him seems to help but the relief doesn't last as long as he wants it to. He's always in a good mood, though. I'm glad I can be of some help."

Just looking at Tsiyi's gnarled, arthritic fingers made Julia's ache. His knuckles were twice the size of hers and it was a wonder the man could bathe himself. His knees weren't much better, swollen and almost impossible to bend when he ventured outside for a walk across the path to Onacona's cabin once a day. Despite all this, she'd never seen a more cheerful man. The tales that he wove while they were all seated around him in the late afternoons were spellbinding, his deep voice radiating out and calling other families to listen, as well. He spoke of the beginning, of how the tribe surrounding them had come to be. With his soft white hair pulled back in a loose braid and his eyes taking in the heavens above them, he was a mystical force to be reckoned with.

Since Onacona had taken on a more prominent role in the tribe's leadership, he hadn't been able to help his brother as much as he wanted to. Having Matthew stay with Tsiyi had been a blessing, Julia could tell. Atsila said the worry lines that had dug deep trenches on Onacona's forehead had smoothed considerably since their arrival and Julia was glad for it.

She just hoped it wasn't too much work for Matthew. She had heard his axe chopping wood all morning, the familiar swish and slam fading into background noise as she'd helped Atsila weed the plot that would become the family's small corn field. Even now, she could see the sweat plastering his hair to the back of his neck and the way he rolled his shoulders made her realize how stiff his job had made him. His shirt sleeves were rolled halfway up his forearm and she could see a couple of scratches where the wood had come up and nicked his skin. She tried not to stare at his nearly bare arms, his muscles hard ridges straining against the fabric.

"I'm sure Onacona appreciates your hard work. Do you need some ointment for your arm? You wouldn't want to it to get infected," Julia asked, taking in a particularly deep gash on his elbow when he shifted his arm around the other way.

"Oh, I hadn't even seen that one," he said in surprise, a trickle of blood beginning to skate its way down his arm toward his wrist.

"Come in through here. I'm sure Atsila has something that could help," she said, leading him to the cabin's back entrance and into the kitchen area. There was a bowl of water perched on one of the ledges and Julia was able to find a tanned piece of deer hide that she could dip into the water and use to dab at Matthew's elbow. She could feel him wince as the material made contact with his skin and tried to be more gentle, tried not to pay attention to the warmth creeping up her own arm and nestling in her chest as she worked to clean his wound.

She kept her eyes focused on the bowls of different powders Atsila had walked her through the first night, trying to find the turmeric. Atsila had told her the plant was a natural antiseptic and that she always kept a ground bowl of it close by. She finally saw the tell-tale bright orange powder clinging to the rim of one of the bowls nearest to the door. Eyeing Matthew's arm to make sure the bleeding was under control, she grabbed what she needed and began applying the powder to his gash.

"You really know what you're doing," he said as whatever bleeding had been there stopped almost instantly. Julia found some cloth and wound it around his elbow, securing it snuggly with a little bow in the center.

"I'm just a fast learner. It's a good thing turmeric has such a distinctive color because I probably wouldn't have remembered otherwise." Looking over at the bowl of water and seeing it had taken on an unmistakably pink hue, she picked it up with both hands. "Do you want to go with me to dump this? I need to get some fresh water from the stream."

"Of course. Tsiyi is asleep now, too, and won't need me for another couple of hours. Lead the way."

Julia wondered if she should yell to Atsila and let her know that she was leaving. But Waya's cries on the other side of the blanket that separated where the family slept from the kitchen and common area didn't show any sign of letting up and she didn't want to add to the din. They went out the way they'd come in and she dumped the dirty water into the grass on the edge of the path to the stream.

The water bubbled and tripped over the rocks like it hadn't a care in the world, the tinkling melody of its downhill journey a soothing backdrop to the pair's impromptu meeting. She hadn't been alone with Matthew since their arrival so she hadn't gotten the chance to ask if he was cursing her for dragging him here or if he'd gotten something, anything out of his experience. She stooped down on the bank to rinse out the basin and fill it with fresh water, thinking that beginning with the admiration she had for his work ethic would be a good place to start.

"I've asked a lot from you, traveling down here and working so hard. And now you're hurt," she glanced at his bandage. She straightened and walked over to a boulder, sitting on it next to the basin that she'd settled in the tall grass at the great rock's base.

"It's nothing serious, Julia. It'll heal in the next week or so."

"It's not just that," she replied, feeling bold enough to be honest. "You're pretending to be someone you're not for me. I know almost nothing about what I'm doing here or what's going to happen after we go back. But I'm trying to understand and you've become integral to that."

"I will admit that how we got down here was unconventional but you need to know something."

He looked down at his boots with uncharacteristic shyness and she felt as if he was about to share a part of himself that he rarely showed anybody else. Her heart picked up speed as he fixed her with his steady gaze again.

"I want to help other people, always have. I've . . . I've just gotten lost somewhere along the way. It feels like I've been trapped in a whirlwind since my parents died and Henry took me in. I've gone from what used to be my home to law school to clerking for your father's practice all in the span of three years. Coming back here, it feels like I never left. I didn't expect to have missed it so much."

"So, you're not angry that you came?"

"No, I couldn't say that. In fact, it's been an eye-opening experience for me. I can see why you were so angry with my uncle for his potential part in tearing families from their homes. And for you to see what challenges this tribe and the ones surrounding it are facing for yourself . . . it's only increased my admiration for you, if I'm honest."

His gaze grew in intensity and she felt completely exposed all of a sudden as she met those blue eyes. There had been hints, little rumblings that what they shared went beyond a budding friendship but the vulnerability of that last sentence, the way his voice had faded out at its conclusion sent tingles shooting up the back of Julia's neck. She felt like she was watching herself from above as she rose and walked over to where Matthew stood.

"You . . ." she croaked out, not sure what else she wanted to say. That she admired him, too. That she felt like someone really understood her and what she was trying to do. It was a powerful feeling and she wasn't quite sure what to do with it, what it would lead to in this moment. It may have been her imagination but she swore that Matthew was leaning in toward her and she didn't want him to stop if he was. She didn't get the chance to find out what would have happened next, though.

"There you are-" Atsila's words cut through the rush of the stream and Julia put as much distance between herself and Matthew as she could without being too conspicuous. She could feel the warmth blooming on her cheeks, spreading to her forehead. Even her nose felt uncomfortably hot as she turned to see Atsila on the bank, arms folded over her chest.

"Atsila! I tried to . . . Matthew and I . . ." Why couldn't she speak in coherent sentences? Atsila wasn't blind; if Julia couldn't get ahold of herself, she would become suspicious and learn the truth. And Julia wasn't ready for this experience to end, to be sent away in disgrace.

"I'm sorry we didn't tell you where we were going. I hurt myself chopping wood and my sister was kind enough to patch me up. We needed to get you some new water," Matthew explained smoothly without a hint of embarrassment. He tilted his head toward the abandoned basin at the foot of the boulder for reference.

How does he do that? Julia wondered, the frightened fluttering of her heart finally starting to die down. Matthew was so unflappable under pressure that she wondered if anything took him by surprise, if any situation could rattle him.

"Thank you," Atsila replied, still eyeing the pair with a hint of suspicion. "I just got a little worried when I couldn't find the two of you. Julia, could you bring that back with us? We still have a lot of work to do in the garden."

Julia nodded, not trusting her voice quite yet. Propping the basin against her hip, she fell into step with Atsila, throwing an apologetic glance Matthew's way as he fell a few steps behind the two women. He bid them farewell when they reached Atsila's cabin and he strode back over to Tsiyi's home. She could tell he wanted to say something more to her when he passed but Atsila stood close by.

"Are you sure you're all right, Julia? You looked like you were going to be ill when I found you two," Atsila said when Matthew was out of earshot.

"Of course. I just don't like seeing my brother hurt."

The lie stuck like tar in her throat and she wished more than anything that she could tell Atsila the truth. When had she allowed lying to take over her relationships with other people? As they went back to clearing the land for planting the first corn crop, Julia worried that this had become her new way of interacting with other people and tried to lose herself in her task.

CHAPTER 22

The peaks of the mountains on the far side of the valley were softened by the early morning fog, rising up to meet the clear, orange-streaked sky the next morning. Cold beads of dew clung to the grass and underbrush as Julia trekked to the outskirts of the village, listening to the birdsong overhead. It was amazing how much she could pick up on in the silence; she could hear the bounding paws of a rabbit that whizzed in front of her seconds before she saw its furry body. She had become so accustomed to living in the city with its constant flow of people and clatter of carriages that the comparative quiet of the forest seemed almost deafening.

Julia took in the beauty around her as she sat on a log bench, pulling the warm blanket snuggly around her shoulders. In the few days since she had arrived, one of the unexpected things that surprised her was how chilly mornings rapidly gave way to warm, humid afternoons. Boston was still holding onto winter when she had left, little piles of dirty snow pocketing the streets' edges and a thin sheet of ice filming up the harbor. Here in North Carolina, she wouldn't need her blanket for much longer and the starched sleeves of her blouse would be rolled up as far as they could go by the end of the day.

The homespun fabric of her skirt rubbed uncomfortably against the skin above her wool stockings but there was cure for that. A bemused grin pulled up the corners of her mouth as she imagined being out here in one of her ball gowns, the silk spattered with mud and decaying leaves clinging to a tattered hem. The rounded toes of her sturdy boots were also a far cry from her dainty dancing slippers. *It feels like I've been thrown into an entirely different world.*

Twigs broke behind her and she snapped her head around to see who was joining her. When she saw Matthew ambling toward her, she moved over on the bench to make room. Smiling up at him as he sat next to her, Julia wasn't sure what would happen now that they were alone together again. Their last meeting had ended on a frustrating question mark of a parting and she wondered if he could forget how close they had come to altering their relationship.

Her fingertips were beginning to crack from all the loom work she had helped Atsila with the previous night and her arms still ached from lifting wood planks to help with the meeting house repair but she felt invigorated by the difference she was making. Seeing the exhaustion lining Matthew's face, she was again afraid she'd demanded too much of him, traveling down here and working tirelessly alongside the other men.

"You're up early," Matthew observed, settling down beside her. They looked toward the horizon where the rim of the sun was beginning to shine between the mountains, rapidly dissipating the fog. She could sense a tension that hadn't been there the previous day.

"Well, when a baby gets up before the sun, generally you do too," Julia replied. Waya was undeniably adorable during the waking hours, all gummy grins and curious fingers. The evenings spent before the fireplace were especially entertaining as Atohi, Atsila's husband, would bring out his drum and the boy would pound on the top, trying to imitate the sounds his father made with his reed stick. Julia and Atsila would dance to the beat and the expression of unbridled joy on the baby's face made Julia melt. He was not so endearing, however, when he woke up before dawn broke, already bouncing with energy.

Matthew smiled softly and she felt some of the tension in her shoulders ease. She could honestly say she'd never experienced the awkwardness that followed a missed romantic opportunity and she was grateful that he didn't seem to be embittered.

"How does your arm feel?"

"I'm very much on the mend, thank you. Though it seems working in an office has made me idle," Matthew quipped, running a hand through his thick hair. "Considering how sore I am now, you'd never know I used to haul those big flour bags into the store."

"You seemed like you were having a good time playing lacrosse with Atohi and the other men. That looks like it requires a lot of stamina."

"Well, it's different when it's fun, isn't it?" Matthew graced her with a mischievous half-smile and Julia felt her stomach dive down to her toes and bounce back up again.

"Yes, it would be, wouldn't it?"

"I found a field of wildflowers on my walk yesterday. Do you want me to show you?"

"I'd like that very much."

They rose from the bench, venturing further into the forest surrounding the village. In another quarter of a mile, the forest gave way to an expansive field dotted with lavender, soft yellow, and deep blue hues made all the more brilliant by the now risen sun.

"This place is so beautiful."

"I know," Matthew answered, as they skated the edge of the field. "I'll be sad to leave it tomorrow."

She shared that sentiment wholeheartedly and hoped that his departure from their group didn't raise too many questions, especially from Abigail. But that was tomorrow and she wanted to focus on what was happening right now. In a move that would no doubt have scandalized Eliza,

Julia stopped and leaned against a willow tree, catching Matthew's hand in hers.

Glancing back in the direction of the village as if to make sure they were alone, Matthew brought her hand to his lips. Julia suppressed a gasp and felt a shiver lace up her arm at the feel of his skin against hers, knowing she couldn't blame the cold. She looked up as he released her hand and the intensity of his gaze drew her closer until her forehead was grazing his. This was really happening and there was no one there to interrupt this time.

"Julia," he whispered. The hint of longing in that one word sent more shivers running through her. She felt like she should be more apprehensive about her first kiss but all she could think was how much she wanted to remember this moment. The way the sun filtered through the branches overhead, the solidity of the tree trunk against her back, the faint smoky scent of Matthew's hair, every detail. Closing the remaining space between them, Matthew's mouth captured hers, his fingers cupping her chin.

The kiss was slow and sweet, his lips a gentle pressure that made Julia dizzy with exhilaration. Her cheeks rosy and her eyes sparkling, Julia looked to Matthew as he broke the connection and drew away from her slightly, her thoughts whirring as his hand fell inaudibly to her neck. She could see the question in his eyes.

"It's alright," she heard herself say, though she didn't recognize her voice. It had taken on a breathy quality that was foreign to her own ears. His fingers were soft against the slope of her ear.

Then his lips came crashing down on hers' again and every thought escaped her, every insecurity vanished and she succumbed to her feelings whole-heartedly. His arms wound about her waist and her hand caressed his stubbled cheek. She wanted to stretch these few stolen minutes together out for as long as she could.

Matthew was the one to pull away first but he made no move to let her go, making her block out why she was so far from home in the first place. For a moment since she'd arrived, the hopelessness of knowing that this vibrant community could be forcibly removed and leave all they had ever known didn't twist her stomach into knots. As she looked up into his bright eyes, all she could see was his quiet strength and something she'd seen flashes of before: his affection for her.

"It's probably best that we head back," Matthew said. "Atsila's probably on the verge of sending out a search party."

"I suppose so," Julia said reluctantly, stepping out of the circle of Matthew's arms. They turned and walked back up the path out of the forest and toward the village. Her spirits soared when he took her hand, his thumb tracing gentle circles along her palm. They parted ways when they came to Atsila's cabin, Matthew shooting her a half grin over his shoulder as he walked away briskly. She was sure he was on his way to wash up and join the other men.

She came through the door as quietly as possible, leaning against its back after she'd shut it. It was impossible to keep the delighted smile she was trying to hold back from spreading across her face.

"You look like you've already had a productive morning," Atsila said from her place by the hearth, making Julia jump with surprise. She raised an inquisitive eyebrow as she lowered the mending she'd been working on. "What kept you? Waya's already gone back to sleep."

"I . . . uh, lost track of time on my walk," Julia answered, her cheeks heating up as she took the seat facing Atsila. "The forest is so lovely and I wanted to keep exploring."

"It seems your brother felt the same way. I saw him go into the woods not long after you headed out." The emphasis that she put on the word *brother* and the mischievous tilt of her head stopped Julia from taking up her own project from the day before. *How did Atsila know that? I didn't even know he was going out there.* Her eyes shifted to the window cut out of the logs on the other side of the cabin, the gingham curtains lifting up in the breeze blowing in from outside.

"Well, same habits, you know," she said lamely, the excuse sounding weak even to her own ears. She attempted to continue with her work, willing her hands not to shake as they smoothed out the fabric. Atsila's eyes were boring into the top of her head and she finally looked up, trying to keep the guilt of her deception from marring her face.

"Julia, I'm not blind. I've seen the way you look at each other," Atsila said gently, reaching out to stay her hand. "Matthew's not your kin, is he?"

She considered refuting Atsila's observation, of laughing it off as some ridiculous assumption. But she couldn't mislead Atsila anymore, especially considering how close they'd grown in such a short period of time. Before she knew quite what was happening, the whole story spilled out of her in a torrent of fumbling words. Julia couldn't meet her friend's eyes as she detailed her desperation to travel down here and the lengths she had gone to ensure her trip was successful.

"I'm so sorry for deceiving you, all of you. I hope you won't think less of me," she said, finally gaining the courage to look up at Atsila. The other woman's face was unreadable for a moment and Julia felt her heart speed up with a rising sense of panic. She was about to start running through the names of other families she could stay with for the remaining day of her mission should she be tossed out when Atsila graced her with a glowing smile.

"You were willing to do anything to meet with our tribe. I thought nearly everyone on the outside had given up on helping us." She came over to sit next to Julia and wrapped her an unexpected but not unwelcome hug. When she released her, there were tears in the corners of her eyes. "Of course, I wish you hadn't lied to me but the hope you've given me is more important."

"I don't want to sound ungrateful for the missionaries who've come down here for so many years," she continued. "They mean well and they work diligently alongside us. But they only seem concerned with our conversion and not the real danger we're facing now. No matter how much they push, I'll never give up my beliefs because they're a part of me. My father has tried to convince me to give up those beliefs but that's one thing I cannot do for him.

From where I stand, we don't want you to save us. Our nation can take care of our own and survive. What we do want is for you all to listen to us, to recognize who we are."

Atsila's voice had taken on a hard edge and Julia could feel the pain radiating from her. "And I'll never give up my home to those who don't honor our treaties and try to rip us from all we've known."

The conviction of her new friend's words solidified Julia's belief that she was where she was meant to be. At the same time, her blood boiled with indignation at the stranglehold the government had on Atsila and her people. Their very lives and communities were being directed by a power that was beyond their control.

"I'll do whatever I can to help you. When my father hears what I have to tell him about my time here, I'm sure I can get him on my side."

Atsila gave her a sad smile, much of her earlier fight seeming to have left her. *She's probably heard this all before,* Julia thought. *How can I make her see that I mean to change things?*

"I know your heart is in the right place, Julia. But it's going to take more than one politician to stand up for our nation, no matter how esteemed your father is."

"Oh, it would be more than just my father. I've spoken with Mr. Clay and he's sympathetic, too. If he gets elected again, I'm sure others will-"

"You put too much faith in these men, I'm afraid. I appreciate your enthusiasm but experience has taught me not to get my hopes up when it comes to the politicians in Washington."

"Well, I'll make sure there's one more ally on your side. I won't give up on this, Atsila. I can promise you that."

"I know you'll do what you can and I appreciate that more than you know. I just hope that you won't be too disappointed when you're faced with the reality of our situation."

Julia squeezed Atsila's hand, trying to impart some of her own optimism onto the other woman. Even if this legislation passed, there would be a fight against its implementation and she knew she was going to be a part of it. And she was going to convince her father to join the fray as an ally if it was the last thing she did.

*   *   *   *

She's in the kitchen at home once more, the haunting strains of the piano floating out from deep in the belly of the house. She would be afraid but she knows that melody and she runs down the hall, trying not to get her hopes up.

It can't be, she tells herself, preparing for the disappointment at finding no one at the piano. But she turns the corner anyway and there is a woman at the instrument, a beauty in her velvet housecoat, her fingers flying over the keys at an unnatural speed.

Her eyes fill with tears and she cannot bring herself to enter the room. She just stands at the threshold, taking in the sight of her mother, vibrant and so achingly alive. It's hard to tell how long she stays there, taking in the sight. It could be a moment, it could be a lifetime.

But, eventually, her mother seems to sense that she's there and she turns, a warm smile bringing a glow to her face. She's aged to what she was before she died but her beauty still shines through, her serenity a balm in a world too overrun with sharp edges.

"I'm so proud of you, she says", her voice seeming to come from under water even though they're in the same room and there is no pond here. She rushes over and embraces her mother, the faintest whiff of lilac tickling her nose.

The parlor suddenly shifts and she's with her mother in the forest outside of the Cherokee village. She can see Atsila out in her garden but when she tries to call out to her, a croak is the only sound that escapes. She looks up to see if her mother is still there and she is. But she seems to be fading away, a ghost floating away into the sunflowers. There are tears in her mother's eyes, though, and she wants to beg her to stay but she's lost the ability the speak to anyone.

"Don't you ever give up, my love," her mother breathes and then she is gone.

Julia woke with a start, sitting up in her cot. Too real tears ran down her cheeks and dripped from her chin on to her shift. She hopes she hasn't cried out in her sleep but the cabin seems still in the pre-dawn gloom and she breathed a sigh of relief. Lowering herself back down, she turned on to her side and wiped at her cheeks, not quite sure if she was gutted or hopeful or somewhere in between.

She heard the baby's soft, rhythmic breathing and eventually, the pounding in her chest slowed to a reasonable beat and she closed her eyes. As she drifted back off to sleep, she knew that her mother would be proud of her and that is all she needs in that moment.

CHAPTER 23

The next morning brought fog that couldn't seem to let go as they packed up their belongings and watered the horses. Julia still hadn't gotten a glimpse of the chief but Onacona had been summoned to a council meeting so she assumed that he and the shaman had returned. Atsila stood near one of the mares, feeding the creature oats while Waya bounced in the papoose on her back. After she made sure the saddle was secure, Julia joined her and combed Waya's curls back from his forehead one last time. The boy smiled expectantly at her and she wished she didn't have to leave so soon. Everything seemed much more uncertain than it had the previous day now that she was going back. She decided to push her doubts down and gave Atsila a reassuring smile.

"I'll write to you, I promise. I've checked with Abigail and the mission can help me get any letters I have sent down to you."

"I look forward to it. Be careful going back up to Boston." There was a sadness in her eyes that was different from the previous morning and Julia felt it, too. Their interaction had been brief but Julia felt as if she was parting with a dear friend she'd known for years, not days.

The melancholic air that hung between them lasted another minute until Atsila's lips curved into a conspiratorial smirk that could only mean trouble as she said loudly, "I'm sure your brother's presence will be greatly missed on your way back, too." Julia coughed into her fist to keep her giddy smile hidden.

"Yes, we'll all miss him terribly," she choked out, shooting a good-natured glare Atsila's way.

Matthew had already departed a few hours ago to Abigail's great, though understandable, consternation. Julia and Matthew had agreed that it would be better to feign an unexpected development rather than telling the O'Connors outright that he wasn't traveling back to Boston with them. What difference could one more lie among many others make?

"But, but you can't leave now," Abigail had spluttered as Matthew had gotten his own horse ready in the dim light of early morning. They hadn't seen much of Abigail and Jacob since they'd arrived, though they'd all pitched in on the repair of the meeting house. She'd looked a bit like a perplexed porcupine as she'd hovered near Matthew, her hair nearly standing on end in some places as she tried to convey her distress in not following the rules to a tee.

Julia had felt guilt roll through her at the sight but it couldn't be helped. Matthew needed to settle the final loose ends concerning his family's estate and he also couldn't return to Boston with them. It was too risky as she half expected the actual Fletcher to be waiting for them at the stagecoach station, railing against her impertinence for all the world to witness.

"I'm sorry but something has come up at the college that I must attend to immediately," Matthew had answered. His words had been tinged with just the right amount of panic to convey how important it was that he leave before them but not so much as to reduce Abigail to hysteria. *If he wasn't already a lawyer, he would make a very talented actor,* Julia had thought.

"It really can't wait until we leave later this afternoon?"

"No, ma'am, I'm sorry. They need me back sooner than I was anticipating. I must leave now if I'm to make good time on my own."

He'd hoisted himself up on to the animal's back and looked down at

Abigail with kind eyes. "I trust you and your husband with Julia. I'm sure the family will be reassured to know I left her in your capable hands." And before Abigail could protest further, he'd trotted out of the village without a backward glance.

"Well, I didn't expect your brother to be so impertinent," Abigail said now, looking much more put together as she joined Julia and Atsila. "What if your stepmother holds Jacob and I responsible for his actions? Imagine, leaving you here to fend for yourself."

"My parents won't hold you responsible for Matthew's rashness, I can assure you," Julia said, knowing she would never allow the O'Connors to bear the blame for her boldness. This had been her doing and her doing alone.

This seemed to make Abigail feel better and she turned to Atsila. "Please tell your father how grateful we are for giving us a place to stay while we were here. I know he's at a tribal council right now and can't see us off."

"I will, don't worry," Atsila replied. Looking up through the fog that the sun was beginning to burn away, she continued. "You better be off if you want to reach Asheville by nightfall."

"Right, right," Abigail said, all business again. She went over to her mare and Jacob helped her up while Julia gave Atsila a firm hug. She then swung herself up onto her horse and the three of them started off, taking the path that circled the village instead of the one that lead directly into its center.

After a few moments, she looked back and saw that Atsila was just a smudge against the landscape now, a tiny ant in a sea of tall, green grass. The lump in her throat and her growing sense of dread had only partly to do with the uphill battle it take to help Atsila and her community. What ramifications would her web of lies result in when she returned to Boston and her family?

*　　　*　　　*　　　*

"You must be excited to see your family again," Abigail chirped two days later as the Webster estate came into view. Julia could only answer with a quick nod and a tight-lipped smile she was sure couldn't hide her panic.

Her anxiety had reached an apropos crescendo as the O'Connor's carriage crested the final hill that led to her home. She'd been able to hold onto her wits in the stagecoach up north and she'd fully been expecting a crimson faced Fletcher to descend on them the minute they were due back in Boston. When he hadn't been there as they unloaded their luggage and located Abigail and Jacob's carriage, she'd taken it as a foreboding sign. A publicly furious Fletcher was preferable to a version of her brother who had had time to stew and bury his anger to keep up appearances. He was going to explode on her in the comfort of their own sitting room and it was going to be dreadful.

As they got closer, she saw his tall frame materialize at the foot of the drive leading up to the house and her mouth went dry. There was no running from what she'd done anymore.

"Whoa, whoa," she heard Jacob say to the horse as they came to a jolting stop. Fletcher stocked out the edge of the lane, his eyes zeroing in on Julia through the pane glass of the carriage's door. She noticed that his chin was rough with scruff, though he looked as put together as he always did in every other respect. *No, not good at all.*

Julia decided it was best to face her brother and his ire head on. She would not cower before him like she might have when she was younger. So she opened the carriage door and stepped out, hoping their meeting would be obscured from their neighbors' view from across the way.

"How kind of you to return to us, Julia," Fletcher said tightly, barely keeping his temper in check. She saw the clench of his jaw and that his hands were balled up into fists. "We were beginning to think you may have left us for good. Edward would've been heartbroken."

At the mention of their younger brother, Julia whipped her downcast eyes up to Fletcher's blazing ones, so shocked by his cruelty that tears cloyed at the corners of her eyes and began to fall before she could stop them.

"I would never-" she began but was suddenly interrupted by Abigail, who had seen the sudden change in Julia and had come swooping in to her aid.

"Who are you, sir? I've never met you before and I can't say I like the tone you're using toward my charge."

"I'm sorry to tell you this, Mrs. O'Connor, but I'm Fletcher Webster. And I need to talk with my sister immediately." His face softened when he took in Abigail's obvious confusion, Jacob's utter silence from the driver's box. "It seems I'm not the only one who was lied to."

"But you can't be her brother. He was with us the whole . . ." Abigail's voice trailed off and her eyes found Julia, sharp as needles. All sympathy stripped away in an instant. "You. You lied to us?"

Before Julia had a chance to apologize, to explain herself, to do anything of significance, Fletcher had taken her arm firmly and was pulling her over to his side of the lane.

"We will take care of this, Mrs. O'Connor, I assure you. I'm so sorry you and your husband were caught up in this."

She didn't dare to glance behind her as she met Fletcher's brisk pace and walked down the path leading to their home's entrance. Not a word was shared between them as she swiped at the tears still tracing canyons down her cheeks and they climbed up the stairs.

After the front door had closed, the barely calm demeanor Fletcher had put on for the O'Connors' benefit melted away to reveal an unyielding rage underneath.

"What were you thinking?" he hissed as he took Julia by the arm and led her into the parlor with newly materialized Caroline in tow. He turned to their stepmother and said in a tight voice, "You may speak with her after I have. I'll let you know when we're done here."

He shut the door in Caroline's shocked face with a bang, making Julia flinch. Taking in his ruddy cheeks and finding herself on the other end of his piercing glare as he brushed past her made her feel about as big as a baby field mouse.

"Julia, you've done some questionable things before but this blows them all out of the water."

She'd never seen her brother this upset before and the fact that his anger was directed squarely on her was frightening. He was seething as she watched him pace back and forth along the length of the front bay window.

"We had no way to contact you. Do you know how worried we all were? You could've been anywhere in the country and we wouldn't have known where. Eliza in particular was beside herself."

"I wasn't galivanting around the country," she squeaked, trying to sound brave. The fact that she'd made Eliza worry so much broke her heart but she needed to defend herself in this moment and so she forged ahead. "I went on the trip I would have gone on if you'd been there to accompany me."

"How can I believe anything you say? For all I know, the O'Connors were in on the whole thing." He scoffed and gave her an incredulous look. It was clear he didn't believe her and a part of her knew that sentiment was entirely justified. But he had brought the O'Connors into this and seeing his suspicion of two innocent people in her scheme made her bolder. She couldn't have him think that she'd secretly been working with them.

"Please do not drag Abigail and Jacob into this. You saw their reactions out there. They had nothing to do with my plan and would've returned me to Caroline if they'd known I wasn't being truthful. I made the decision to go entirely on my own. I felt like if I didn't go now, I would've wasted my opportunity to make a difference."

"Then why didn't they bring you back when they learned you were travelling with them by yourself?"

His question gave her pause but she knew she couldn't betray Matthew after all he'd done for her. There was Louisa to consider, too. She'd been dragged into this mess by association and Julia would defend her to the last. That's why she decided to be as vague as possible when she answered her brother.

"You heard Abigail. I lied to them, too," she said in a flat voice. Which was the truth but only just. If Fletcher pushed her further, she would need to spin another web and that was the last thing she wanted to do.

Fletcher pinched the bridge of his nose, closing his eyes in what could only be described as exasperation. "What have you done, Julia? I hardly recognize you anymore."

This was said in almost a whisper and she sensed that some of his initial rage had subsided. She approached where he stood with trepidation, settling a few feet aware from him as he glared pointedly out the window.

The sudden image of Eliza's worried face took her back to what Fletcher had said a few minutes ago and she said in an equally quiet voice, "I know that I've damaged my relationships with you and Caroline and Eliza. For that, I'm incredibly sorry."

He turned to look at her with renewed fire in his eyes. "You're sorry? That's all you have to say for yourself? Julia, if this gets out, your reputation will be in tatters. No one from your family was there to accompany you and people have active imaginations. If they know you were essentially alone, rumors will fly about what you did down there. And our family could suffer by extension. That includes Caroline and Eliza."

"Doesn't that tell you something, Fletcher? I know I shouldn't have deceived you all and I feel guilty about what I had to do. But I did the right thing by going down there and seeing what the situation truly is for the Indians."

He cleared his throat indignantly, "How could you say-"

She rushed on before he could launch into a diatribe and she lost her nerve to stand up for herself. This would be the only chance she would have to make him listen.

"I was boarded with a family nearly the whole time I was there and I saw how they were so much like us, how much they relied on one another. How much they loved one another and how strong their whole community is. That is all likely to be taken away from them and it's unbearably cruel, especially now that I've seen how connected they are to their home. How can I be punished for educating myself by a society that doesn't care a whit about them? That's what's really wrong here."

"It is regrettable what is happening, Julia," Fletcher returned in a patronizing tone that made her want to hurl one of Caroline's intricately embroidered throw pillows in his face. "But you cannot lie and risk reproach because you think what you're doing is right. There are protocols that need to be followed and you broke those. For that, you must face appropriate consequences."

"Fine. I will accept whatever punishment you and Caroline cook up. But it won't change my thoughts on what is going on underneath all of our noses that no one talks about. Nor can I let go of just how awful it is."

Fletcher opened his mouth as if to retort but stopped himself, his lips pulling together in a grim line. Without another word, he stalked over to the door and opened it. Caroline was on the other side where they'd left her, the color high in her cheeks.

"I'm sorry, madame. She's all yours," Fletcher said to their stepmother as he hurried past into the belly of the house. She turned her attention to Caroline as she entered the room and was taken aback when the other woman didn't say anything for some time. When she finally spoke, her tone was as icy as a northern wind blowing in off the harbor in winter and just as cutting.

"I cannot look at you right now. I want you to take a couple days with Eliza and try to make amends for your behavior while you are there. In that time, I'll talk with your brother and come up with an appropriate punishment for you. And decide what exactly I'm going to tell your father when he returns. Let me get my things together to take you over there. *Your* bag is already packed."

Julia didn't dare to contradict her but simply followed in her wake, picking up her discarded bag from the entryway while Caroline pulled on her wrap for the short journey. The ride over to the Lee home was silent and the sun shone brilliantly through the glass pane, clearly unaffected by the tension within the carriage.

When they pulled up in front of the home and she had descended down to the street, Eliza came out the front door without even bothering to hide her relief as she hurried down the front pathway to the gate separating them and opened it with a clang.

"Julia, I was so worried. Are you hurt? What happened?"

"No need to worry about her, Eliza," Caroline's cool voice emanated from within the carriage. "She'll explain everything to you. I'm just not sure how sympathetic you'll be when you discover how she lied to us all. I will pick her back up promptly on Saturday morning."

With that, Caroline signaled to James that they could disembark and they bounced away over the cobblestones. Julia felt like she'd just been shunned by a ruthless queen who didn't have the time of day to deal with rebellious courtesans.

"What is she talking about, Julia?" Eliza shot her a questioning look, the first hints of doubt tinging her concerned expression. Julia had known this would be the most unbearable conversation to have when she returned. She knew it would be difficult to contend with Fletcher and Caroline after what she'd done but she knew deep down that her decisions would affect Eliza the most. Kind, gracious Eliza who had always been there for her and was her most staunch supporter.

Caroline is already punishing me, Julia realized with a heavy heart. She was going to have to tell Eliza of her betrayal of trust on her own and she was dreading every minute of it.

"We need to go inside," she replied, looping Eliza's arm in hers and evading her glance. "There's so much I need to tell you and I'm sure most of it will make you think less of me."

CHAPTER 24

That evening, after a tense dinner, Julia perched on the edge of her bed, feeling like she was going to burst out of her own skin she was so tense. A book lay open and unread beside her and she kept thinking back on the hour long talk she'd had with her cousin that afternoon, the hurt and disappointment on her face. At the sound of the door scrapping against the floor, her head snapped up and she felt an uncustomary twinge of dread at the sight of Eliza.

In the soft light emanating from the fireplace and the sun slowly setting outside the window, Julia could almost imagine that this was just another night here, another leadup to one of their customary talks about what had happened that day. But the sadness she could feel pouring off of Eliza wasn't normal and she hated that she was the cause of it.

"I think of you as a daughter, Julia," Eliza finally began, her voice small but strong, her eyes focused on her neatly folded hands. "When your mother entrusted me with your care, I took her faith in me very seriously. I know that your father loves you but he hasn't been there for so much of your life. I have been. That's why your disregard of my feelings cuts so deeply. You couldn't trust me with what you were planning to do. And considering that I can't . . ."

Her cousin's voice caught and she had to cut herself off when her eyes suddenly glistened with tears. Julia wanted to go to Eliza and wrap her arms around her. She wanted to assure her that she trusted her beyond measure, that she'd felt that misleading her was her only option in the moment when Fletcher was held up and everything was spinning out of control. But, as she watched Eliza pull back her shoulders as if gathering her strength and took in what she said next, all she could do was listen with horrified astonishment.

"I'm unable to have children of my own, Julia. It's been the most difficult realization of my life, knowing I can't carry a baby and watch that child grow. It's one of the many reasons why you mean so much to me." At the look of guilt and pity contorting Julia's face, Eliza rushed on. "I don't say this to make you feel guilty. I've made as much peace with it as I can. But I want you to realize how much I love you."

She thought she'd known everything about Eliza. How naïve she had been to assume that there weren't hurts and hopes, heartbreaks and desires that the other woman had kept from bubbling to the surface. She was suddenly taken back to when she was small, of faded memories of whispers and tears from her own mother who had lost children, too. Though faint, she could still remember her mother holding her tightly against her, her tears falling on Julia's forehead as she kissed her and promised she would always hold her this way, that she couldn't lose her, too. It made her feel all the more self-centered.

"That's all I want you to consider before you make more decisions when it comes to this fight. Because I know you and that you're not going to give up no matter what the outcome is. Your determination is admirable but I want you to think of the consequences before you act."

With that, Eliza turned and closed the door firmly behind her. She may as well have slammed it the way it made Julia start. She didn't even try to keep the tears from rolling down her cheeks, turning over the damage she had done to her bond with her cousin until she couldn't see anything beyond the hurt etched on Eliza's face.

She knew she'd done the right thing in going down to North Carolina but her heart ached with the full realization that the trust Eliza had put in her was shattered. Their relationship would likely be piece mailed back together over time but it would never be as interwoven as it had been before Julia's schemes and one almost unforgivable lie.

When she was spent, she wiped her damp cheeks and stared out the window, barely registering the sun disappearing beyond the horizon and the stars suddenly twinkling into existence in the purple hued peripheries of the sky. This rift between she and Eliza was something she knew she would carry with her for a long time.

The next evening, her last in the Lee home after a day spent in nearly silent tension, she went down the stairs quietly. Barely noticing the late afternoon darkness that was beginning to overtake the house's nooks and crevices, she saw light seeping through beneath the parlor door. Assuming Eliza was in there talking with Thomas, she veered off in the opposite direction toward the kitchen.

As she approached the door, she could hear the murmur of whispered voices. Doubling back to avoid interrupting an obviously private conversation, she stopped short when she picked up on Louisa's familiar tone. Suddenly, all she wanted to do was talk with her closest friend, to try to work through the unforeseen effects of her betrayal. She walked forward and was about to push against the slightly ajar door when she caught a glimpse of who Louisa was speaking with.

Peter's strong back faced her and curved down toward Louisa's barely visible frame. When his hand came up and gently cupped Louisa's cheek, Julia knew she needed to back away and leave them be. They certainly weren't discussing the next day's menu. But before she could slink off, she watched as Louisa rose up on her tiptoes to meet Peter's lips with her own. The way her hands wrapped around the back of his neck and the ease with which he took her into his arms made Julia realize that this wasn't the first time this had happened. She didn't know whether to be elated or incensed but she did know that she was too drained to confront Louisa about any of this tonight.

Her intention to sneak back to her room without Louisa and Peter discovering her was for naught, though, as she unwittingly slammed into the hall table as she was backing up and it bucked into the wall. She was barely able to catch the tea tray that was on it before it crashed to the floor and alerted the whole house to where she was when Louisa dashed out the kitchen door. Her face reddened when she saw Julia returning the tray to its rightful place and her eyes darted back to where she'd come from in panic.

Taking Louisa's hand swiftly, she led the way back up to her room, easing the door shut as the other girl started a fire in the grate with shaky hands to ward off the unexpected chill, the logs hissing as the small blaze intensified. When the room was bathed in light, she turned to face Julia with an uncharacteristically resolute expression.

"Are you gonna turn us in?

Julia was taken aback by Louisa's suspicion that she would turn on her like that. How could she think she would put Louisa and Peter in harm's way?

"Why would you even ask that? Of course I'm not going to betray you." Julia considered her next words carefully, trying to strike a balance between empathy and voicing the very real hardships Louisa and Peter faced. "But what you're doing is dangerous. What if you and Peter get caught? I don't think even Eliza would have a choice about what happened next."

"Don't you think we've turned this whole thing over and over 'tween us? My uncle is goin' to blow a gasket if he finds out who I've fallen in love with. It terrifies me every day when I see them constables patrolin' the streets when I go home. I feel like they can see it all over my face and will arrest me on the spot. We've tried to bury our feelings, tried to go on like nothin' has changed. But that's impossible now and I don't want to deny it." Louisa seemed on the verge of tears but she blinked them back before continuing in a small voice. "I feel hollow when I'm apart from 'im. I don't know how I let myself fall so deeply so quickly."

Julia could see what a struggle this all was for Louisa to confess. She couldn't imagine how agonizing it would be to love someone that she couldn't even be seen in public with. So much had come to light since her return to Boston that she felt like she was underwater, drowning in the secrets that her actions had unexpectedly brought to the surface. When she glanced at her friend again, she wore the steely look of determination.

"I lied for you, Julia, and I would do it again. I know yer heart was in the right place and I know you didn't mean to hurt Miss Eliza. Now I'm askin' you. Can I trust ya with my own secret?"

She could honestly say that she'd never seen this side of Louisa before. The woman before her wore a resolute, if slightly wary, expression that convinced her she wouldn't give Peter up even if Julia begged her to. Stepping forward, Julia took her small hands in her own and squeezed them with all the reassurance she could muster.

"I promise I won't tell a soul," she whispered, hoping that she was making the right decision. The relieved expression on Louisa's face made her feel better but she couldn't entirely shake the feeling of foreboding that crept up her spine. The three of them were all playing with fire now. She now had experience with secrets and how destructive they could be once they spiraled out of control.

*　　　*　　　*　　　*

"Where are you going?" Julia asked Caroline two weeks later when her stepmother came into the sitting room in full travel attire. Caroline had decided to go with a lightweight, maroon traveling cloak and a hat to match; even her sturdy boots held a tinge of the color. She was certainly the queen of her castle and wanted to make sure Julia knew it, too.

This past fortnight had seen Fletcher's brisk departure a day after she'd returned from Eliza's, his cold eyes conveying how disappointed he was in her. The days since had been filled with tense, stop and start conversations that didn't seem to go anywhere with a stepmother who was taking pleasure in seeing Julia taken down a peg . . . or four. She had only left the house in Caroline's company and that had only been to call on matriarchs she hardly knew to begin with.

"I'm surprising your father in the capitol. He's working so hard that I thought a couple days of distraction would do him good."

"Oh. I didn't know you were planning on going down. Is anyone going with you?" She fought hard to maintain a placid expression. Caroline hadn't even consulted her about whether she wanted to go and it cut her to know that her lies had cost her time with her father. It was another unforeseen consequence of doing the right thing but going about it all the wrong way.

"My older brother. He'll be here in the next fifteen minutes. I'll be back before Saturday but I expect you to stick close to the house while I'm gone. I've told Doris to keep an eye on you."

Julia nodded, resigned to another few days of imprisonment. Although it wasn't completely for naught; the number of books she'd read had her hopeful that she could plow through the rest of the pile that had been sitting on her end table for months. And she had nearly perfected her upside down cake. Maybe she could even convince Eliza to call so that she could beg for her forgiveness.

"You're going to tell him what I've done, aren't you?"

She had been waiting for the letter from Caroline to go out since she'd come back, for the hammer to fall and the punishment to come full circle. This would certainly be a golden opportunity for it.

"No, I've decided I won't tell him of your actions while I'm down there. He deserves some peace and quiet before the recess. But I will tell him of your gross lapse in judgement when he comes home in June and I suggest you prepare yourself for his reaction. It's sure to be far from pleasant."

We can agree on that, she thought, envisioning what was either going to be a bombastic explosion that would be intense but could peter out quickly or a more subtle disquiet that could follow her around for days, if not weeks.

She didn't know which one would be worse.

"I still don't understand how you were able to convince the O'Connors to go down to North Carolina with you without your brother," Caroline said, bringing Julia back into the present. "They're upstanding people; she's even sent me a letter of apology for what transpired."

This was so unexpected of a statement that Julia didn't have time to mask her surprise. Fletcher had been too distracted by the impudence of it all to really question how she had pulled her scheme off and though her stepmother had questioned her about it after her brother's return to Harvard, she'd been able to skate around the inquiries. That had all changed now. Caroline picked up on her slip right away and narrowed her eyes; Julia could almost see the wheels turning behind them.

"You didn't go alone, did you? You wrangled someone else up to go in Fletcher's place."

"Well, I . . ." She didn't know if it was better to try to keep dodging Caroline's questions or come out with it outright. All she knew was that her stepmother wouldn't rest until she found out who it was and the last two weeks of animosity had exhausted Julia more than she'd known. She was tired of being under a metaphorical magnifying glass.

"Who do you know that you could have tricked the O'Connors with?" Caroline was thinking out loud now and seemed to have forgotten Julia was even in the room. Then, her face lightened with recognition and she turned to Julia again.

"Matthew Eaton? It was him, wasn't it?" Julia's traitorous cheeks flared to life and gave Caroline all the answers she was looking for. "I would have thought he'd have more sense than that."

"I convinced him to go. He didn't want to when I first asked him, I can assure you. But he wanted to help me, too, and that won out. You can't hold him responsible, it was all me."

"He still should have known better. What were you both thinking?" Caroline's eyes narrowed further. "Did he . . . did he take advantage of you?"

She thought she'd been mortified before but this was the pinnacle of embarrassment. Why did Caroline have to make everything sound so tawdry? It had just been a couple of kisses, nothing more. She wouldn't have let it go down that road and she was convinced Matthew wouldn't have, either. He was older than her, yes, but he also respected her and wouldn't take advantage of her. She'd seen his goodness first-hand and Caroline barely knew him.

"No, Caroline, he was a perfect gentleman the whole time. He only wanted to help me because no one else could or would."

"Oh, Julia, you were half in love with him already before you went down south. You don't understand the implications this has for you. He could say anything happened between you and you wouldn't have a leg to stand on."

"As I just said, he would never do that. He's too decent of a man."

Caroline still regarded her with some skepticism but the conviction of Julia's words seemed to have gotten through to her.

"Well, your father needs to know about this, too. Matthew works at the law office, for goodness sake."

"I'll tell him. Please, Caroline, let me have this courtesy. I know I probably don't deserve it but I want him to hear this one piece of what I've done from me."

Caroline scrutinized her with an exacting expression and she was sure she'd gone too far. But then, the other woman's eyes softened just a bit.

"Alright, you can be the one to tell him. This is something that needs to be discussed between the two of you without my interference. I'm afraid I know what it's like to be half in love myself."

Before the conversation could go any further than that, they both heard a hard knock on the front door and Caroline was all straight edges and hard lines again.

"That will be William. I expect to hear an exemplary report of your behavior when I return."

Julia nodded and watched Caroline leave briskly. She then sank back into the chaise, wondering not for the first time how she'd allowed circumstances to get so tangled.

CHAPTER 25

"I can't believe Papa's coming in today," Julia said, attempting to engage her stepmother. The first week of June had finally arrived and the two women had been in New York City for a whirlwind couple of days. She could sense how Caroline was keeping her at arm's length now that all the preparations for her father's arrival were settled. Though Julia was anxious to see her father again for the first time since January, her stomach roiled with the knowledge that he would likely see her differently after Caroline told him what she had done. He was a staunch advocate for standing up for one's beliefs but she knew she'd crossed a line and didn't know if he would be particularly quick to forgive her defiance.

Her father had also informed her through his sporadic correspondence that Congress was dangerously close on deciding whether the Indian removal bill would pass and that the debate continued to be intense. Julia could only pray that Congress made the right decision.

"He'll be so happy to see you," Caroline returned tightly, sinking into one the lodging house's comfortable chairs. "His carriage was due to arrive a half an hour ago so he should be here within the next fifteen minutes. The station is not too far from here."

"How did he look when you went down to Washington a couple of weeks ago?" Julia asked, pacing the expanse of carpet in front of her stepmother; she was too riled up to think of sitting down.

"He looked exhausted," Caroline answered through thin lips but her expression softened when she must have seen the worry on Julia's face. There had been an uneasy truce established between them since Caroline's return now that each knew where the other stood. Caroline had even apologized for not telling her that she was making that aforementioned trip to Washington without her. "But don't worry. I'm sure it's nothing serious. It's likely just the strain of his time in the capitol. He seemed better by the time I left."

"I hope so," Julia whispered, trying not to let her fear overtake her.

"There he is, Julia," Caroline said, catching a glimpse of her father from over Julia's shoulder. She turned toward the front doors to see her noticeably slimmer father walking toward her. A wide smile broke out across her face as she was enveloped in her father's arms. The familiar hints of cigar smoke and old books clung to his clothes, filling Julia's nostrils and she hugged him tighter still.

"Hello, my dear," her father said softly into Julia's ear and they reluctantly let go of each other. "How have you been?"

"I'm fine, Papa," Julia countered as she took in his appearance. There were dark circles under his eyes and his clothes hung from his body considerably, making Julia instantly concerned for his health. "You look like you haven't eaten in days, though. Are you well?"

"I've been better," he admitted, an ironic smile breaking over his cracking lips. "But we can talk about it when we get home. I have the carriage ready; are we ready to leave for Boston?"

Caroline looked up sharply at this news. "We're not staying here overnight, Daniel? I thought that's what we'd discussed doing. You've already been traveling all morning."

"Yes, I know my dear. But I've decided I can't stand to stay in another uncomfortable bed for one more night. I want to be home as soon as I can."

"You make a good point, love. Just let me talk with someone at the front desk." Caroline strode over to the check in desk and began talking with the slim, bespectacled man behind it.

Julia, in turn, picked up the luggage she and Caroline had brought with them. "Papa, what about the Indians?" she blurted out, unable to control herself. Her father turned and looked at her, his eyes unreadable.

"We'll discuss that when we get home, Julia," he replied tiredly. "Right now, I just want to get this last leg of travel over with." Caroline returned to them after what looked like spirited negotiations between she and the clerk and the three of them left the lodging house, stepping into the humid city air. An overwhelming sense of dread overtook her as she watched Caroline help her father into the carriage and then hoisted herself in. She feared that her father's health was not the only distressing news.

* * * *

"Miss Julia, you're off to an early start this morning. The flower beds out front weren't enough for you? Now you're helping with the vegetable garden, as well?"

At the sound of Doris's questions, Julia started a bit. She'd been concentrating so hard on pulling roots from last year's empty vegetable patch that she hadn't heard the housekeeper's approach. She was too jittery to try baking anything so she thought gardening would be a welcome distraction. The dirt between her fingers and underneath her nails grounded her in a peculiar way, as if she felt like she didn't have very far to fall. It felt good to be useful.

"I needed to get out of the house and do something constructive. I'm not Caroline's favorite person right now." *And I likely won't be for a very long time,* she thought, wondering when her stepmother was finally going to tell her father what she'd done. The waiting was almost worse than what she assumed his reaction would be.

"She'll come around eventually, miss. You lying wasn't kind but the reason you did it was very brave. You saw something that was wrong and you stood by your convictions. You're your mother's daughter through and through."

Doris's unexpected support brought tears to Julia's eyes. The older woman had been so loyal to their family all these years and had grieved Grace's death right alongside them. To hear that she understood and even approved of what Julia had done was a gift.

"Thank you, Doris," she replied, swallowing the lump that had formed in her throat. "For you to say that warms my heart." She paused, the sudden flash of memory of her mother in this very same garden, bent over and working the soil like she was now bringing a pang of grief. They should've been working alongside each other now, reminiscing about all that had happened this past year.

Without thinking, she said wistfully, "I miss her so much."

"So do I, Miss Julia," Doris replied, looking forlorn for a moment as she stared off beyond their garden to a copse of trees in the distance. She started then, seeming to jolt back to the present. "Oh, I've forgotten to check on the pies Mrs. Webster wanted for tonight. Please excuse me, dear."

She watched Doris walking back toward the house, sighed, and then resumed working on the garden, her apron already spattered with wet dirt. The sounds of Edward playing with the new kitten in the other corner of the yard made her smile and vow to make this a good day as she began yanking at the stubborn weeds. His return from school the previous day had been a saving grace for her.

After at least ten minutes of working on a particularly deep seeded patch, her arms were beginning to burn. The back door of the house banged against the outside wall, likely caught in the breeze that had whipped up suddenly and added an unexpected chill to the early June day.

Julia turned to ask Doris to grab the spade that was out of her reach but the words died on her lips as she realized it was Matthew coming toward her. She barely had a minute to collect herself when Edward whizzed past her and came to a halt before Matthew. Wiping her hands on her apron, Julia suppressed a smile as she watched her brother attempt to cover up the fact that he was certainly about to throw his arms around Matthew's waist. He'd been trying hard to act more grown up now that he was a couple months away from his tenth birthday.

"Matthew, I'm so glad you came to call on us," Edward said with an affected air. Julia had to put a hand to her mouth to keep from laughing; she didn't dare look at Matthew's expression. "We didn't see you arrive. Would you like me to let Papa know that you're here?"

"That's very kind of you, Master Edward, but I've already spoken with your father." When Edward's bravado fell a little bit, Matthew interjected, "I only arrived a sort time ago. Don't worry, I was greeted with great hospitality."

"Oh, we didn't see your horse coming up the road. Or did you come here on foot?'

"Ah, a gentleman never reveals his secrets. But I'm lucky enough to have a fast horse who also happens to have quiet hooves."

"Is she in the stable? I'll help James give her a rub down."

"I think Lucia would be very glad to see you again. I'm not sure which stall she ended up in, though."

"Don't forget Patches," Julia reminded him as Edward took off in the opposite direction. He changed course and ran to where the kitten was cleaning its tiny back in the grass, scooping him gently up into his arms before continuing on his journey.

"He seems much improved," Matthew said as they watched Edward practically gallop toward the stable.

"It's good that he's back home. And that Papa let him keep that kitten. He found him outside mewing in the bushes. We don't know where he came from but he's brought Edward out of his shell."

They both turned quiet after that. There was no one else there to distract her from the fact that this was their first time alone since North Carolina.

“We should go inside to the parlor,” she said as another gust of cool air ruffled the curls on her forehead and she untied the apron.

“Lead the way. I've something important to tell you.” Julia took him around the side and through the front door of the house, trying to settle on what Matthew needed to tell her. It could be any number of things but the pit in her stomach told her how anxious she was for his news.

"Why did you come to see my father?" she asked as they settled in the front sitting room, bathed in late spring sunshine.

"I told him I'm leaving Boston," he said. His tone was matter of fact, as if he had told her he was simply moving across the way. Her head shot up involuntarily, any attempt to temper her emotions abandoned.

"You're . . . you're what?"

Matthew at least had the decency to look uncomfortable, shifting back and forth in his chair. "Well . . . I've decided to move down to Washington."

Julia could feel her mouth hanging open but couldn't find the wherewithal to snap it shut. Of every scenario she had envisioned, this one hadn't crossed her mind. She took in his relatively calm demeanor and had to fight to keep from jumping up and pacing the room. Or shouting. Or bursting into tears.

"What, if you don't mind me asking, is in Washington? You can't be thinking of working with your uncle. Are you?" She told herself that couldn't be, that he had to have had a transformative experience when they went down south just as she had. But she had learned that one shouldn't infer too much about what someone else was feeling.

His eyebrows shot halfway up his forehead and he looked at her incredulously. "How could you think I would support my uncle after what he's done? After he couldn't be bothered to hear about what we experienced?"

"I'm sorry . . ." she said but Matthew didn't seem to hear her. He rose and settled in front of the window that looked out over the front lawn. She noticed his hand jiggling at his side as he let out a marked sigh. After a few minutes, he turned back to face her and only then did she notice the worry lines furrowing his brow.

"My uncle has cut me off," he said, so softly that she was sure she'd misheard him. She leaned forward as if she could grasp what he was saying if she was physically closer to him. When he didn't make any effort to clarify his new circumstances, Julia rose from her own chair, not sure if she should go over to Matthew or keep her distance. She chose to stay with the latter.

"Cut off. How could he do something like that?"

"He's furious with me. There's a firm down in the capitol that's working with a number of the tribes to fight the removal law. I sent a query a couple of weeks ago and they've asked me to come aboard. I leave tomorrow to try to get myself settled."

Julia tried to get her bearings as she took in all of what Matthew said, feeling as though she'd been sideswiped by a runaway carriage. He was leaving and she didn't know when, if ever, he would come back to Boston. The selfish part of her wanted to demand that he stay, to insist that they could work together right here. But there was a much more significant part that was awed by his sacrifice. He had erased any doubt she had about his commitment and she felt partially responsible for the bridges he'd burned to follow his convictions.

"Your uncle isn't half as brave as you are," she assured him, striding over to where he stood. Glancing toward the doorway to make sure no one was watching them, she took his hand in both of hers. "I didn't know how much this meant to you," she continued softly.

"His stance on this had bothered me for a long time but I kept pushing those doubts aside. He was such a rock for me after my parents died and he hadn't experienced what I had growing up. I thought he would take what I had to say seriously. But the way he dismissed me when I came back. . ." he trailed off, looking into her eyes with the intensity that she'd come to expect from him. In so many ways, he was refreshingly straightforward but she knew there were also parts of himself that he refused to share with her.

"I never meant to drive a wedge between you two. I wasn't thinking of the repercussions when I forced you to accompany me."

"Julia, this isn't your fault. In fact, I'm glad I went back to North Carolina. You gave me the push I needed to break away from him. You were right. I can see now how far my uncle is willing to go for the president and his politics."

"Do you think there's any chance of helping the tribes? All I can see when I let myself think about this are Atsila and her family." She had tried not to dwell on the hopelessness of it all but it was difficult to remain optimistic when the circumstances were so precarious and the probability of her friend's displacement was so high.

Matthew's expression turned grave and he pulled her closer to his side. "I don't want to give you false hope. This is going to be an uphill battle. But I'm going to do everything I can to make these lawmakers see reason."

"I know you will. Promise me you'll write as often as you can," she said, closing her eyes and resting her head on his shoulder. He rested his cheek against the top of her head in affirmation and they remained pressed against each other for as long as they dared.

"You didn't tell your father that I was the one who went to North Carolina with you, did you?"

Her heart began to thump at his unexpected question and she was afraid he could hear the pounding in her chest he was so close. His voice was quiet from above and she was glad he couldn't see her face.

"No, I didn't," she whispered back. "But I'm going to tell him soon. I promised Caroline I would." She didn't want his opinion of Matthew to change on her account. They got on so well and she didn't want their relationship to dissolve because of what she'd dragged Matthew into.

"Julia, you should have told him by now. I'll write to him when I get down to Washington. I can't have you taking all of the blame for this."

"Please don't," she said, lifting her head off of his shoulder so that she could look at him. "You never would have gone if I hadn't begged you to. Why risk damaging your connection with him over something that wasn't really your choice?"

"Because it's the right thing to do. It was my choice to make and I need to face the responsibility of it. You didn't hold me at gunpoint and I could have said no. It turns out that it was the kick that I needed."

Before she could argue her point further, a muffled commotion outside broke them apart and Julia cringed when she heard Caroline's voice wafting in through the front door. She scurried to the sitting room entrance and watched as her stepmother closed the door with a loud crack and huffed off in the direction of the dining room.

"You'd better leave before she realizes you're here," she said, turning back to Matthew. He gathered his hat and riding gloves from the chair and Julia led him into the entryway. As he made to open the door, she was overcome by a new wave of panic. This was the last time she'd see him for weeks, or more likely months. The time for holding back had passed.

She squeezed in between his body and the door, gripping the lapel of his coat. He looked at her with a questioning expression, she nodded, and then his lips were pressing insistently against hers. Heat seared through her as she moved her hands to his neck, his shoulders, his back and finally intertwined them in his hair. His arm wrapped around her waist, pulling her up against him until there wasn't a whisper of space between them. This was what she wanted to look back on when she thought of their last moments together, what would keep her hopeful during their lengthy time apart.

When he broke away, she tried to regain control of her breathing. It was intoxicating and slightly terrifying, this need to be near him. His cheeks were pink, too, and she wondered if she had the same effect on him as he did on her. He leaned into her and kissed her forehead with a tenderness that made her heart ache and realize that there were certain times when words weren't necessary. He finally gathered himself and she had to fight her instinct to run after him as he slipped by her and out the door.

As she watched Matthew make his way to the stable and tousle Edward's hair, she brought her hand to her mouth and smiled. The past few months had taken some unforeseen turns but this one was completely unexpected. She could never have guessed she'd fall in love with such an upstanding man.

CHAPTER 26

"Julia come here, please."

She heard the edge in her father's voice as it wafted over from his study and she knew that Caroline had finally told him. It was the day following Matthew's unexpected visit and departure and she was in the sitting room with Edward pretending that everything was normal. Edward had been playing around with Patches but he stopped mid yarn pull when he heard their father's tone.

"What did you do?" he asked as Julia rose from her seat and made her way to the doorway.

"None of your business," she told him playfully, sticking her tongue out at him before venturing into the lion's den. She didn't want him to know quite yet what she'd done.

Taking a deep breathe, she knocked on the door frame and entered when she heard the gruff permission to 'come in'. There were two lit candles on the windowsill and an oil lamp was burning on the desk to keep the thunderstorm-induced darkness of the room at bay. Her father sat behind his large desk, a stony and disapproving expression contorting his familiar features into a mask she had trouble recognizing. She'd only ever seen him like this when Fletcher had misbehaved in primary school and she could count on one hand the number of times that was. Having it directed at her was terrifying.

"Sit. Now." She nearly scampered over to the imposing chair on the other side of his desk, stuffing her hands under her legs to keep them from shaking.

"Caroline has just told me something quite extraordinary. You might find it so, too. It seems a daughter of mine lied to everyone who has her best interests at heart when her brother wasn't able to chaperone her down to North Carolina. She went anyway, can you imagine? Oh, and she also wasn't truthful with the missionaries who only wanted to help her. Can you think of who this misguided, foolish girl could be?"

Julia raised her eyes just enough from her lap to find him staring down his nose at her as if she were a fox that had found its way into the henhouse. She had reverted back to childhood and felt herself withering under his piercing stare.

"I wasn't thinking-"

"Well, at least you're speaking the truth now. It's evident that you weren't thinking about the people who love and protect you. It's a wonder I didn't get a frantic message from Caroline or your brother. It seems they handled everything and kept it all under wraps just fine without me. Don't you realize the danger you put yourself in? Try and make me understand, please."

"I was desperate, Papa. I'd put so much time into preparing for this and wanted so much to learn even more. You can understand that, can't you?"

Her father gave a *humpf* but she could tell she'd struck a chord with him. If nothing else, her father was the consummate student, always wanting to gain more knowledge and better himself. So she plowed on.

"I was perfectly safe. The O'Connors were committed to looking out for me. As was the family I stayed with. They were kind beyond measure.

And Matthew . . ."

Too late she realized she'd let possibly the biggest secret of all slip out. Without any pressure from her father at that. How could she be so clumsy?

"Matthew? Eaton? What does he have to do with any of this?"

She watched the confusion melt away and morph into recognition on his face. She could tell he knew what she was going to say before she squeaked the words out.

"He was the one who went with me. I told Abigail and Jacob that he was Fletcher."

Any headway she had made in the last few minutes completely evaporated. Her father was well and furious now, she could see it in the rising color in his customarily pale cheeks and the way he sucked in his breathe as if he was trying to keep his expletives at bay. It was far worse than when she'd told Caroline.

"You . . . you've taken things too far, Julia. I had that man in here yesterday. I actually felt sorry for what he was going through with that blasted uncle of his, admired him for his courage to break away and do what he thought was right. Now you're telling me I shared a brandy with the very individual who could leave your reputation in tatters if he wanted to?"

"It wasn't like that, Papa. He's not an opportunist. I begged him to-"

"Don't you dare defend him. He's older than you, he should have known better. You think you know a man . . ."

Her father wasn't listening, he was too far gone in his disgust. While he got up in a fit of agitation and began pacing behind his desk, she wished she could take it back. This was exactly what she'd feared, that Matthew's relationship with her father would be altered, possibly irreversibly so. Her father would forgive her eventually, she was certain of that. The same couldn't be said for poor Matthew.

She just sat there, feeling powerless as her father worked out his aggravation in starts and stops of movement and strangled exclamations.

"Do you love him?"

The question was so unexpected that she thought she'd imagined it. But her father was looking at her expectantly and so she answered with the only logic response.

"Yes. Yes, I do."

"Well, you're going to have to rethink your affection, Julia. This is unbelievable."

Before she could be properly outraged and tell him how wrong he was about Matthew and his intentions, all of the fight seemed to go out of him and he walked to the chair, clutching the back as if he was the one who needed propping up now.

"You were foolish to risk it all, I'm sorry to say. It grieves me to tell you that all of your efforts wouldn't have change the vote anyway. Though I voted against it, too many others voted for it. The Act passed."

This conversation was giving her whiplash. She had known this was the likely outcome, knew she couldn't have stopped the vote even if she had burst into the Capitol building with Atsila at her side. But her father's quiet words still made her feel as if she'd been punched in the stomach and she had to make a conscious effort not to double over. It was all too much and suddenly far too warm inside this room, this very house.

Without another word, she turned and flew through the door of her father's study with surprising force, needing desperately to abandon the thick, humid air threatening to engulf her senses. The disturbing news her father had just given her still rung in her ears. As she pushed through the back pantry door into a cascade of raindrops, she finally felt relief as the cool rain pattered on her burning cheeks though her heart continued to beat hard against her chest as her rage intensified. Peering up into the intertwining branches of the oak trees in the backyard, her thoughts were as complex as the network of tiny branches, each fighting to win dominance over the other.

How could this happen? she thought, barely able to swallow the tears that burned her throat and threatened to become intermixed with the rain. *How can people be so cruel?* Now thoroughly soaked through, she returned to the heat of the pantry leaning heavily against the door, though its strength did nothing to still her shaking or provide any comfort.

She could hear Doris asking her concerned questions but Julia felt like she was muffled, like she herself was underwater and, try as she might, she couldn't come up for air.

"I'm sorry, Doris," she heard herself say. "I just . . . just think I need to go lay down for awhile. That's all"

She let her body take over as she passed through the kitchen and went up the stairs to her bedroom. Closing the door behind her, she listened as the rain pounded on the roof over her head, an unrelenting deluge. Only when she realized she was shivering from her foray into that very same rain did she step away from the doorway and unlace her boots. She didn't even bother to change out of her wet things, just pulled back the quilt and nestled into the familiarity of her sheets, wondering listlessly if anything would ever feel right again.

*   *   *   *

"I know that you're upset, Julia," her father acknowledged the morning after he had broken the news of Congress's passage of the Indian Removal Act. The hard edge was gone from his voice and he squeezed her hand as they sat together on the bench out in the garden. After such a violent storm the day before, the brilliance of the sun hurt Julia's sensitive eyes.

"Your reaction yesterday says it all," he continued. "But you have to get past this; I don't want this to worry you. The decision was out of your hands."

Julia knew her father's assurances were meant to make her feel better; however, they only made her feel powerless. *I could have done more,* she thought, keeping her red-rimmed eyes downcast. *I could have worked harder, found out more about the people in Congress and petitioned somebody.*

"I just don't understand, Papa," she finally replied. "How could so many people support this? It seems like a waste of effort to try to change peoples' minds."

"Don't sound so hopeless, Julia," her father insisted, hooking his finger under chin and lifting her face up so that they were eye to eye. "You may have not have been able to reach every member of Congress but you reached me. I think your passion for this cause was the main reason why I voted against it."

Julia regarded her father with astonishment. While he had mentioned his decision to vote against the bill, this was the first time she had heard him speak of any influence she may have had in it. A cautious smile lifted up the corners of her mouth as she studied her father's face.

"Really, Papa?" she questioned, still not fully able to believe she had had such a profound effect on her father.

"Of course," her father replied. "It began with the valid points about the Indians. And you may have a hard time believing this but both Eliza *and* Caroline wrote to me to let me know how dedicated you became to doing what you could." He stroked her hair comfortingly and took her hands in his. "How could I disappoint you by voting for that bill?"

"Thank you, Papa," Julia choked out. "Thank you for taking what I had to say seriously. Even though the bill passed, I think you made the right decision."

"I think you're right." He grew serious then. "It will take time to repair the damage you've done and regain our trust after the lies you told. I cannot forget that nor do I think anyone should. I'm confident that you've discovered you went about some of this horribly wrong. But I also can't forget how you saw the injustice of this wretched situation and you kept fighting to be heard. You remind me of my younger self in that regard."

She sunk into her father's side, astonished by his praise. How could he continue to be rightfully upset with her and still make her glow from within? They stayed like that for a awhile until she could feel his body go lax with sleep, his light snores reminding her of when she used to sit on his lap as a little girl and he would doze off reading her a bedtime story.

There were so many she still needed to make amends with. Caroline, Eliza, Abigail and Jacob. Maybe even Fletcher, too, if she was in a particularly charitable mood. And she would work with all her power to do that. But she wasn't going to be silent anymore, either. She had found a battle she was willing to risk so much for and she wasn't going to give in just because the odds seemed insurmountable.

She *was* Daniel Webster's daughter, after all.

HISTORICAL NOTE

As was the case for many of the children of prominent political figures of the time, not much was written about Julia Webster, though you can find three of her diaries at the Massachusetts Historical Society in Boston. These are from her adult years.

Due to this fact, her character and motivations in the novel come primarily from my imagination. I also aged her several years as she was actually born in January 1818. Matthew Eaton is also a completely fictional character, though John Henry Eaton was, in fact, President Jackson's Secretary of War during the time the novel is set.

The political issues and powerful policy makers mentioned and explored in the novel were all true to life and I tried to stick as closely as I could to the historical record in that regard. Sadly, the Indian Removal Act was passed in 1830 and though its implementation was delayed for several years, it did lead to the removal of the five indigenous nations (Cherokee, Creek, Choctaw, Chickasaw, and Seminole) referenced in the book. This removal led to the Trail of Tears and immeasurable suffering for those who were forced from their land.

A primary endeavor of mine in writing this novel was to shed light on the grotesque treatment of indigenous people by the citizens and government of the United States during that time in history. There is a direct correlation between the tragedies of the past and how indigenous people live and are treated in modern day America. My hope is that my readers gain more knowledge of one of these tragedies and this leads to a desire to learn more and be more thoughtful about marginalized groups.

If you would like to learn more about Daniel Webster and/or Andrew Jackson, I would highly recommend historian Robert Remini's works, particularly *Daniel Webster: The Man and His Time* and *Andrew Jackson and His Indian Wars.*

The 1619 Project: A New Origin Story also features a powerful essay by prominent African American historian Tiya Miles entitled 'Dispossession' that is also an excellent read. The essay explores the dual trauma of both indigenous people and African Americans in early America up through the 1830's.

ABOUT THE AUTHOR

E.P. Livingston is a native of northwestern Pennsylvania and a graduate of Gannon University's History program. She has always been fascinated with stories of the past and writing historical fiction, particularly centered on little explored eras in the space, brings her much joy. When she's not working, researching, or writing, she's wrapped up in a gripping book, devouring YouTube videos, or going on adventures with her partner and the three boys they share between them. *The Senator's Daughter* is her debut novel.

ABOUT NEXT CHAPTERS

Do you have a dream of being a published author, but don't have the motivation or time to write an entire book on your own?

We have you covered.

Next Chapters' authors participate in our crowdsourced novels, where writers add their own chapters to works in progress, which are open for any of our writers to contribute.

Log into our writer's platform and see what stories are being written, you may find one you're excited about adding your own voice to as it continues to completion! Or start your own idea and work with the world to see your words mature into a full book, ready for publication.

And best of all, an author writing chapters contained in any of our crowdsourced novels shares in the profits if the book makes money!

You can become a published author.

We're excited to have you come write with us at NextChapters.com.

- Tim Vickey
  Founder, Next Chapters

Made in United States
Orlando, FL
19 April 2023

32240230R00150